FINAL LOOK

A Christine Lane Mystery

Dianne Scott

Danforth Press

FINAL LOOK

Copyright © Dianne Scott, 2022

This is a work of fiction. Names, characters, places and incidents are either the product of the author's imagination or are used fictitiously. Any resemblance to actual persons, living or dead, events, or locales is entirely coincidental.

Cover Design: Lance Buckley

978-1-7776042-0-2 ISBN Paperback

978-1-7776042-1-9 ISBN Ebook

978-1-7776042-2-6 ISBN Large Print Paperback

Danforth Press

diannescottauthor.com

To my father, Peter Scott, whose stories of policing Toronto Island
inspired the creation of Christine Lane.

And to my mother, Rose Marie Scott, who supported my creative
endeavors.

Chapter 1

June 1968

Through the patrol car window, Policewoman Christine Lane spied two boats on a collision course to Ward's Island Dock. The ferry's horn bellowed as the vessel plowed through the lake, frothing water curling from its prow. The eight-person water taxi raced the ferry from the periphery, peppering the air with its staccato horn.

"Stop the car!" yelled Christine to her sergeant behind the wheel.

Sergeant Bard slammed his heel into the brake and she pitched forward into the glove compartment, bracing herself with her arm. The car slid to a halt in a spray of gravel stones two hundred feet south of the dock.

"They're racing!" she said as she sat back in her seat.

Her sergeant looked at her, unruffled.

Fine. She would take care of it herself. She shouldered the car door open and then hurtled across a swath of grass toward the ferry dock, hiking her uniform skirt to go faster, her police-issue purse bouncing against her hip.

She thumped onto the wide wooden dock. "Slow down!" she shouted, waving her hands above her head to get the attention of the ferry captain in his second-story cabin.

The captain spotted her, pausing the throttle.

The water taxi emitted a jubilant beep as it cut in front of the bigger boat and steered toward the side dock allocated for small watercraft.

Christine staggered as the ferry butted the row of tires lining the dock, engines churning in reverse as the wake slopped over the worn rubber treads. What the heck were the drivers doing? They had passengers on board, for goodness' sake. She pointed a finger at the bearded ferry captain and motioned him down with a cupped hand. When she saw him move away from the window, she hurried along the dock toward the water taxi.

A leather-faced man stood in the taxi's hull with a cigarette dangling from his lip, helping passengers disembark.

"Sir, I need to speak with you," she said over the chatter of the passengers.

Squinting at her from underneath his sun-bleached hat, the boat pilot scanned her six-foot length, from her derby hat down the brass buttons of her dark navy serge jacket, to her skirt, beige nylons and polished black oxfords.

He helped the last passenger onto the dock and then hopped out of the boat. He barely came up to her shoulder—in fact, he was looking straight down the V of her starched white blouse.

She stared at him until he lifted his eyes.

"Who the hell are you?"

Christine turned. It was the bearded ferry captain. He stood in the middle of the dock while ferry passengers with bikes and wagons of groceries flowed past him.

She pulled her memo book from the purse strapped across her shoulder and took a step toward him. "PW Lane—Toronto Police. Your name, sir?"

"Who the hell is she, Sammy?" he asked the taxi driver.

Sammy shrugged his narrow shoulders. "A stewardess? Island Airport?"

"Goddamn, they're making them tall," the ferry captain said. He was compact and muscular, hair a deep barn-red, a good three inches shorter than Christine. Sammy was another five inches shorter than him.

"I'm a policewoman," she repeated, pointing to the metal badge with the number sixteen on her hat brim. "Toronto Police Force. Both of you were carelessly operating your vessels."

"Is that so?" The ferry captain crossed his thick, freckled forearms.

"Hey, Sammy. Mike."

Christine turned at the sound of Sergeant Bard's voice. *Thank goodness. Backup.*

Her sergeant's round face shone under the midday sun as he ambled toward them on the dock. He nodded at the last trickle of passengers, greeting a young family by name.

Turning to the men, Sergeant Bard said, "Ruffling the new hen's feathers?"

"She's yours?" said Mike, the ferry captain.

"A fresh recruit."

"I've been a policewoman for four years," she said. "And in Records two years before that."

"She's a woman," Sammy observed.

"Don't I know it." Sergeant Bard tugged a white handkerchief out of his pocket, pulled his police hat off and swiped his face and then his bald spot. He plunked his hat back on, stuffing the linen into his pants pocket. "She's caused me a heap of problems already."

Christine clenched her jaw, schooling herself to ignore his comment. "Sergeant," she said, "they were driving recklessly."

Sergeant Bard sighed. "They're not cars, PW," he said. "Didn't they teach you anything at the Women's Bureau?"

Mike snorted. Sammy grinned, showing tobacco-stained teeth.

Christine ignored the two sailors. "It's a 221, Sergeant. Operating a vehicle in a manner dangerous to the public."

"Harbor Police enforce watercraft violations. Nothing to do with us landlubbers." He turned and started walking toward the Island, his heavy footsteps vibrating the dock planks.

"Call the Harbor Police, then," she said to his retreating back.

Sergeant Bard said over his shoulder, "See you gentlemen tonight."

"Can't wait to relieve you of your money," Mike said.

"You won't be getting a royal flush two weeks in a row," Sergeant Bard retorted as he stepped onto land.

Poker buddies. It figured. The residents Christine had met her first week of Toronto Island patrol were all old school chums, sailing club members, church parishioners or related in an obscure way. Or, evidently, gambled together. And for some reason, they were immune to the laws that applied to the rest of Toronto's citizens.

She hurried along the dock and across the grass to the police car, irritation spurring her to outpace her boss, even with her stride shortened by her A-line skirt. Not only was she stuck working in this backwater island station, but transgressions were also ignored with a wink and a slap on the back. She got into the car and slammed the door shut.

Sergeant Bard strolled along, the air behind him blurry with heat, as if the city skyline was a mirage. He heaved himself into the driver's seat with a grunt, the vehicle swaying with his weight.

She could sense him looking at her, but she stared ahead at the waterfront buildings lining the Inner Harbor, the green-blue water like a moat dividing the city from Toronto Island. What she would give to be working in a downtown station, where regulations were followed and culprits apprehended.

"Don't get yourself in a snit," he said. "They're just having a bit of fun."

She looked over at him. "What if they had collided? Or rammed through the dock?"

"Mike and Sammy have been at each other for fifteen years. The Islanders expect it. Adds excitement to their day." He patted his bowling-ball stomach, which strained the threads of his uniform buttons. "Time for lunch. Have you been to Clergy House?" This was a restaurant housed in an old rectory.

After a pause, she shook her head. She had to learn to hold her tongue, adapt, follow her sergeant's lead. This wasn't the Women's Bureau, where female officers were given more leeway for discussion.

She reached for her purse. She hadn't expected to lunch out. Her cheese sandwich, apple and bottle of milk were sitting in a brown paper bag in the fridge at the Center Island Police Station. Thank goodness for the emergency five dollars tucked into the back of her wallet. Clergy House would not be cheap; the refurbished church building was the only proper restaurant on Toronto Island, apart from the pizza, pretzels and hot dogs sold at the Centerville Amusement Park.

Her sergeant eased the car into first gear and drove slowly along the gravel pathway, four-way signal lights flashing. Three minutes later, they'd parked and were following the stone path beside the old residence to the backyard. Reaching the patio, Sergeant Bard hailed a waitress, who pointed to an empty table away from the other patrons.

They wove a course between the cast-iron tables and sat in silence under the shade of the arched poplar trees. Past the patio, she could see a couple walking along the wooden boardwalk that edged the southeastern side of the island. Farther past the pair was a vista of gray-blue water: Lake Ontario. Christine made herself take a deep breath and exhale, letting her anger seep out of her and the velvet green of the leaves calm her.

No more stomping around in front of her superior officer. That would just earn her a poor performance review. Policing was different on Toronto Island. She needed to accept that.

"It's beautiful back here," she said. She thought of her Women's Bureau friends inside the old brick building on College Street, their side-by-side desks surrounded by hulking filing cabinets. Toronto Island certainly was a different assignment.

Sergeant Bard smiled at her. "A hidden paradise." He waved at a waitress laden with a tray of food. "A frosty one, Ginny dear," he called out. He passed Christine a menu.

Geez, things were expensive. Hamburgers were over a dollar, the steak three dollars. She looked around at the clientele: gray-haired ladies in sun hats, a few couples clasping wine glasses, a group of young women in flowing beach dresses, several families. Tourists, she guessed, at least some of them, here to visit the car-free community or tan on a beach.

"Islanders ever eat here?" she asked.

Sergeant Bard nodded. "During the winter, or midweek dinners. Summertime, it's the tourists and mainlanders that keep the place afloat."

"Here you go." Ginny placed the frosted glass in front of him.

Beer. He was drinking beer. On duty. She had heard of station officers who drank at local pubs when on foot patrol or from metal flasks hidden in their inside jacket pockets, but she had never seen it at the Women's Bureau. Her colleague Julie kept a whiskey flask in her bottom desk drawer, but that was reserved for birthdays. Or celebrations, like when they finally caught the creep who had been exposing himself to children on playgrounds.

Sergeant Bard tipped his head back for a long draught, then clinked the glass down on the metal tabletop. "Saw your dad on TV, Ginny," he said to the waitress.

Ginny's brown hair fell in a shield in front of her face, the tresses highlighted by the sun. "I don't watch the news."

"He gave a speech on saving Island homes from the wrecking ball," he added.

She tucked a swath of hair behind her ear. Her eyes were glacial blue. "My mom and I don't watch him." She turned to Christine. "Can I take your order?"

"Hi," Christine said. "I'm PW Lane. I'm new to Island patrol."

Sergeant Bard said, "Ginny's family has lived here for four generations."

"Five," Ginny said, not looking at him.

"Water, please," Christine said. "What's your soup of the day?"

"Cucumber."

Christine had never eaten that, but it was the cheapest thing on the menu. "It's cold?" She was sweating along the cinched line of her utility belt, her radio holster heavy on her hip.

"Yes."

"I'll take that, thank you."

Her sergeant ordered the surf and turf. Clearly, he wasn't minding his finances or his waistline.

His eyes followed the waitress inside. "Her father's Daniel Rogers—the news commentator. He has a house with his second wife and their kids on Algonquin Island."

"Does Ginny live with them?" Christine said. The young woman looked eighteen. Maybe she was still in school.

"Nah. Messy divorce. First wife is Nancy Hamilton, who lives on Ward's Island. Ginny's been with her since the split seven years ago. Ginny works here at Clergy House, babysits, sells her art."

"So, were the islands always connected?" she said. Toronto Island was a chain of fifteen islands, the largest being Ward, Center and Algonquin.

"More or less, either by bridge or land, except Mugg and Forestry. They're boat-access only."

After a few minutes, Ginny arrived with their food. The officers ate without talking. The breeze blew inland, bringing the smell of the freshwater lake and the squawks of arguing seagulls. Christine's soup was cool, creamy and delicious—as it should be, for a dollar.

When they finished eating, she reached for her purse.

"Put your money away." He stood, hitched his pants and walked away.

"We have to pay for our food," she called after him. And her sergeant's beer. He continued walking and disappeared out of sight around the stone building.

She clutched her wallet with two hands. Did he expect her to pay for his meal? Why hadn't she eaten her packed lunch in the station kitchenette as planned? She could buy her stepbrother Wayne a new baseball glove for the price of today's meal.

She walked into the restaurant through the open back door. Ginny was leaning against the bar, tallying a bill on the counter, fingers adorned with silver rings, shoulders freckled under the yellow straps of her dress. Like many Islanders, she was tanned right down to her toes, one foot encircled by a beaded anklet.

Christine said, "May I have the bill, please?"

Ginny looked up, brow furrowed. "Cops don't pay for their food."

No, thought Christine, *police*men *don't pay.*

"This one does," Christine replied. She unfolded her five-dollar bill and placed it on the counter. She added a two-dollar bill on top. "This should cover everything. Thank you," she said and headed toward the door.

Sergeant Bard was drumming his fingers on the car's steering wheel. "Why do you lady folk take so long?" he said through the open window.

Biting her lip to prevent a retort, Christine got into the police vehicle. It was going to be a long deployment on the Island—two years before they'd consider her transfer to a downtown station, where she would patrol city streets and collar hardcore criminals. Seven hundred and twenty-three days left to go.

"Lots of people out," Christine said to her sergeant the next day on patrol. Groups and pairs dotted Cibola Avenue, heading toward Ward's Island. "Is it because it's Saturday?"

"Something's up." Sergeant Bard swerved the patrol car onto the grass and pulled on the parking brake. He flagged a passerby. "Danny!"

A man in khaki pants and a plaid, short-sleeved shirt jogged over, a clipboard tucked under his arm. Christine recognized Daniel Rogers from seeing him on television—and remembered Sergeant Bard talking with the Clergy House waitress yesterday about her famous father.

"Our man in blue." Rogers shook the sergeant's hand. "Are you joining us?"

"What's going on, Danny?" the sergeant asked.

"Who's this?" Rogers said, bending down to look into the car.

Christine leaned forward in her seat. "Policewoman Lane."

Rogers reached in to shake her hand. "Nice to meet you," he said, looking at her with deep blue eyes. "It's good to see a woman with a badge."

"You want her?" Sergeant Bard said.

Rogers smiled, then his face became serious. "They're tearing down more houses."

"Metro Council gave the order?" the sergeant asked.

Rogers nodded. "It's that damn parks commissioner, Tommy Thompson. He's bulldozed homes from Hanlan to Center. Now he's after the two communities left."

"What are you going to do?" Sergeant Bard said.

"Stop him," Rogers said, meeting the sergeant's glance, then hers. She could see why the camera loved him; his gaze felt like he was looking right into you.

"If you'll excuse me," Rogers said. "We're gathering at the community center." He gave them a quick smile, then turned and caught up with a group of people walking toward Ward's Island.

"Let's check it out," said Sergeant Bard to Christine.

"Expecting a problem?"

He shook his head. "Most of the Islanders are peaceful: artists, nature-lovers, summer cottagers with kids. But there's a few hotheads. It's an emotional issue. Eviction. Demolition. Some families have been here for generations. Now their leases are up, and the government wants to mow down their houses and send them packing." He turned the ignition, and the patrol car slowly followed the line of people walking to Ward's Island.

Christine heard the crowd before she saw them. Holy smokes. Four hundred people had gathered across the width of the field, bracketed between the community center on one end and the baseball diamond on the other. Daniel Rogers stood in front of the community center talking to a tall, thin man with a gray goatee—Gary Owen, the head of the Toronto Island Residents' Association. Christine had met him last week.

Sergeant Bard parked on the far side of the building, and they meandered into the crowd. The sergeant knew many Islanders by name, including the children who were using the field for summer camp.

A group of young men with shoulder-length hair sat at the back of the field, hand-written placards resting against the home plate fence that read: Down with Fascist Governments and Power to the People.

"Gentlemen," Sergeant Bard said as he stopped in front of them.

"Look!" the hippie with the oatmeal-colored goatee said. "It's Papa Pig." His two friends snickered. The bearded man glanced over at Christine. "And Mama Pig too." A few more titters.

"What's your business here?" Sergeant Bard said. His voice was calm, but his face was an unhealthy shade of red.

"Why? Are we under arrest?" the bearded man asked.

The sergeant crossed his arms. "Break any laws?"

The man shook his head. "Just hanging low." He gestured to the crowd with one arm. "Enjoying the Island with my friends here."

The young man pushed himself upright and walked over to Christine, stopping six inches away, staring at her through his overgrown bangs. They were the same height. She could smell him: a combination of body odor, marijuana smoke and patchouli. She looked back at him without blinking. At the Women's Bureau, she had heard every suggestive or abusive line you could imagine—from prostitutes she searched before they were jailed, drunken teenagers she arrested at a dance and men who hollered out of car windows during her crossing guard duty. This guy didn't intimidate her.

"Hey, Mama Pig," he said in a soft voice. He opened his arms wide and called, "Mama Pig, Mama Pig, let me come in."

Loud laughter from his friends. A few heads in the crowd swiveled to look at them.

"That's enough!" Sergeant Bard wedged his portly body between Christine and the man, forcing her to step back. "What's your name, son?"

"I'm the Wolf." He leaned to the side to address Christine. "Want to blow my house down, sister?" More laughter. She pressed her lips together and said nothing. She had to let her sergeant take care of the situation.

Sergeant Bard stepped closer to the young man. "I'll ask you one more time, and it will be the last. What's your name?"

"Be cool," he said, raising his hands in surrender. "Kevin Lamprey."

"Where you from, Kevin?" the sergeant asked.

Kevin gestured to the crowd. "Somewhere, everywhere."

"You're not an Islander," Sergeant Bard stated.

Lamprey shook his head.

"I'm looking for a specific address."

Lamprey paused. "Thirty-seven Russell Hill Road."

Sergeant Bard snorted, slapping his thigh with the meat of his hand. He turned to Christine. "Mr. 'Down with the Man' lives in his daddy's mansion in Forest Hill."

The smile left Lamprey's face. Sergeant Bard chuckled, shaking his head.

"Good afternoon," boomed a voice. Gary Owen was standing on the community center steps, megaphone in hand. People settled on the grass, on blankets and beach towels, hushing each other.

Sergeant Bard said to Christine, "Keep your eye out for anyone who's not local—n'er-do-wells looking for trouble."

Christine thought of the anti-Vietnam demonstrations that had taken place in front of the American embassy on University Avenue. They were mostly peaceful, but several rallies had turned violent, with youth throwing bottles at police and overturning the barricades, resulting in arrests.

Sergeant Bard continued, "Take the front. I'll stay back here." He jerked his head for her to get going.

She threaded her way toward the community center. Lamprey and his buddies were probably harmless, more likely to be spouting beatnik poetry or picking up a blonde in a miniskirt than inciting violent revolution. Still, she didn't like to leave Sergeant Bard alone with them. She parked herself under a tree in the field's corner, where she could view the young men and monitor new arrivals.

"Welcome, Islanders," Gary Owen said. "Friends, allies and concerned citizens. This is a crucial time. Metro Council is determined to kick us off Toronto Island!"

People booed.

"Ten years ago, our main street was lined with hotels, restaurants, grocery stores and businesses. There were houses all along Lakeshore Avenue, on Center Island and Hanlan's Point. Under the direction of Parks Commissioner Tommy Thompson, they demolished our shops and livelihoods. They bulldozed our hearths, set fire to our homes. And they want to do it again." Cries erupted from the audience. "But we will not let them!" His fist punched the air. The crowd roared.

People streamed in. Christine nodded at Ginny, the waitress from Clergy House, who was holding the hand of a young, mustached man with long, dark hair.

Owen passed the megaphone to Daniel Rogers.

"We've written letters, called our politicians and made presentations to council," Rogers said. He shook his head. "It is not enough. We need our protest to expand. We must have the citizens of Toronto on our side."

A tow-headed toddler climbed the three stairs and Rogers picked him up. "Dada," the boy said into the megaphone. A spatter of laughter from the crowd.

"People need to see us as fathers, mothers and neighbors," Rogers continued. "We have jobs and families. We pay taxes." He put his son down and the boy climbed down the stairs to his waiting mother.

"We live in one of the most beautiful places in Canada." Rogers spread his arms wide. "From the time John Hanlan set up a fishing hut a hundred years ago, we have been stewards of this place. Our neighborhood is a living, breathing example of Toronto's history.

"We have to take this vision of our community to the television screen, broadcast waves and newspapers. To our tennis clubs, churches, libraries and workplaces. Torontonians must know about us, see us, recognize themselves in us. We cannot be silent. Look what that got us." He pointed toward the uninhabited side of the island. "We can be silent no more."

A surge of applause. People stood up cheering, the noise thunderous.

Christine looked around for Sergeant Bard but couldn't see him through the throng.

What did this protest mean for Islanders? For Island patrol? For her?

Chapter 2

"Teeny, telephone," Donna announced from the bedroom doorway. Christine's little sister was still in her pajamas, wiry arms showing in the short sleeves of her dress.

Christine checked her watch. It was seven thirty in the morning. "Who is it?" she asked her stepsister.

"It's a man."

Christine walked down the hallway to the kitchen. "Hello?" She cradled the black telephone receiver in both hands.

Donna sat down at the kitchen table to eat her bowl of cornflakes. "PW Lane?"

"Sergeant Bard!" Christine straightened her cotton top and miniskirt.

"All hands on deck. I need you to come in."

"Yes, sir."

"Damn Metro Council. They ferried demolition equipment over to the Island last night. A construction crew is going to take down 42 Lakeshore within the hour."

It must be a house on the boardwalk, near Clergy House restaurant. "Is it vacant?" she said.

"No," he replied. "The Whitmores are removing their belongings as we speak. They've paid no attention to the eviction notices."

Christine pictured the Ward's Island meeting. "Is there a crowd?"

"The Islanders are rounding up as we speak. A siren's going off and they're knocking on doors, gathering people. Those damn hippie protesters arrived five minutes ago. I don't know how they heard about it so fast. There's about fifty people, but that's changing quickly. Pilkington's here. I've called in Morano and Fillingham. A water taxi will pick you up city-side and take you to Ward's."

"I'm on my way." She hung up. In the living room, her ten-year-old stepbrother was still sleeping on the pullout couch.

"Donna," Christine said as she sat down at the kitchen table kitty-corner to her sister, "I've been called into work. You and Wayne need to go to school on your own this morning. Mom's sleeping—it's her day off."

Donna's spoon halted halfway to her mouth. "I don't want to go with Wayne. You said you would take us."

On Christine's day off, she usually walked her siblings to school; that way, she could navigate them around the occasional drug user or old man yelling to himself.

"I know," Christine said, placing a hand on her sister's leg. "It's an emergency. I'll be back to pick you up after school. How about we drop by Farley's for some penny candy?"

Donna frowned but nodded. Christine kissed her on the head and ran to get ready.

Hoping the sergeant would reimburse her, she used the emergency money in the tin on top of the fridge for a taxi to the ferry docks; from there, she hopped in a water taxi. After she disembarked at Ward's Island dock, she spotted a bike leaning against a tree trunk; she hopped on, hoping the owner wouldn't mind.

She pedaled quickly toward the Ward's Island Community Center, her legs pushing against the bias of her skirt. Residents were running across the field from their homes, children trailing behind mothers, men buttoning shirts, calling to each other to hurry. Christine biked through the throng filling the path, calling, "Excuse me. Police!" as she headed toward 42 Lakeshore.

As she turned onto the wooden boardwalk, she heard the rumble of heavy machinery. Geez, they were starting the demolition.

Christine slowed down as the crowd thickened near the gray clapboard house. A hulking yellow excavator sat beside the cottage, its claw like a snakehead. After tucking her bike behind a tree, Christine headed toward the line of police officers.

Sergeant Bard stood ten feet from the excavator, his arm around a woman's shoulders, her two adolescent children by her side. The Whitmores. Behind them were stacked boxes, a desk, kitchen table and two mattresses. A heavy, two-inch diameter rope hung across the width of the property, bisecting the yard. Pilkington and Morano were standing at either end of the rope, corralling people behind it with large, swinging arcs of their arms. A short, blond police officer was positioned in the middle. Must be Fillingham; she hadn't met him yet.

Over a hundred and fifty people were penned behind the rope. Gary Owen was gesticulating wildly, screaming at a man with a clipboard, his words swallowed by the excavator roar. Beside him stood the manager of the Algonquin Island Yacht Club, his face red from yelling, then Ginny from Clergy House and a few more restaurant staff Christine recognized. She saw Mike, the ferry captain, and several other ferry workers. People were holding hands, singing lyrics that couldn't be heard over the machinery. Half of the crowd was anxious parents with children clinging to their legs. Near Pilkington were the three bearded protesters from the community meeting, their fists raised, chanting in unison. Kevin Lamprey punched a sign into the air with thrusts of his sinewy arm.

Christine ran over to Fillingham and tapped his shoulder. He looked up at her for a second, eyes flicking to the badge on her hat brim, then moved over to make room for her. Christine grabbed the thick, heavy rope in both hands, arms spread wide as bodies pressed again the barrier. The cordoned group was spreading, amassing all the way to the dump truck, bulldozer and trailer parked at the back of the property—the equipment to haul the debris away later.

A wail erupted from the crowd. Christine turned around.

Sergeant Bard was holding up two fingers. Two minutes until demolition. Mrs. Whitmore began rocking back and forth, her arms clutched around her body. Her children huddled closer. People were running in from the boardwalk, the lake an Aegean blue behind them. The crowd was no longer contained behind the rope; they spilled out in a broken circle around the house.

Christine ran over to Fillingham and leaned down to cup her hand to his ear. "We should call it off!" she yelled.

He pointed to the house.

She turned. The excavator bucket lifted off the ground. The machine rolled closer to the house. Christine felt its vibrations through the ground, zipping up her legs to her spine. She tensed as the arm rose higher. The claw stopped, tilted, then swooped down and pierced the roof. Roof shingles, two-by-four planks and red bricks tumbled down.

Mrs. Whitmore fell to her knees, mouth open in an unheard wail. Christine felt rather than heard the screams from the crowd behind her.

The claw descended again, tearing through a wall to reveal a bedroom with green ivy wallpaper, framed paintings still on the wall. The house resembled an opened sardine can.

Sergeant Bard started running away from the house toward the crowd, pushing people to the side, belly shaking as he ran, his face distorted with effort. When he reached Christine, he pushed her hard in the chest. She tripped over Fillingham's foot and fell on her back, Fillingham crashing down beside her.

She gasped, the wind knocked out of her. The dump truck from the back of the property careered by, plowing through the middle of the crowd, who were pushing and lunging to get out of its way. She could see the driver through the passenger window, his mouth drawn back in a grimace, arms pulling at the wheel.

Christine scrambled to her feet and watched the truck lurch over the boardwalk and drive through the sand straight into the lake. It shuddered to a stop thirty feet from shore.

The excavator rumble stopped, like it had been unplugged. People were standing, their faces slack with shock; others were lying on the ground, looking around in confusion.

Someone tugged her jacket sleeve.

"Help her." It was a mustached young man with long dark hair. He looked familiar. He pulled her over to a patch of nearby grass.

Ginny Rogers lay on her back, one leg splayed at an awkward angle, dirt smudged in a line across her clothes. Fillingham reached Ginny at the same time as Christine.

"Ginny!" Christine said as she fell to her knees beside her. The young woman opened her eyes, which were a startling blue in her pale face.

Fillingham pulled his radio from his belt as he kneeled on Ginny's other side: "Dispatch, 52-25, PC Fillingham. Requesting an ambulance." His chin lifted as he scanned the crowd. "Four ambulances to 42 Lakeshore; 10-78. I repeat, 10-78."

Christine touched Ginny's hand. "Help is coming. Hold on."

Ginny looked at her, her glance questioning, then past Christine to the birds soaring above the lake. Her eyelids slowly closed.

Where were the firemen to help with first aid? Their station was down the street. They should be here by now for crowd control. Standing up, she peered through the dazed crowd.

A stream of young men ran into the lake, splashing through the water to the partially submerged dump truck. Christine recognized Kevin Lamprey in the lead. In their hands were bricks and planks of lumber. One man batted the side of the truck bed with a two-by-four while the other threw a brick against the passenger window. Lamprey stepped up on the running board of the truck and pried open the driver's door. Grabbing the trucker by the shirt collar, Lamprey pulled him out of the cab and threw him into the water.

Christine ran toward the lake, stumbling in the sand. Water splashed up her nyloned legs, shockingly cold, as she waded in. The men were hooting and swearing as they kicked the water in a tight circle, churning it frothy, their faces alight with glee.

She pulled her billystick from her purse and squeezed the leather handle, feeling the buckshot shift inside.

Something hit her right temple and knocked her into the waist-high water, her billy shooting out of her hand. Everything went black.

She took a deep breath, inhaled water and sputtered, then inhaled again, swallowing more water. Suddenly, she was yanked upright by her loosened hair. Stumbling on the uneven sand, she coughed out lake water. Fillingham grabbed her upper arm to steady her. He was hatless, and his blue shirt stuck wetly to his chest.

Behind him, Morano pressed Kevin Lamprey's face hard against the truck cab, slamming Lamprey's head twice before handcuffing him. The other two protesters waded toward Sergeant Bard, who was yelling at them from shore. Sergeant Bard grabbed the first young man and pushed him down on his knees, then kicked him in the back so he landed flat on his stomach with an "Ooomph." Kneeling heavily down on one knee, the sergeant wrenched the man's arms back and handcuffed him. The other protester quickly lay down beside them and was handcuffed. Sergeant Bard barked at the two to get up, and they rose awkwardly to their feet. Morano and Sergeant Bard walked the men up the beach back toward the half-demolished house.

Christine wiped the wet hair out of her face. Her hand came back bloody.

"Where's the truck driver?" she asked Fillingham. He shook his head, his blue eyes widening.

She plunged underwater where the circle of men had stood, her arms and legs spread-eagle, feeling for his body. Coming up for air, she saw Fillingham dive into the water several feet away.

She submerged and resubmerged, her breath holding for fewer and fewer seconds. Although she tried to be methodical, search a section at a time, the lake was cloudy from the stirred-up sand, and she couldn't always tell where she had searched. She ventured farther into the lake, her feet sinking in the soft bottom as she scanned the top of the water.

Something dark bobbed at the surface and disappeared. There! There it was again. Christine dogpaddled toward it, never looking away, her arms and legs churning the water.

She swam to the spot, circling. Something banged her shoulder, and she lunged for it, submerging. It was him. She rolled him onto his back, grabbed the collar of his shirt, and started to swim back to shore. She kept sinking and then kicking up for air, then submerging again as she pulled his weight. A flicker of fear tickled her gut as she tried to touch bottom but couldn't. Fillingham surfaced beside her and held the man's face above water as they swam toward shore. When she felt sand under her toes, she grabbed the man under the armpits and Fillingham lifted the driver's legs. They stumbled toward the shore and dumped the construction worker on the beach. His mustached face was gray and still. He looked like a morgue photograph.

Fillingham kneeled on the sand and thumped on the driver's chest with his palms. Christine stood panting beside them, trying to catch her breath, counting Fillingham's compressions. Sixteen. Seventeen. Eighteen.

The driver's face grimaced, then gray liquid projected out of his mouth, over his workman's navy shirt now darkened to black. Fillingham quickly turned him on his side. The driver finished vomiting onto the sand and lay gulping air, eyes closed.

"Thank God," she said. She looked toward the demolition site, looking for Sergeant Bard, scanning for the boxy outline of an ambulance or fire engine.

Fillingham looked up at her: "You need a doctor."

"I'm okay," she said, although her forehead tingled like it was on fire. And she was having trouble seeing out of her right eye. "The girl—Ginny. Did the firemen treat her?"

He looked down at the sand. She waited, but he wouldn't meet her eyes.

No. It couldn't be.

Ginny Rogers was dead.

Chapter 3

"Help's arrived," Fillingham said, waving to someone behind Christine.

She turned toward the sound of an engine droning. A large wooden boat charged toward them from the west, a Canadian flag snapping from the transom, a Harbor Police officer standing in the cockpit while another shadowy figure steered the craft inside the windowed cabin.

The engine idled as the boat neared. Fillingham pointed to the truck driver lying on the sand, chest rising and falling in quick pants. The officer in the boat's stern opened an equipment cabinet and extracted a wooden rescue board.

The boat cut its engine. Fillingham waded into the water, grabbed the backboard from the officer and held it over his head as he walked it in and placed it alongside the truck driver. Kneeling, Christine and Fillingham lifted the driver onto the board. He was dead weight. They buckled him in at the knees, waist and chest.

Christine stood up and immediately toppled over, falling to one knee, fingertips digging into the sand. Gosh, she was dizzy. She tried to push back onto her heels to right herself, but she couldn't. It felt like her elbows were made of spaghetti.

"Stay there," Fillingham said. He motioned to the boat.

The Harbor Police officer slid into the waist-deep water and headed toward them.

Christine watched the two men lift the stretcher off the ground, using the slots around the board edge as hand holds. "Give me a second," she said.

They ignored her and waded into the water, the board wobbling as they raised it to keep the driver dry. When they reached the boat, they slid the backboard onto the hull's edge. Fillingham held it there while the officer hauled himself into the vessel. The construction worker disappeared into the belly of the boat.

Fillingham returned to shore. "You're next," he said to her.

She couldn't leave now. She had to help with the injured, isolate the accident scene, check on Ginny, in case Fillingham had made a mistake. She shook her head. A bolt of pain shot through her temple.

"Hey, PW, over here!" a loud voice called. She turned. A man in a wrinkled suit held up a camera, and Christine blinked at the blinding flash of light, white spots dotting her vision.

"What the hell!" Fillingham stomped across the sand to the man holding the heavy black camera, its round, silver flash as big as a grapefruit. Fillingham stood chest-to-chest with the photographer, livid, police uniform clinging wetly to his lean frame. "This is a crime scene," Fillingham said. "No civilians." He pressed a finger into the man's chest. "Unless you want me to arrest you right now for interfering with an investigation, get the hell away!"

The man's mouth twitched. He was five inches taller than Fillingham and looked fifty pounds heavier, but he turned and walked across the sand to the boardwalk, his equipment bag slapping his leg.

Fillingham watched him for a few seconds, then turned back to Christine. "You're going to the hospital," he said, motioning with his thumb to the police vessel.

"We have to find out what's going on," she protested. "Assess injuries. Take witness statements."

Fillingham retrieved his utility belt with attached radio and gun holster from underneath a shrub. Unlike Christine, he must have hidden his gear before running into the water. Depressing the black button on his radio, he said, "Dispatch, 52-25. PC Fillingham. Harbor Police has arrived at 42 Lakeshore. Requesting transportation of injured civilian and injured PW to the mainland. Over."

Before Dispatch responded, a crackle: "52-25. Sergeant Bard. Detail injuries of PW. Over."

"52-25. PC Fillingham. Head injury, contusions, no obvious broken bones. Walking ambulatory. Over."

"I don't need to go to the hospital," Christine repeated, still on one knee. She wanted to tell him to give her a second, then she would be able to return to the demolition site to help, but she couldn't get the words out.

Fillingham ignored her.

The radio crackled. "Dispatch to 52-25. Civilian and PW transport verified via Toronto Harbor Police THP 11. Ambulance directed to the ferry dock. Toronto General Hospital notified you are en route. Over."

Fillingham hung his utility belt over one shoulder and pulled her to her feet. She staggered and leaned heavily on his other shoulder.

"Jesus, you weigh a ton," he said. He grabbed her under her armpits and steered her toward the water. She tried to help, make her legs walk underneath her, but her knees kept giving out. They stumbled the first ten feet until they were waist-deep and he could pull her along in the water. Looking down, she realized she no longer had her purse or shoes, her soaked radio sat ruined in its holster and her nylons were shredded like webbing around her legs.

The officer in the boat helped her up the metal ladder overhanging the hull; her knees buckled inside the cockpit, and she slid down on her side beside the truck driver, like a netted fish. Fillingham pulled himself into the craft, and the two men stood in the cockpit, water pooling in the hull from their wet clothes. The engine gunned. Christine rolled toward the driver as the boat turned. It straightened and accelerated; she was jostled as the boat smacked the waves.

Her stomach churned. She tried closing her eyes, shutting a curtain on the day's clear blueness to curb the nausea, but she kept getting flashes of Ginny's bent leg, of her troubled final look. Christine swallowed. She tasted bile and the metallic tang of blood. Groaning, she pulled herself up by a metal cleat on the gunwale, leaned over the side and vomited into the foamy wake, her long brown hair whipping around in the wind. Someone held on to her by her belt as she leaned over the side and threw up twice more. Finished, she slid back down to the floor and closed her eyes.

She woke up in the ambulance as the attendant listened to her heartbeat, the two of them connected by the blue tube of his stethoscope. Behind the attendant, Fillingham came in and out of focus.

"What day is it?" the attendant said.

She knew what he was doing—a neurological check—and it was a simple question. No problem answering. Except that her blurry vision was confusing her thinking. What had he asked? About the weather? Her mom's name? The siren wailed; she couldn't think with that sound penetrating her skull.

"It's sunny," she said during an ebb in the siren howl.

The attendant turned and said something to Fillingham in a low voice.

Inside the hospital, a nurse directed the three of them into a cubicle in the emergency ward. They lifted Christine onto the narrow bed, and the nurse shooed the men away. After horseshoeing the curtains around the bed, the nurse approached Christine with scissors.

"I'll cut off your clothes," she said. "It's easier."

"No," Christine grunted. Police officers were granted one uniform every two years. And she had to have hers custom-made because of her height. "I can take them off."

"They're pretty stained," the nurse said.

Christine looked down at the sodden wool, the dark blotches on her tunic and skirt—bloodstains. "That's okay." As the nurse helped her out of her clothes, Christine squeezed her eyes closed against the pain. Grunting, she shifted sideways so the nurse could wriggle her skirt off. The nurse dressed her in a faded blue hospital gown, easing her arms into the sleeve holes the way Christine used to dress Donna for bed when her sister was younger.

Christine lay back exhausted, her mind flickering to the demolition, replaying ten-second reels of the morning: Sergeant Bard running toward her; Ginny's boyfriend grabbing her sleeve saying, "Help her"; Kevin Lamprey and his buddies gleefully kicking the submerged truck driver; Ginny lying broken on the grass, like a daisy run over by a lawn mower.

Christine swallowed, closing her eyes to stop the replay. She raised a shaking hand to her face and felt the swollen lump of her eye.

"Don't touch," the nurse commanded. "I'll clean you up before the doctor comes in." She inclined the bed.

Christine felt the nurse clasp her wrist, pressing her pulse point. She smelled the alcohol before it touched her face. Stinging. Stinging. Christine sucked in her breath. She must have a cut above her right eyebrow. Her eyes watered in response, and she blinked the tears away. Her head pounded. The nurse spoke to Christine, but her words sounded muted, like she was speaking underwater.

The police force's physician came in and introduced himself as Dr. Jim. He was energetic and cheerful, used to attending to the broken bones and minor injuries police officers were prone to when on street patrol. He asked her to follow his finger, say her name, the new prime minister's name. When she whispered, "I have a headache," he scribbled something on a clipboard, patted her on the shoulder and left with a swish of the curtains and a reminder he would check on her after her X-ray.

The nurse brought another blanket and tucked it under her armpits. "This will make you feel better," she said, holding up a syringe, then inserting the needle into a blue vein in the V of her arm. Everything got softer, blurry. Christine yawned. God, she was tired. And hollow—like an emptied-out house. Like the Whitmores' home, with the hole in the second-floor wall and furnishings tumbling out like it had been disemboweled.

"Christine. You awake?"

Christine blinked against the glare of the fluorescent lights overhead. A policewoman leaned toward her from her perch on a wooden chair beside her hospital bed. She looked so serious, shaped brown eyebrows knitted together over wide, brown eyes, red-lipsticked mouth pulled into a frown.

"Julie!" Christine said, surprised to see her friend from the Women's Bureau.

Julie smiled, her lips lifting into a cupid bow.

Pushing herself upright, Christine froze as a bolt of pain in her temple immobilized her. She fell back against her pillow with a groan.

"Glad to see your brain is still working," Julie said. "You had us worried there for a bit. Hold on." She got up, opened a slice of curtains and stuck her head out. "Sailor boy!" she called. "She's awake."

Christine gingerly touched her face. Her right cheekbone felt so tender, like it was broken. A lump of gauze covered her right eye; a cotton pad was taped above her eyebrow near her hairline. They must have bandaged her cut, the one that bled all over her face and uniform, after stitching it. She tried to comb her fingers through her hair, but the strands were knotted with sand and crusted blood. The rest of her body—her arms and legs—were sore. The bottoms of her feet felt were scratched, cut on rocks after she lost her shoes. But nothing seemed broken. Just her face.

Julie closed the curtain and came to the head of the bed, arms crossed. "You look like hell."

Christine regarded her pretty friend, who always kept a tube of crimson lipstick tucked into her uniform pocket. "How did you know I was here?"

"Your mom called the Women's Bureau."

Christine frowned. "Why?"

"Someone told her there was an officer down on Toronto Island. She couldn't get an answer from the Center Island Police Station or Dispatch, so she called the WB to see if we had heard anything. Gail, Sarah and I asked if we could check on you in person. Sergeant Baker agreed to free one of us, so here I am." Julie touched Christine's arm. "Do you want your mom? We could send an officer to pick her up."

Christine shook her head, then stopped when it caused her face to throb. She didn't want to scare her mom, plus it was Phyllis's day off. "Tell her I'm fine. I'll see her later at home."

"Christine, I'm not sure Dr. Jim is going to let you—"

"Knock, knock," a male voice said from behind the beige-and-white-striped curtain.

"Come, in," Julie sang, tucking her white-blonde bob behind one ear.

Fillingham pulled back the curtain. A hefty, dark-suited police officer accompanied him—an investigator. Both men looked at Julie, who gave them a wide, red-lipped smile.

Fillingham turned his attention to Christine. "Do you know who I am?" he said.

She surveyed his gray track pants and white t-shirt, short blond crew cut, light blue eyes and honey tan. He must have found a change of clothes. He looked like an ad for a college athletic program.

"My new tennis coach?" she offered.

Julie burst out laughing. The investigator's lips twitched.

Fillingham smiled. "I don't think we were formally introduced. Geoffrey Fillingham. I've been working the Island for the last year." His expression turned grave. "Nothing like the mayhem of today."

Immediately, Christine envisioned the excavator claw tearing through the Whitmores' roof, the frantic diving of the crowd as the dump truck rumbled through. She swallowed. "Christine Lane. Thanks for helping with the truck driver, for resuscitating him." She paused—talking was tiring. "And for getting me in the boat. I still think I should have stayed—to help the injured. To secure the scene."

The tall man announced, "Investigator Ron Allen, 52 Division." His dark hair was threaded with gray and combed to the side, his paunch held up by a black leather belt. "I need to speak with PW Lane alone."

Julie stood. "I'll come back later," she told Christine. With a wave of her fingers, she followed Fillingham out.

Bracing herself, Christine knuckled both fists into the mattress to push herself up.

The police investigator asked her to recount the day's events while he scribbled into his memo book. When she had finished her summary, he bombarded her with questions, asking some twice: "When did the demolition start? How did you get there? What did you see? What were the other officers doing? Where did the truck come from? Why had the crowd gathered? Did you see the deceased get injured? What were you doing when the truck drove through the crowd? Describe the actions of Kevin Lamprey." She tried to answer honestly, to be clear, not to worry if she responded with "I don't know" to too many questions. Recounting the demolition scene was the hardest. She had to look away, staring at the curled fold of striped curtain as she described the excavator noise, the crowd streaming into the yard, Sergeant Bard pushing her out of harm's way, the truck chugging into the water. Her voice thinned to a whisper as she described Ginny's injuries and her final look before her eyes closed.

A nurse stepped into the room to take Christine to X-ray, and she exhaled in relief. The investigator pocketed his memo book and said he would talk to her later. Eyes closed against her sledgehammering headache, Christine lay back on the pillow. The nurse unlocked the wheel brake and rolled her bed out of the cubicle. Opening her eyes, Christine spied the clock above nurse's station. Three o'clock. *Oh, no!*

Knifejacking to a sitting position, she grunted against the pain. "I have to phone home," she said to the nurse navigating her bed through the emergency ward. Christine had promised to take Donna and Wayne to the candy store after school.

"Let's have your head looked at first," the nurse responded as she continued walking.

"Stop!" Christine said.

The nurse continued pulling the bed. "They're waiting for you in—"

Christine swung her legs over the side of the bed.

"Whoa, whoa!" The nurse stopped.

Fillingham and Julie appeared beside the trolley. "What's going on?" he said.

"I need to call home. Now." Christine had meant to sound commanding, but her voice trembled. Why wouldn't they let her use the phone?

Julie touched her leg and turned to the nurse. "I'm sure the X-ray can wait another minute or two. We have a policewoman who needs to let her mother know that she's okay after being injured on the job. I'm sure that's not too much to ask." Julie smiled at the nurse, her large brown eyes level and unmoving.

The nurse hesitated, then nodded. "Fine. Wheel her to X-ray," she gestured toward a hallway, "when you're done."

"Where can we find a phone?" Fillingham said. The nurse pointed to the wall beside the desk counter. Christine lay back down, and Julie pulled the trolley beside the black wall phone, dialed the number and handed Christine the receiver.

"I'm fine. I'm fine," Christine said to her mom on the line. "Just a bump on the head. No, no. Don't come down—they're checking me out. Don't worry, I'll be home soon. Mom, I told Donna and Wayne I would pick them up after school and buy them penny candy at Farley's. I won't make it in time. Can you do it?"

She turned her shoulder away from Fillingham and Julie and spoke in a quieter tone. "It's twenty-five cents. You don't have to use your bingo money. I'll pay you back. Just meet them at the school and take them to Farley's."

She held out the phone for Julie to hang up, not meeting her friend's glance, and turned to Fillingham. "You two can go. I'm fine."

He shook his head. "Sarge told me to stay here with you. It's protocol with officer down."

"I wasn't down," Christine said, "just—"

"You were floating unconscious on the lake," he said. "I thought the brick had killed you."

"A brick hit me?"

He nodded.

"Who threw it?" Christine said.

He shrugged. "I saw it sail through the air, but I didn't see who tossed it."

"She needs to get to X-ray," Julie said. She gave Fillingham a sideways look. "Coming?"

He grinned. "Absolutely."

Julie and Fillingham grabbed opposite sides of the trolley and rolled it forward.

"She weighs a ton, you know," he told Julie. "I had to lift her into the boat." A smile played around his lips. His teeth were so straight, so white, they didn't look real in his golf-tanned face. He and Julie were like a couple from an Eaton's advertisement.

"She's all muscle and brain," Julie said in a loud stage whisper.

Christine frowned. "I'm right here."

"A bit staid," Julie added, patting Christine's leg under the blanket, "but we love her anyway."

"Listening to you two is worse than a brick in the head," Christine mumbled. It was like being stuck in an episode of *The Dating Game*.

"Is she always this testy?" he asked Julie.

"Pretty much," Julie responded. She outlined a square with her two index fingers.

Christine wished they would both go away. She didn't have the energy for banter after this morning's events, and her head was splitting. Why hadn't Gail or Sarah come? They wouldn't flirt with policemen. Sarah was married, and Gail didn't seem interested in men. "I'm sorry I'm not the life of the party." Her tone was sarcastic.

"You're forgiven," Julie said. She looked over at Fillingham. "How else would I have met the Island's finest?"

Christine closed her eyes as Julie and Fillingham's laughter echoed in the narrow hallway.

When the three returned to the emergency ward, Fillingham left to check on the truck driver.

After settling Christine back in a cubicle, Julie pulled out a compact and examined her heart-shaped face in the mirror. "You may have to stay in the hospital for a few days," she said as she blotted her nose.

Christine stared at her. "I can't do that."

The compact snapped closed. "Christine, your siblings have a mother."

Christine felt her face warm. "She needs my help."

Julie said, "Dr. Jim will be by in twenty minutes. Talk to him about how long you want to stick around, but I don't think he'll be happy about you leaving. If you do get discharged, I'll have to sneak you out back."

"Why?"

"There's a horde of reporters and photographers camped outside the emergency entrance."

"What?" Christine said.

"You know those newspaper guys: Jack Brace, Ken Talbott. They listen in on the police frequency. Officer down—a PW down—that's big news."

Humiliating, Christine thought.

"Plus," Julie's face sobered, "that poor girl died. Did you know that she's Daniel Rogers' daughter—the TV newsman? Geoffrey said five other people had broken limbs or contusions. And there's the driver who almost drowned. The demolition is a big story."

The curtains tugged open. Fillingham entered. "Hello again."

"How's the truck driver?" Christine said.

"He looks better than you do."

Christine glared at him with her good eye. Was everything a big joke with him?

He pulled up a chair beside Julie. "No brakes on the truck. He started it up, put it in gear, drove ten feet, tried to brake—nothing. He pumped and pumped, but the truck kept going."

"How about the parking brake?" Julie said.

Fillingham shook his head. "He said that was shot too."

"Do you believe him?" Christine said. But she remembered the driver's open mouth, his wide, frantic eyes.

"I do," he said. He pulled a handkerchief out of his pocket and showed them a rust-brown smear on the damp cotton. "The truck trailed this all the way to the water."

"Where'd you get that?" Christine said.

"I saw the oily fluid on the grass after the truck went by, so I swiped it with my handkerchief. The cloth got wet in the lake, but the stain's still there."

Julie leaned in to touch the rusty-looking smear with her thumb, then held the material up to her nose. "Brake fluid," she said. Christine sometimes forgot that Julie was smart, because her friend spent so much time being pretty.

"His brake line snapped?" Christine said.

He raised his eyebrows. "Most likely cut."

The women looked at him.

"That makes Ginny's death intentional," Julie said.

"And a homicide," Fillingham added.

Chapter 4

Julie pushed Christine's wheelchair down the corridor toward the back of the hospital where the delivery and garbage trucks parked. Visitors stared at Christine's bandaged face as she rolled by in her men's hospital scrubs—the only clean clothes they'd been able to find that fit her. Her damp, stained uniform lay in a paper bag on her lap.

Outside, Julie had illegally parked her poppy-red Mustang beside a cleaning company truck.

As Julie opened the passenger door, Christine said, "I can get in myself." Holding on to the car door frame, Christine pulled herself up and out of the chair. She teetered; Julie grabbed her under the armpits and lowered her into the seat. Christine sat in the bucket seat with a grunt, her head resting against the red leather upholstery.

After running the wheelchair inside, Julie returned. "We'll fill your prescription on the way home." The engine growled awake.

"You're being so nice," Christine whispered, eyes closed. Julie was acting more like Sarah, who had been a social worker before joining the police force.

"It's hard not to," Julie replied as the car gained speed, "after the day you've had."

Christine didn't respond. She was using her mental energy to suppress her carsickness. After a few minutes, Julie pulled up in front of a row of stores on King Street.

"Stay put," she said.

As if Christine were going anywhere.

Ten minutes later, Julie returned with two paper bags. Extracting a bottle of pills, she handed Christine two chalky white tablets.

Christine obediently popped the pills into her mouth.

Julie showed her the open mouth of the smaller bag. "Gauze, antibiotic lotion, surgical tape, face makeup. And these." She pulled out a bag of caramel hard candies.

Christine managed a smile—her WB friends knew she loved butterscotch.

"You're all set." Julie placed the paper bags on the back seat with Christine's soiled uniform. "I know a good dry cleaner. I'll take him your uniform."

The drive home wasn't bad compared with the fatigue of shuffling up the path to her apartment and climbing the flight of stairs to her door. Christine hung on to Julie's elbow like an octogenarian being helped into church.

Julie knocked on Christine's apartment door. They heard voices inside and the door opened.

Donna stood in bare feet in a green t-shirt and shorts, eyes wide with alarm as she regarded her sister. "Teeny?"

"It's me," Christine said.

"Just a bit knocked about," Julie said. She gave Christine a gentle push and they followed Donna's pattering steps down the front hall into the kitchen.

Mom and Wayne stood behind the melamine table, her hands on his bony shoulders like a tableau of mother with son. "Did someone beat you up?" he said incredulously.

Donna stood beside her brother. The trio regarded Christine's bandaged face with horror.

Christine let go of Julie's arm and grabbed the back of the metal kitchen chair. "Just an accident—someone throwing stuff around. My head got in the way."

"Did you arrest him?" Wayne said, frowning.

"Don't worry," Julie said. "The bad guys are in jail." She turned to Christine's mom. "Hello, Phyllis."

Phyllis returned the greeting. Her mom took two quick steps and pulled Christine into an embrace, hugging her daughter around the middle.

It took a second for Christine to respond; she couldn't remember the last time her mom had given her more than a brief squeeze. Christine could feel her mom's ribcage under her palms, the thin wiriness that Donna and Wayne had inherited.

Phyllis coughed and stepped back. "I called the Center Island station; no one answered. Dispatch couldn't tell me a thing because you hadn't signed on to duty. Nobody even knew if you were on the Island."

"Everyone's safe now," said Julie. "Dr. Jim says it's a mild head injury, with a bit of bruising and a cut. Nothing broken. All Christine needs now is quiet and rest. Can everyone manage that?" She looked at Donna and Wayne, who both nodded.

"I picked up dinner, Phyllis," Julie continued. "Cold roast beef and potato salad. And soup for Christine." She handed Phyllis a brown paper bag of groceries.

Wayne grabbed a folding chair from the closet, and the five sat down at the kitchen table. Julie asked Phyllis about her work in the Records Department and then quizzed Wayne about playing first base on his baseball team. Donna sat mesmerized by Julie's quick laughter and the crimson gleam of her lips. When asked, Donna happily described her school volcano experiment and ran to get her sketch book to show Julie.

Christine listened with a small smile on her face, not really following the conversation, molars clenched against the throb in her forehead.

Julie refused to stay for dinner. "Got a date." She looked at her watch and stood up. "Better head out."

Christine shuffled down the hallway to walk her friend out, despite Julie's admonitions for her to stay put.

"You need to go to bed," Julie said. "Right now. That's an order."

"I will." She touched Julie's uniform sleeve. "Thank you. For coming to the hospital and driving me home. Picking up groceries and the pain medication." She swallowed, feeling tears welling.

"Stop sounding so surprised. The WB takes care of its own." Julie leaned in to give her a brief hug. "We're the Fearsome Four, remember." That was the moniker the four female cadets had given themselves when they first met at police college.

Christine closed the door and sagged against it. She could hear Julie's feet tripping lightly down the stairs.

There was the squeal of a water faucet. "Christine!" Mom called from within the apartment. "Bath!"

Julie must have said something to Phyllis, directed her to take care of Christine. On the count of three, Christine pushed herself off the door. Holding on to the wall with one hand, she walked herself around the corner into the lemon-yellow bathroom, the smell of lavender greeting her entrance. Her mom had used some of her birthday bath salts in Christine's bath.

Alone inside, Christine let her trousers drop onto the one-inch yellow and white tiles. With her fingertips, she carefully lifted her shirt off, mindful that the material didn't brush her face. She folded the scrubs over the towel rack, intending to wash and return them to the hospital. Her skin smelled like the lake, and she had a flashback to diving underwater, the choking fear as she searched for the truck driver. At least that part of the story had turned out. One piece of the day hadn't ended in tragedy.

She lay in the warm, lilac-colored water, her neck braced by her mom's inflatable pillow, her arms floating, legs and torso heavy, hearing her own deep, slow breathing. Her unfocused stare rested on the dainty yellow tulips painted on the border tiles, the corner tile chipped where Wayne had banged it with his baseball bat while practicing his hitting stance in front of the mirror.

A knock on the door—Mom asking if she was okay. Christine confirmed she was fine. She should hurry and shampoo her hair while she had the energy, while the painkiller was working.

Sliding down the tub, she let her tangled hair immerse in the water, gently turning her head back and forth to loosen the sand and blood, careful to keep her bandaged face dry. She drained the tub and then refilled it, glad that they only paid for heat, not water or electricity. After gently shampooing, she rinsed her hair in the water, then pulled the plug. Enveloped in a towel, she crouched on the bathmat, dizzy and hot.

In her room, she found an extra-large V-neck t-shirt and a pair of soft shorts in the dented wooden bureau she shared with Donna. Pulling them on, she raced against her dizziness and collapsed against her pillow, panting. After a few minutes, her breath slowed and her eyelids drooped, the hard edges of pain now softened by her medication.

Ginny's light blue eyes appeared in her thoughts, and Christine's eyes fluttered open. When Christine left Ginny's side to chase Kevin Lamprey into the lake, the young woman had died. Christine hadn't meant to let go of Ginny's hand—to abandon her....

In her dream, Christine ran down the dark, tunneled corridors of a high school, searching for something, rushing into locker bays, pushing open the heavy doors of the gym. She kept seeing movement out of the corner of her eye, a flash of red, but she never got close enough to see it, to find the thing she was seeking.

Christine woke up with a start. Donna stood at the bottom of the bed in her pajamas, her long mahogany hair pulled into two ponytails, staring at Christine with hazel, unblinking eyes.

"Hey," Christine said, slowly sitting up. She was tired, as if the running in her sleep had been for real, but the razor edge of her headache had disappeared, dulled to the heavy ache of a bruise.

"You look scary," Donna said.

"*You* look scary," Christine replied. She frowned deeply, imitating Donna, but stopped when a twinge of pain stabbed her forehead.

"I don't like that." Donna pointed at Christine's bandaged eye.

"How about you look at this side?" She turned her left cheek toward Donna.

"Mommy says it's bedtime," Donna said.

Christine checked the alarm clock on the nightstand between their twin beds: eight fifteen. "You got fifteen minutes to read before lights out. Is it Ramona tonight, or Dr. Seuss?"

"*You* read me a story," Donna said, her tone aggrieved.

Sometimes Donna was clingy, as if she recalled the numerous times her parents had left her at a neighbor's to go to the track when she was a toddler. Christine wondered if her sister remembered being shuffled into the bedroom closet for a game of Flashlight Patty Cake with her siblings as Phyllis and Eddie fought drunkenly in the kitchen. That was five years ago, just before Eddie left in a whisky-fueled, expletive-laden rant.

Donna walked over to the bookshelf that doubled as their night table and chose Dr. Seuss's *Green Eggs and Ham*. Cuddled side by side with Donna on her bed, Christine was glad she knew the story by heart; one-eyed reading made her nauseous.

After tucking her sister in bed, Christine closed their door against the soft twilight coming through the living room window. Mom was reading in the rust-brown recliner, its vinyl arms rubbed smooth with use. A white line of cigarette smoke rose from behind the *Modern Romance* magazine that had been given to her mom by a friend. Wayne was sprawled across the couch, watching *Get Smart* on the television.

"Bedtime soon," Christine said to him when he looked up. Mom had the other bedroom, so Wayne slept on the sofa couch in the living room. If you didn't check on him, he'd watch TV until midnight.

"Feeling better?" Phyllis lowered the magazine into her lap.

Christine nodded and sat down on the end of the couch near her mother's chair.

"You look like hell."

"Mom! Language." Christine looked at Wayne, who was smiling at something Maxwell Smart was saying to Agent 99.

"You do." Phyllis dropped her magazine to the floor, the pages open to an illustration of a woman with a blonde bob locked in the embrace of a sinister man in a suit. "I don't know why they called you in." She mashed her cigarette out in the ashtray on the coffee table. "Nothing like this happened at the Women's Bureau."

"Mom," Christine said, "I'm a police officer. Even the WB can be dangerous: drunks at the dance halls, teenagers high on drugs, the domestic calls." She had never told her mom about the time a homeless man hit her with a bat because he thought she was going to take his duffel bag. Or when the band of drunken football fans cornered her and Sarah in a dead-end alley.

Mom shook her head, the long gray-brown hair rustling over her shoulders. "They shouldn't call a PW into a riot. You're not equipped for that."

"I'm as equipped as the next officer."

Phyllis knew perfectly well that policemen were put out to pasture on Toronto Island: those near retirement, tired cops, alcoholic cops, cops who couldn't handle the streets. Officers who had made mistakes. Were they any better than her?

Christine said. "Experience on patrol is the only way to get promoted. To make more money." She paused, then added softly, "So we can pay George Ray back quicker."

Her mom looked away.

"Dr. Jim said I had to take a couple of days off," Christine continued. "I'll take it easy."

Get Smart ended. As usual, Agent 99 fixed her partner's fumbled defense of national security. Christine and Wayne moved the coffee table over to the side wall, and Mom pulled the sofa bed open. Wayne's sheets lay in a striped tangle on top of the mattress.

As she shook out the top sheet, her mom said, "If you're feeling okay, Christine, I might catch the last game of bingo."

Christine watched Phyllis tuck the sheet around the mattress corners. It would have been nice if her mom had offered to put Wayne to bed tonight, argue with him about brushing his teeth, make sure that he didn't turn the television back on. But bingo was preferable to the racetrack, and her mom's drinking was better now, too.

"If you're not feeling good, then I'll stay," Phyllis said, meeting Christine's glance. "Donna's asleep. Wayne just needs to hop in bed." She headed briskly toward the kitchen. "I'll warm up that soup Julie brought."

Christine wasn't hungry, but she made herself take a few sips of the hot broth before Phyllis headed out. After the apartment door clicked shut, Christine washed her dish, took a quick peek at her slumbering brother and then headed to bed herself.

The next day, Christine had the apartment to herself. Her mom had left at 6:15 a.m. for her morning shift at Records. Two hours later, Wayne and Donna set off for school. Christine was glad to close the door on all three. She was tired and cranky after spending the night on her back to avoid pressure on her face, constantly shifting to find a position that would allow her to sleep, even for a short time. Every time a stab of pain woke her, her mind ricocheted to the demolition. Only the quiet breathing of her sleeping sister soothed her into sleep again.

Christine went into the bathroom to replace her bandages, her hair brushed into a ponytail to keep it off her face. She removed the bandage covering the stitches at her hairline, revealing the black spider-like threads. Wincing, she peeled the tape from the gauze around her eye. Dropping the dressing in the sink, she stared agape at her reflection. The right side of her face was grotesque: bruised and lumpy, round instead of oval, her eye a swollen egg. Half-moon circles purpled both eyes, as if she had broken her nose. She didn't recognize herself.

Slowly, carefully, she rebandaged her eye and laceration.

Buzz. It was the front door intercom.

Who could that be? She walked to the intercom phone in the front hallway.

A male voice said, "Policewoman Christine Lane?"

"Yes."

"Sam Carmichael, *Toronto Telegram*. Can you describe the injuries you received yesterday on duty?"

Christine was silent. A reporter.

"You're the one who got hurt on Toronto Island, right?" he said.

"One of the injured," she answered reluctantly. She thought of Ginny's bent body, her boyfriend hovering over her. And Fillingham pumping on the driver's chest.

"Aren't you worried about your safety on the job?" he said.

"No." Her hand went up to her face, but she checked herself before her fingers touched her cheek.

"Do the incidents yesterday make you concerned about being a policewoman?"

"No."

"Is your job too dangerous for a woman?"

He sounded like her mother. No one asked a policeman if he thought his profession was too risky.

"I shouldn't be talking to you," Christine said. "Call police headquarters if you have any more questions."

"PW Lane, please…"

Slamming the receiver down, she winced at the noise. She restrained herself from peeking out the living room window to check if the newspaperman had gone.

As she sat at the kitchen table, waiting for the water to boil for tea, she thought about the reporter's comments. Not about being a female officer. But was it her fault she got injured? If she had been more alert, would she have noticed the thrown brick? Was her ineptitude responsible for her injury?

Maybe she should call her policewoman friend Sarah today. Or even Julie. They would understand how Christine was feeling. WB officers responded regularly to calls regarding victims of violence.

Sarah, who used to be a social worker, encouraged policewomen to talk about the tough shifts, saying it was helpful to acknowledge a terrible situation: a wife almost beaten to death by her husband or an elderly man found starving in a rooming house. Pushing down these experiences didn't improve their policing. It was better to talk so you could move on, get rid of the monkey on your back. Or you would end up drinking or angry or cynical, which was the case with too many policemen.

Ginny Rogers had been only nineteen, just five years younger than Christine. Christine remembered Ginny's boyfriend staring down at his injured girlfriend, his hands held to his face in horror.

Christine knew it was better to keep busy—it kept the flashbacks at bay. She washed the dishes that Donna and Wayne had left in the sink, her motions deliberate and careful. In a slow shuffle, she swept the linoleum floor.

The intercom phone buzzed again. She considered ignoring it, but the caller would keep buzzing. Better set them straight.

"PW Lane?" said a deep male voice.

"I'm not doing interviews," she responded.

"It's Deputy Chief Darlow."

She froze, her hand clawed around the white receiver. As a lowly constable, she never spoke with high-ranking senior officers, only viewing them from a distance at ceremonial parades and graduation ceremonies.

"I need to speak with you, PW. May I come up?" he asked.

After a pause, she said, "Yes, sir," and pushed the entry button.

This was bad. Very bad. A home visit by the deputy chief. Maybe they blamed Island officers for letting the demolition get out of hand. For not protecting the citizens.

She looked down at her faded denim miniskirt and the gingham blouse she had buttoned on this morning. Out of her police uniform, she felt naked. Vulnerable.

Rap! Rap!

At the front door, she peeked through the viewing hole. Deputy John Darlow stood on their door mat in full uniform. The three bars on his epaulets marked his rank as one of the four deputies.

She opened the door wide. "Sir!" Christine stood at attention.

He was several inches taller than her. Not lean—but fit, muscular, as if he played tennis. After examining her face, he said, "At ease, PW." When she relaxed her stance, he said, "Can I come in?"

He followed her down the front hall past the kitchen to the living room. His glance took in the faded mustard couch, scratched coffee table, television and old hutch laden with family photos and knickknacks.

At least the room was tidy, even if the furniture looked worn in the morning light. Christine and her mom liked things in their place. Wayne had folded the sofa bed away. Donna stored her games and art supplies in the wooden box by the living room window. Wayne's LEGO was packed into tubs on a shelf, and his sports equipment was crammed into the back of the front closet.

Deputy Darlow stepped into the middle of the living room, polished black dress shoes on the orange and brown braided rug. He glanced over at the school pictures of Wayne and Donna, the military photo of Christine's father and Christine's police graduation photo.

Christine cleared her throat. "Can I get you something, sir?" They had tea or water—meager offerings.

He shook his head. Christine gestured to the couch, and they sat down at opposite ends, the good side of her face toward him. The thinness of the cushion material embarrassed her—the corduroy rubbed flat from wear. She folded her hands in her lap, covering the band of skin that showed above her knees.

He stared at her for several long seconds.

She wished she had applied the makeup Julie had bought—toned down the livid purple under her eye and camouflaged her facial swelling.

"How are you feeling, Constable?"

She exhaled, relieved at the normalcy of the question. "A little sore, sir," she said, "but improving." She smiled tentatively.

A few more seconds of silence ticked away. Was he trying to assess her injuries in order to push her into desk duty? She pointed to her face. "It looks worse than it is. Dr. Jim said mostly bruising. A minor cut." She omitted the doctor's diagnosis of a mild concussion.

The deputy crossed one leg over the other. "How is it going?"

The question confused her. "The investigation? I'm not sure, sir. I haven't followed up with Sergeant Bard. Investigator Allen is in charge—"

"I mean, after a 10-79."

She blinked. Did he think she wasn't tough enough to handle a citizen's death? "I've seen quite a few sad situations at the Women's Bureau: domestics, abandoned children, child prostitutes; 10-79s."

"Yes, I've read your file."

That couldn't be good, she thought. He must be here for a reprimand. She had done something wrong during the protest, was unable to stop the crowd gathering. Should Island patrol have been better prepared for the demolition? Or was she in trouble for her injury?

Please don't make me go on leave, she thought. *Or dock my pay*. The next payment to the loan shark was Thursday.

Deputy Darlow reached inside his uniform jacket and pulled out a folded rectangle of newsprint, which he opened on the coffee table in front of them. "Have you seen this?"

She leaned closer to examine the photo on the front page of today's *Toronto Telegram*. A woman kneeled in the sand, arms wide in supplication, blood darkening one side of her face and down the front of her jacket. Her hair stuck out in tangled clusters, like an unhinged Lady Macbeth.

It was Christine.

In large letters, the headline read: "Can Women Really Serve and Protect?"

Heart fluttering in panic, she stared at the deputy. He was going to fire her.

He said, "Chief Clark sends his regards and best wishes for recovery. I'm sorry I missed you at the hospital yesterday—you were already discharged when I arrived."

Her hands clasped tightly in her lap, knuckles white.

"There is a lot of interest in the case," he continued, "because of the unfortunate death of Miss Rogers, the recognition of Daniel Rogers, the ongoing conflict between Toronto Island residents and Metro Council. And now this." He gestured to the newspaper. "You are under orders to refuse interviews."

Christine nodded vigorously. She didn't want to talk to reporters. If the deputy wanted, she would stand on her head, dance a jig, if it meant she could return to work.

His brown eyes locked onto hers. He tapped the photograph with his index finger. "This cannot happen again." They sat silently until Christine lowered her eyes.

He was giving her another chance. She wouldn't, couldn't mess up again.

He stood up, and she jumped up too, pulling her skirt down quickly. She wanted him to leave before he changed his mind.

At the front door, he turned, hand on the doorknob. "Have we met before, PW?"

She nodded. "You were the senior officer at my graduation ceremony, June 1964. Also," she paused, "you handed me the police application when I was working in Records."

Five years ago, a recruiting team led by Deputy Darlow, a staff inspector at the time, had walked through the civilian departments of the force, handing out brochures to female employees regarding the force's affirmative action mandate to hire more policewomen.

"This situation is my fault?" he said.

"No. Yes." Was he trying to be funny? "No, of course not, sir."

He raised one eyebrow, then turned and left. She closed the door behind him, her heart pounding, awash with relief. She had escaped the gallows, for now.

Chapter 5

Three days later, even Donna knew to let the intercom buzz and the telephone ring until Phyllis or Christine unhooked the receiver. Christine had stayed inside, not just because she looked like a gargoyle, but also to avoid the reporters hanging around the apartment building's entrance. Worried that her siblings might be bothered by newshounds, she made her mom walk them to school. But only one reporter had approached the trio and then immediately turned away when he spotted the kids.

Christine gave herself lots of time to get ready to go out. Dr. Jim had told her to take a week off, and then light duty for two weeks after that. Today, she intended to go into the station on her day off to thank Sergeant Bard for pushing her out of the truck's path and get an update on the investigation. The hammering headache that had clouded thought and impaired movement was gone. She was still tired, though, not just because she was sore, but also because her nightmares were riddled with the sound of machines and screams and the smell of motor oil.

Since she still looked like heck, Christine spent an hour in the bathroom before heading to the Island. While brushing her hair, she was careful to avoid the stitches at her hairline. She applied a thick coat of pancake makeup to camouflage the yellowing bruises and the black shiners circling both eyes. Her right eye, unbandaged, was droopy-lidded and bloodshot, like a lazy eye. She applied lipstick to match her heavy makeup. With so much face paint, she felt like a Las Vegas showgirl. An ugly one.

The waistband of her navy Capri pants hung loose; she hadn't felt like eating since the demolition. She packed two chocolate chip cookies in wax paper and an apple and donned a pair of sunglasses she had found in a kitchen drawer. Flattening the hem of her sleeveless cotton blouse with the palm of her hands, she was ready. Exhausted, but ready.

Christine exited her apartment building into the muggy morning, the bald yolk of the sun throbbing with June heat. Behind the green-tinted sunglasses, she scanned for reporters. The coast was clear. She hurried the three blocks to the streetcar stop on King Street, hedging close to the buildings and the rectangles of shade.

Midday, the streetcar schedule was irregular—it would take her an hour to get into work. As she waited, the heat from the asphalt warmed the soles of her shoes and sweat beaded her lip. Cars idled at the light, and her stomach lurched at their exhaust fumes.

Today, Morano and Pilkington were scheduled to work the day shift with their sergeant at the Center Island station. Pilkington was tall, quiet, mid-thirties with a receding hairline and an overbite. Sergeant Bard said Pilkington didn't like car patrol, so he was assigned permanent desk duty: answering phones, writing up incident reports, penning the day's activity log and buffing the wooden floor until it gleamed.

Morano was another kettle of fish. The first thing he had said to her before their first and only shift together was, "Look. A new piece of ass."

When she stared at him, he said, "Affirmative action slag."

Sitting beside him in the patrol car that day, she felt animosity seeping out of him like leaking motor oil. He was a woman-hater cop, the kind her colleagues had warned her about when she transferred out of the Women's Bureau, who complained about hiring a woman for a man's job and paying her the same wages to boot. In his mind, policewomen ruined policing and made policemen's jobs harder. The force needed brawn, not gossip and lipstick.

Morano's wife had phoned the station three times during his shift with Christine. When Christine answered the phone, Morano's wife berated her, shrieking, "What type of woman works alone with men? With my husband?"

Yuck. Morano would probably have something to say today if Christine saw him at the station: ask pointedly about Christine's injuries, assign her blame somehow, though he had been at the demolition too.

The streetcar was half empty, but the Center Island ferry was packed with families on their way to the amusement park.

She stood on the second-floor deck of the ferry near the rope equipment, the least crowded part of the boat, angling herself to avoid the wind blowing on her still-sensitive face.

"How are you, PW Lane?" asked a voice.

She turned, recognizing Mike Stanton, the ferry captain.

He shook her hand, pumping her arm several times.

"I'm fine," she said between pumps.

He kept their hands clasped. "We were worried about you."

"That's kind of you."

"Glad you're back." He leaned forward, blue eyes intense under auburn eyebrows. "We're not like that here, you know."

No one had been able to identify the person who threw the brick at Christine. Somebody in the crowd. Most likely Kevin Lamprey and his ilk, but the pandemonium that followed the truck's rampage meant they hadn't found a witness.

"I know." She swallowed. Gosh, she hadn't reached the police station, and she was already batting away tears. Pulling her hands gently out of his grasp, she said, "I'm sorry about Ginny Rogers and the injured Islanders."

His ruddy face turned pensive. "A terrible day. One of the saddest in my career, and I've been working the Island for twenty years."

With a nod, he turned around and disappeared into the throng of passengers.

After disembarking, Christine walked past Centerville and the streams of families eager for an afternoon of carnival rides, games and cotton candy and headed over the bridge. As she veered left, the police station came into view.

Darn. She should have taken a painkiller before she left home. She could feel the thump, thump, thump of her pulse underneath her stitches at her hairline. But she had wanted to be sharp in case there was a debrief of Ginny Rogers' investigation.

The doorbell tinkled as she opened the station door, notifying officers of a visitor's entry. She stopped in her tracks, staring. The counter that ran the width of the room was crowded with vases of flowers, potted plants, hand-written cards and ribboned boxes, like an oversized hospital room. Approaching, she spotted a note with her name taped to a wrapped loaf of banana bread. It said: *Thank you for your caring and bravery. We hope you have a swift recovery and return to Island patrol.* It was signed Mrs. Polotov, the old lady on Ward's Island with the lush garden, the one who offered officers tea when they were on patrol.

Pilkington's long face appeared behind a fern plant. "What are you doing here?"

"What's all this?" She gestured to the counter.

"You're not on duty," he said, stepping sideways to view her better.

"I know. I thought I would check in. Help you out at the desk for a couple of hours."

"You're not on the schedule anymore."

"What do you mean?" She lifted the levered section of the countertop and came through into the office. The schedule was thumbtacked to the cork bulletin board above a desk. She removed her sunglasses.

Pilkington was right. Her name was no longer there—for the entire six-week rotation to the end of July. How could that be?

She was returning next week. Had Deputy Darlow spoken to her sergeant?

"Where's Sergeant Bard?" she asked.

"With the investigators at the community center." He pointed eastward.

"I'll talk to him. Clear this up." She picked up a small box from the counter decorated with hand-drawn butterflies. "This is for me?"

He stared at her face, his upper lip curled in horror, exposing his protruding front teeth. "They really beat you up."

This was going to be a long day if everyone she encountered remarked on her injuries. She shook the box at him and repeated, "Is this for me?"

He gestured to the counter. "It's all for you. There's more stuff in the fridge: casseroles, meat pies, desserts." He paused. "Some of it's eaten. We thought you wouldn't..." His glance strayed up to the bandage above her eyebrow.

No one had expected her to come back to work. That was why she was no longer on the schedule. They assumed that after being injured and witnessing a 10-27, a death, she would quit, overcome by the brutality of the job. Or scamper back to the Women's Bureau.

She headed outside to the back shed where the emergency equipment was stored and tossed flares and ropes aside as she looked for a bike to ride. Her headache was making her short-tempered—she had to calm down before she met with Sergeant Bard and asked him about the schedule. Her boss needed to see her as a vital part of Island patrol, eager to return to work. And the investigators needed to perceive her as someone knowledgeable who could assist them with their case.

She pushed aside a sawhorse and a tower of pylon cones. *Shoot.* Nothing. She had spied a bike in here last week, not an official police bicycle, but probably one abandoned on the Island. None of the officers patrolled on two-wheelers. It wasn't dignified enough for them—they always drove the police car.

Fine. She'd get to Ward's Island on foot.

She hurried along the path, afraid she would miss an end-of-shift debrief by the investigators. Fifteen minutes later, the back of the community center came into view. Thank goodness. She was hot and uncomfortable in the midday sun. On the field, summer campers played parallel games of football, a small rubber football for the youngsters and an NFL-sized ball for the teenage supervisors. She wondered how the children could play in the heat. They must swim at Ward's Island Beach after their game.

To her right, three hundred feet away, concealed behind trees, was the Whitmores' plot of land. The hair rose on her arms as she pictured the flattened grass, the scattered furniture, the tire tracks. The house, was it demolished now? She shivered, trying to block the image of a broken Ginny from appearing in her mind. Later, when her head didn't hurt as much, she'd return to the demolition site to see if it helped her remember any details pertinent to the investigation.

After hustling up the steps of the community center, she pulled open the squeaky screen door. In the shaded, curtained room, five pairs of eyes turned to look at her. Fillingham and Morano stood facing the two suited investigators who were sitting on the edge of a long table, Sergeant Bard bracketing the far side.

Christine removed her sunglasses and stepped inside.

"What are you doing here?" Sergeant Bard said abruptly.

"I, uh, I'm checking in, Sergeant."

"Checking in?" Sergeant Bard responded. "You're not working today."

"I thought I'd review the schedule with you," she said.

"You're not working today," her sergeant repeated.

"Was she always this ugly?" the stocky investigator asked. He was bald, with weasel eyes. Beside him was Ron Allen—the tall investigator she'd met at the hospital.

Morano said, "Pretty much."

Laughter rippled around the room. Christine looked at Fillingham. His smile froze as their eyes met, then he looked away.

So that's the way they wanted to play. "I got hit by a brick, Morano," she said. "What's your excuse?"

The two investigators broke out in loud guffaws. Morano glared at her.

Stupid move, she thought. There were only seven regular Islander officers. It wasn't smart to make one an enemy.

"Out you go." Sergeant Bard pointed to the door.

"I wanted to ask about the investigation," she said.

"Out. Now!"

She turned on her heel and proceeded outside. When her sergeant met her at the bottom of the steps, she opened her mouth to talk, but he held up his hand.

"I'm not sure what you're trying to prove, coming to work like this." He pointed to her face.

"I feel fine."

He held up his hand again. "You do not have permission to talk, Constable, until I say so. Is that clear?"

She nodded, lips pressed together.

He crossed his thick arms and contemplated her. "What message does your face give the public?"

She remained quiet, assuming it was a rhetorical question.

"I'll tell you," he continued. "It's a marquee, an advertisement that police are not in control. That the bad guys got the best of us. That we didn't protect our womenfolk."

She didn't need protection.

As if he read her mind, he added, "You are walking proof that policewomen are not up for the job, as the *Toronto Telegram* aptly noted."

She bit her lip to stop a retort.

"Do you understand, PW Lane," he said, "that this is not about you? It's about how the Toronto Police Force is perceived." He nodded, giving permission for her to speak.

"If I were a man," she said, "I'd get a pat on the back for returning to work quickly after an injury."

"Get it through that thick skull of yours that you are not a policeman; you're a PW!" he roared. "Do you not see the problem that this creates? When I saw the dump truck out of control, all I could think about was that you were a woman and my responsibility. And I had to save you."

"Thank you for that, sir," she said. "I haven't had a chance to—"

"While I was saving you," he interrupted, stepping in close to her, "while I was pushing you aside, I wasn't saving Ginny Rogers."

Christine couldn't get her breath; it was as if he had socked her in the stomach. Again, she saw Ginny lying in the yard with her brown hair spread on the grass, leg bent, their eyes meeting.

"You look like a Saturday night punching bag," Sergeant Bard said, glance ranging over her face. "Go home."

Christine blinked away tears, her lower lip quivering.

"She saved the truck driver," a voice said.

Both looked up. Fillingham stood on the top step of the community center, the door closed behind him. He was hatless, blond hair parted to the side, the sleeves of his police shirt rolled up his forearms. How long had he been there? Had he overheard her conversation with Sergeant Bard? Christine winced in shame.

"What did you say, Constable?" Sergeant Bard asked, his voice hard and flat.

Fillingham descended the steps so the three formed a triangle. "I resuscitated the truck driver," he said to Sergeant Bard, "but she found him floating in the water. She's the one who noticed those hooligans pulling him from the truck. He'd be dead if it wasn't for her."

A few seconds ticked by. Sergeant Bard's face stained a darker hue of red. "If she's so goddamn heroic, Fillingham, why don't I make her your partner?"

Fillingham shook his head, half smiling. "I don't need a partner. I was just saying that—"

"I'll make out the new schedule today. Congratulations to you both." Bard turned to Christine. "Don't let me see your battered face for a week." He turned and stomped up the stairs, the screen door banging behind him.

Fillingham shook his head, staring at the closed door. Abruptly, he turned and went back inside the building, not looking at Christine.

She stood there for a full minute, staring at the wide windows of the community center that looked back at her dolefully. Then she turned and walked northward, the excited yells of the playing children a backdrop to her churning thoughts.

What had just happened? Was Fillingham now her partner? And was Ginny's death Christine's fault? Would Sergeant Bard have saved Ginny if he hadn't had to push Christine out of harm's way? Christine's chin trembled as she trudged toward the Ward's Island dock to take the ferry home. Her sergeant's comments made her like a murderer.

If she could keep it together for the ferry ride, for the streetcar home, control herself until she stumbled into her apartment, she would lock herself in the bathroom, turn the faucet on, sit on the toilet and let herself bawl.

"PW Lane!"

It was Mrs. Polotov, a long-time Islander, pushing an ice-blue bike toward her from the Ward's Island cottages.

Christine slowed but didn't stop. She couldn't talk to anyone. Even someone as nice as Mrs. Polotov, who had left her a get-well note and banana bread at the station. Christine had to get home.

"I'm glad I spotted you!" the Islander said as she intercepted Christine along the path. The old woman pushed the kickstand down with her sandaled foot and parked the bike.

"Oh, child." Mrs. Polotov planted herself in front of Christine. Her blue-veined hand gently touched Christine's hair above her ear. The old women's deep brown eyes pulled down at the edges with concern.

Christine coughed, her eyes looking everywhere but at Mrs. Polotov, then burst into a series of staccato sobs, her hand clamping over her mouth to shut herself up, to contain the bawling that shuddered her body.

"Oh, dear. Oh, dear. This way." Mrs. Polotov steered Christine by the elbow to a large log that overlooked the water east of the ferry dock. Shuffling blindly through her tears, Christine kept her hands over her face until she felt Mrs. Polotov pressing on her shoulders, and they both sat down on the tree trunk. Christine sobbed. A tissue appeared in her peripheral vision, and Christine took it and held it over her face.

Mrs. Polotov patted her back. "There, there. A terrible tragedy. So sad. We are all so sad."

Christine's sobs diminished to heaving breaths. She wiped her face with the tissue, streaking it with beige makeup and coral lipstick. After a minute, she said, "You're being so kind, but you should know. I'm responsible for Ginny Rogers' death."

Mrs. Polotov handed Christine another tissue from inside her sleeve, and Christine blew her nose.

"That's nonsense, dear," Mrs. Polotov responded. "It was a terrible thing to behold—a devastating tragedy. Our hearts are broken, but we all know that a truck killed our dear Ginny." She leaned forward and took Christine's wrists in her small hands, pulling Christine's arms gently so that they faced each other on the log. "The person who tampered with the truck, that's the one who killed our Ginny, meaning to or not. And that's the shame of that."

Word had gotten around fast, or someone else had noticed the red-brown liquid that had trailed across the lawn to the water's edge.

Mrs. Polotov held Christine's wrists for several seconds before letting go. "I was on my way to the police station to see you, actually. I heard you were asking about a bike, and this old girl was taking up space in my shed. I use my three-wheeler now for groceries and getting around, so I thought you might find it useful for work."

She stood up, then gently walked Christine over to the bike. The front basket and panniers were festooned with vines of multicolored plastic flowers, white tassels hung off the rubber hand grips and a red rose was hand-painted on the bike bell.

Mrs. Polotov gestured to the bike. "Five gears, baskets to carry supplies, padded seat; there's a hook if you want to pull a wagon."

Christine blinked back a new rush of tears. "It's—it's beautiful."

"You can take it now." She proffered the handlebar. "Which way you headed?"

"I'm going home." She straddled the bike obediently. Mrs. Polotov had raised the seat and handlebars so it was only a bit too short for Christine.

"Looks good on you!" Mrs. Polotov said. "Off you go, then." She patted Christine on the back, then stepped away.

"I'll drop by the police station first," Christine said, "pick up the things people brought for me. And thank you so much for the loaf."

"We Islanders take care of each other." Mrs. Polotov waved her off.

Christine pointed her handlebars west toward the Center Island station. She'd be darned if she was going to let the likes of Morano, Sergeant Bard, Pilkington or the investigators get their hands on her poppy seed loaf or hydrangeas. She'd clear out the fridge too, casseroles and all, even if it meant she had to make two trips.

Chapter 6

After a few days of afternoon naps and leisurely baths, Christine was restless. The lasagna and casseroles from the station had been refrigerated or frozen. She and her mom wouldn't have to cook for two weeks. The flowers and plants added splashes of color to the apartment and made her think of the kindness of Islanders each time she passed a bouquet.

Although she was sore and her facial injuries were still painful, it was difficult to heed Dr. Jim's recommendation to take it easy. It wasn't in her nature, and when she tried to relax and read a magazine or a book, the lines of text blurred. Even watching TV gave her a headache.

So between naps, she cleaned. She was slow and often broke into a sweat, her head pounding whenever she bent over, but she washed the kitchen floor, waxed the linoleum and wiped down the cabinets. While her siblings were in school, she vacuumed the living room and gave all the shelves and furniture a good dusting. Exhausted after each exertion, she would plop down on the couch and rest until she felt sufficient energy for the next task. She changed the bedsheets, getting Wayne to help carry the hampers of dirty linens to the basement, where she ran three loads of laundry. At night, she played Go Fish and Battleship with Donna and Wayne.

Wayne thought her injuries were cool. "You look like Terrell after fighting Muhammad Ali," he said. Donna was a bit of a concern. She hadn't been so clingy in years, since Mom's gambling days, and never seemed farther than an arm's length away from Christine when they were in the apartment together. If Christine went into another room, in a minute she'd hear: "Teeny?" Christine read stories with her sister, drew pictures, and played cards. Donna insisted Christine walk them to school, although they were used to doing it themselves when Christine and Phyllis were working, which meant Christine had used half the foundation makeup Julie had purchased. At least the swelling had gone done, and her right eye was fully open, albeit bloodshot.

On the morning of Ginny Rogers' funeral service, Christine polished her work shoes, inhaling the scent of black polish as she worked it into the leather creases, giving her Oxfords a final buff with the clean edge of a chamois. She carefully ironed flat the collar of her uniform blouse, then pressed a razor-edge pleat down the length of each white sleeve. After taking her uniform out of the dry cleaner's bag—Julie'd had it cleaned, and it was miraculously unstained—she slowly got dressed.

The service was at eleven. She'd ferry in for the funeral and stay on after that. Dr. Jim had given his approval for her to work the afternoon shift with Fillingham.

Christine had called the station that morning to get an update on the investigation and got an annoyed Pilkington at the end of the line. With his voice lowered to a furtive whisper, as if he were worried about being overheard, he replied that the police mechanic concluded the truck's brake line was cut with a hacksaw. The emergency brake wire was snipped as well. Whether the perpetrator meant to wreck the equipment or had purposely set out to endanger people was up for debate, according to Pilkington. Any which way, Ginny Rogers was dead.

The funeral was held at St. Andrew's by-the-Lake Church, a white clapboard building with brown Tudor edging and arched windows that had supported the Islanders' liberal Anglicanism for eighty years. The building had been moved fifteen years ago, floated on a barge to its current location beside a lagoon not far from the Center Island police station.

Arriving at the Center Island police station promptly at ten o'clock, Christine found it already crowded with the entire Island police staff: Pilkington, Sergeant Bard, Fillingham, Morano, Ulster and two older constables Christine hadn't met: Andrew Reynolds and Robert O'Donnell. They looked like thinner versions of Sergeant Bard, with ruddy complexions and salt-and-pepper hair.

The officers gathered on the civilian side of the counter, a few of them sitting on the benches that hugged two walls, others chatting in pairs, their backs to Christine. She overheard Fillingham tell Morano about a bonfire party he had broken up the other night. Fillingham's suit was freshly pressed, a knife-edge pleat down his pants. She wondered what he felt about their new partnership. Mentally shrugging, she reminded herself that she could not control his reaction. What she could do was focus her efforts on finding Ginny Rogers' killer.

Sergeant Bard stood behind the counter as if he were a blackjack dealer serving up the next high-stakes game. He cleared his throat and the room silenced, all eyes turned toward him. Their boss thanked them for their attendance and for offering their condolences to Ginny's family. Officers would be posted to the front and back of the church to protect the family from journalists, but word was that reporters and photographers were going to lay off out of respect for Daniel Rogers, a brother in the industry.

Sergeant Bard reminded them that the homicide case was active. Officers were to monitor the crowd, looking for strange or out-of-character behavior. The Identification photographer would be there in plain clothes with a zoom lens. The killer might attend the funeral to keep close to the drama. Intentional or not, Ginny's death was a homicide, a 222 according to the Criminal Code. And the investigators were betting that an Islander had done it.

"What about Kevin Lamprey and his friends?" Christine said. "Are we ruling them out?" Lamprey's father had hired a battalion of lawyers to defend his son against the charges related to the truck driver; it looked like none of the allegations was going to stick.

Sergeant Bard stared at Christine for a few ticks. Was he going to ignore her, like everyone else? She squared her shoulders and stared back. She had taken the time off as ordered and now she was back on the job for her scheduled shift. It was a legitimate question.

Eventually, he shrugged. "I haven't ruled out those spoiled sons of bitches." He scanned the room. "Let's keep an open mind and open eyes and ears during the funeral. For those on shift afterwards, Fillingham, Lane, you'll continue searching the community for the hacksaw that was used to cut the brake line." He checked his watch. "For now, it's time to head out."

Everyone shifted. The benched officers stood up, and the group exited the door in single file, except for Pilkington, who would remain on desk duty. Christine wanted to ask why Pilkington always stayed behind, but she was afraid her question would spur Sergeant Bard to switch her to desk duty instead. Most PWs assigned to police stations were destined to type reports, file and answer phones. She didn't want to be chained to a desk because she was female and could type eighty words a minute after her two years in the Records Department. And today, she wanted to pay her respects to Ginny and her family.

The group walked in pairs along the gravel pathway—Morano and Fitzpatrick, Fillingham and Reynolds, and O'Donnell and Ulster. It was a beautiful June morning, hot but dry and gusty, the buttercups and wild irises bordering the lagoon dancing with the morning breeze.

Sergeant Bard caught up to her.

"Sergeant," she acknowledged, hoping he would pass by. She kept thinking about their last meeting, his livid coloring revealing that he wanted to throttle her. The *Telegram* photo had gotten her in a lot of trouble—with the brass, with her mom, with Sergeant Bard. She couldn't afford to mess up. They had barely let her back on

Island patrol. Her goal was to remain low-key, under everyone's radar. Particularly Sergeant Bard's.

"How are you?" he asked.

Christine tried to read his expression, but he was staring at the straight backs of the uniformed officers walking in front of them. Did he want her to take more time off? She didn't look that bad any more—way better than last week when she saw him at the community center. Her cheekbone was slightly swollen, but the bruising was camouflaged and her stitches were covered in flesh-toned medical tape. One eye was still bloodshot, that was all. She'd used more pancake makeup this morning than she ever had in her life, and mascara and lipstick as well. There was no way he could send her home because of her appearance.

"I feel fine," she said, trying not to sound defensive.

"One time I got knocked in the head." He pointed to the top of his hat. "I had ringing in my ears for weeks. Drove me crazy."

Was he trying to be nice to her, after accusing her of being responsible for Ginny Rogers' death? She hadn't forgotten that allegation, despite Mrs. Polotov's protest that the person who had tampered with the truck shouldered the blame. Sergeant Bard and Christine walked on in silence, the shadows from the blowing trees shifting leaf patterns across their path.

"No more reporters or photographers?" he said, squinting at her in the sunlight.

Did he think she had invited the photographer to take a picture of her on her knees, blinded by her own blood? "No." She paused. "Deputy Darlow visited me at home to remind me to keep my counsel."

His eyes widened. "He did, did he?"

"I thought he was going to fire me," she said with a choked laugh.

"There's still time," her sergeant said. He moved ahead to join Parker and O'Donnell.

The church was packed, people spilling out of the propped-open doors, down the stairs and onto the grass. Tables covered in white linen were set up on the church lawn; collapsible chairs were set around the yard. Families handed off dishes of cold pasta, tuna casseroles and upside-down cakes to a team of women organizing the post-funeral refreshments.

Seats had been reserved for officers inside. Christine found hers in a pew midway down the aisle. Sergeant Bard sat up front, behind the rows reserved for family, while Fillingham sat in the back with the investigators. The rest of the officers were posted outside.

Ginny's white casket was set on the raised dais of the pulpit, flowers draped over it. Christine was glad it was closed. She did not want to see the pale, marbled face, Ginny's perfect frozen youth, a reminder, a rebuke that the police—Christine—had failed to protect her. It wasn't true, of course, that Ginny's murder was Christine's fault. She knew that. The killer had pushed the first domino piece by sabotaging the truck, which then became the murder weapon. But Christine had been right there—seen Ginny's final look—and felt the responsibility for the young woman's death like a stone weight around her neck.

Christine scanned the crowd: children buttoned into their Sunday best, some of the older women sporting hats and white gloves, men freshly shaved. A few spoke in whispers, but most were silent, children held in the noose of their mother's unsmiling embrace, fathers with small frowns between their eyebrows. Everyone's eyes were sad.

The investigators thought the murderer might be in attendance today, sitting amidst the congregation. An Islander who had killed one of their own. Did it make him feel powerful to see the pain he wrought? Or did he feel guilty? Were his eyes averted from the coffin, too?

Down two stairs from the dais, an enlarged photograph of Ginny sat framed on a wooden easel. She was smiling, freckles sprinkled across the bridge of her nose, blue eyes almost translucent, brown, sun-streaked hair blowing sideways in the wind. She looked younger, carefree, happier than when Christine met her waiting tables. Green flower stems wound around the easel frame, and sprays of purple and white freesias edged Ginny's photo. Beside the easel stood a cello and guitar, a lectern, a chair and two large ceramic pots filled with tall ferns.

Christine regarded the dark oak ceiling beams that contrasted the white walls, the stained-glass windows that narrowed to a point as if directing the eye heavenward. An ethereal stream of light reflected off the front face of Ginny's casket so that it seemed to glow, to radiate whiteness.

Three musicians entered the church from the back door and walked past the casket to stand beside the easel. The man with long hair picked up the cello and sat down in the chair. The gray-haired woman lifted a flute to her mouth, and the young woman in the flowing skirt placed a violin on her shoulder. Christine checked her watch. Five minutes until eleven. After a few taps of the violinist's foot, the trio launched into a classical piece. The chords swelled, filling the space, rising high into the air of the peaked roof, the tune at first airy and then melancholy.

"Excuse me."

Mrs. Polotov. Christine angled her knees sideways to let the older woman slide into the seat beside her, which had been reserved by the placement of a crocheted shawl. The Islander must have been helping with the food. Christine felt the warmth of a blush on her cheeks as she recalled blubbering in front of the older woman after Sergeant Bard chastised her and sent her home. How could Christine garner the locals' respect if she so evidently couldn't handle the job?

"You look much better, dear," Mrs. Polotov said, patting her knee with an arthritic hand.

Christine nodded but said nothing. Lucky for her, she had broken down in front of Mrs. Polotov and not Morano or her boss. Later, she would thank Mrs. Polotov again for the bike and her reassurances. For now, Christine had to be professional. She was attending the funeral as an officer. As part of an investigative team.

She would offer her condolences to the family, but her primary purpose was to help catch Ginny Rogers' killer.

When the performance ended, the two younger musicians sat down, leaving the older woman at the lectern. She nodded at the organist, who began playing the chords of a slow hymn. The congregation rose to their feet, songbooks in hand, joining the woman in singing "Abide with Me."

Daniel Rogers' family filed in from the far pulpit doorway. The singing continued with all eyes on the grieving father. He held his youngest son in his arms, both dressed in sober black suits, white shirts and dark gray ties. Surveying the families packed in the pews, the people standing five deep at the back of the church and the bodies pressed against the side walls, Daniel gave a small smile of acknowledgement. He paused at the casket, almost staggering to a halt beside the shiny-white, garlanded box. His wife came up behind him, holding the hand of a blonde girl who looked to be five as Daniel stared at the casket. After a minute, his wife tugged his hand, and the three stepped down from the dais to the front pew. An older woman, who looked to be Daniel's mother, followed the trio.

As the organist played the final chord of the hymn, Nancy Hamilton, Ginny's mom, entered the pulpit, a female friend on either elbow, followed by the minister. Nancy leaned back as she walked as if she attended against her will, clutching a bundle of dried leaves to her chest. Her wide brown eyes looked unfocussed, her glance darting from the parishioners to her ex-husband to the coffin. Christine wondered if she was high or medicated—but that thought was uncharitable. The woman was grief-stricken.

The minister walked over to the lectern, his flowing white vestments embroidered with black and red thread at the cuff and neckline. Nancy and her supporters sat down in the front pew on the right side of the aisle, Daniel's family on the left. Davy Morgan, Ginny's boyfriend, walked past Christine to the pew directly behind Nancy. Dressed in a black T-shirt, pants and cowboy boots, his eyes were hidden behind tinted sunglasses. She wondered why he hadn't dressed more formally. Or sat with either of Ginny's parents. Was there bad blood between them? Or maybe they couldn't handle each other's grief—Morgan had been right beside Ginny when she died.

Opening his arms wide, the minister welcomed the assembly. He seemed to know Ginny personally, naming the people the young woman had loved: her friends and family, her boyfriend, the coworkers at Clergy House, others she had babysat or befriended.

He spoke about Ginny as a young girl, her artistic talents, her roles as friend, daughter, student, employee, girlfriend and sibling. He acknowledged her love of the Island, not only its beaches, waterways, and gardens, but also her rootedness in its history, her pride in her family's ancestry, her desire to remain on the Island to live and work. Finally, he talked about the solace of God, when there seemed no reason or rhyme for a young woman to be taken away. How we find comfort in the God in all of us, our central goodness, as seen by the neighbors who brought food today, the musicians and singers who gave of their talent and the Island community who filled the pews. He concluded by inviting them to band together, to mend the hole Ginny's absence had created, to resew the material to make it whole once more.

The minister sat down in a chair at the back of the pulpit. The male musician rose, retrieved his guitar and introduced the next song as Ginny's favorite, Leonard Cohen's "Suzanne." As Christine listened, she thought the woman in the song sounded like Ginny: creative, free-spirited, living by the water. It surprised her that the church allowed a contemporary song. The funerals that Christine had attended featured prayers and hymns. As she reminded herself, Islanders were a different breed.

When the last chord sounded, two men walked up the middle aisle and turned to stand in front of Nancy Hamilton. The younger man, a broad-shouldered Indigenous man with braided hair, took the bundle of dried leaves Nancy held out to him. He lit one end with a lighter, and a line of pungent white-gray smoke rose to the ceiling.

Christine tensed.

"It's sage, dear," Mrs. Polotov whispered. "An Indian tradition that Nancy requested."

Christine nodded, relieved. The older man regarded the congregation and then spoke in his native language. In English, he said, "Oh, Creator. We light this sacred medicine to open the way for Ginny as she journeys from this island you have named Menecing to the stars in the sky. May her passage be safe."

The younger man held the bundle of burning gray-green sage up high to the peaked ceiling and then lowered it to brush the ground. Straightening, he offered the smoking herb up to each of the four directions, then placed the sage inside a shell dish on the coffin. Turning in unison, the men acknowledged Nancy with small bows and returned to their seats, the younger one glancing at Christine as he passed.

Daniel Rogers handed his toddler, who had been sitting on his lap, to his wife. He walked to the lectern and gave the eulogy.

The newsman was a skilled orator. He described Ginny's childhood on the Island with Lake Ontario as her backyard: swimming, biking, summer camp, beach fires and Saturday-night parties at the community center. In the winter, skating and ice sailing. A true Island brat—independent, opinionated and careful about the Island and its usage. He even got Nancy Hamilton to laugh when he recounted the Mother's Day when Ginny burned the pancakes so badly that their neighbor called the fire department about the black smoke streaming out their kitchen door.

"She was a talented artist and an avid animal lover," Rogers said. "And smart. Working at Clergy House was a way for her to stay on the Island, with Davy," he looked at Ginny's boyfriend, "and Nancy. She had other aspirations too, things she wanted to do with her life. She was trying to figure out the next steps."

He paused for a second and wiped a tear away. "Ginny's life wasn't perfect. Or necessarily easy. She didn't always want to talk to me, to be part of my life, as she was part of her mother's." He smiled at

Nancy, who was staring at him, silently weeping. "Ginny and I didn't see eye to eye, and I wish now I had worked harder at connecting. I thought it would blow over." His voice was tremulous. After a pause, he said, "I thought I would have more time. I knew we loved each other, that we would eventually work things out. And now she's gone." His voice caught on a sob. His wife stood, but he motioned her to sit.

"She was well loved," Daniel continued, "by two families, by her friends, coworkers and her boyfriend, by all of you Islanders who help raise our children. So today, hug your daughter, your mother or your friend, someone you haven't reached out to in a while. Hold them tightly. And let them know you want to connect, to be part of their lives. And work hard at it, harder than I did."

He reached into his suit pocket. "Ginny died trying to protect the community that she loved. She had this button pinned to her purse." He clipped the two-inch yellow button onto his lapel, featuring the outline of a brown house and the words *Save Island Homes.*

As if on cue, the congregation pulled out identical buttons from their bags, pockets and purses and pinned them to their shirts, blouses and suit lapels.

A red-haired waitress from Clergy House joined the musicians by the lectern and motioned for everyone to stand up. Accompanied by the guitarist and flutist, the waitress sang in a clear, powerful voice, "People get ready, for the train to Jordon." Christine recognized the gospel song, the one they played at Martin Luther King's peace rallies.

Congregants curled arms around each other's waists, swaying in the pews as they sang together.

As the song ended, Sergeant Bard turned and met Christine's glance, eyebrows raised.

This tragedy, she thought, the demolition, the fight with Metro Council, it hadn't ended. Ginny was now a martyr to the cause—her death the battle cry.

Chapter 7

After giving her condolences to the family, Christine mingled with the congregation outside, introducing herself to Islanders she had not yet met and fielding concerns regarding her injuries. Many had seen the *Toronto Telegram* photograph. An occasional low rumble of laughter erupted from the subdued group as people filled plates with jelly loaf, deviled eggs and potato salad. A line of people sipping lemonade stood in front of a display of Ginny's beadwork, macramé and paintings. A family friend had made a collage of photographs of Ginny: as a toddler, skating on the Inner Harbor; with her mom at a Gala Day bonfire; as a high school graduate holding a dozen crimson roses; paddling a canoe with Davy Morgan.

There were no reporters in view. The Identification photographer must be concealed as well. Daniel Rogers had agreed to be interviewed at Mount Pleasant Cemetery on the mainland after Ginny's interment; the journalists were keeping their pledge to grant the family privacy until then. Daniel and his wife Bianca stood by the church stairs, greeting people for forty-five minutes after the service, then left with most of the crowd for the mainland gravesite.

Each person Christine spoke with during the reception had a nugget to share about Ginny: how she had won the three-legged race every year in camp. At sixteen, Ginny had launched her own art show in the community center. Last year, she fostered a dog for the Humane Society. How she was a helpful companion to her mom.

Nancy Hamilton fluttered around the yard in a white, lacy cotton dress, her face a pasty contrast to her tanned arms. She paused often to have a brief conversation with an Islander, allowing the person to hold her hand or give her a hug before moving on. As she approached, Christine could see her wide, unfocussed eyes and twitching fingers. Christine had worked enough dances and had searched enough drug addicts and prostitutes to recognize the dilated pupils and distraction. Whether it was drugs or booze or a combination, Nancy Hamilton was on something. Christine would ask Sergeant Bard if Nancy had someone to take care of her, a boyfriend or sister, like Daniel Rogers had with his wife. Nancy was unraveling.

Christine spied Fillingham chatting with two young women in short skirts and big Jackie Onassis sunglasses.

"Excuse me, Constable," Christine said.

He turned, his smile slackening.

"I'll see you at the station at 2:45," she said.

After a slight incline of his head, he turned back to the women.

Only a quarter of the original congregation remained; most of the Islanders had dispersed to the cemetery or had gone home to gather in smaller groupings. Nancy was nowhere to be seen.

Christine checked in with Sergeant Bard and then hurried back to the station to retrieve her bike, intending to patrol on her own before shift. As she rolled Mrs. Polotov's bicycle out of the shed, she smiled—her first smile of the day, it seemed. The bike was a silly thing, like a banana split with all the toppings—the plastic flowers and tassels, the snowflake-blue color and painted bell. It was so unlike Christine, personally and professionally, more like something Julie would ride with pride. But it marked her as a true Islander, and darned if she wasn't going to use it in the spirit it was given. The added benefit was that no policeman would ever borrow it.

She pedaled back past the church, where a small group of women were storing leftovers in plastic containers and men were stacking chairs, heading toward Ward's Island ferry dock. Steering south, she retraced her path on the day of the demolition, from the point where she had grabbed the bike resting against the tree, past the community center, tennis court and lawn bowling green. The field on her left, usually dotted with summer camp children or picnickers on a weekday morning, was empty except for a single family sitting under the shade of the big willow.

Christine's shoulders tensed as she steered onto the wooden boardwalk, planks clacking underneath her tires. Her fingers gripped the rubber handlebars tightly. Eleven days ago, she had ridden this path through a throng of alarmed Islanders heading to the Whitmores'. She could see the demolition site ahead. Muddy tire tracks zig-zagged across the wooden boardwalk. To her left, deep grooves gouged the sand where the tow truck's tires had dug in for traction to extract the dump truck from the lake.

When she reached the Whitmores'—or what used to be the Whitmores' and now was Metro Council property—she set her bike down on a lump of turned-over sod. This must be what war looked like, what Vietnam looked like with its bombed, pockmarked fields and villages. The Whitmores' house was gone, leaving a rectangular scar of soil embedded with broken bricks. In the corner was the rock foundation of a demolished fireplace. Blackened timber dusted with gray ash lay in the yard on a scorched circle of grass—the residue from the burned studs and beams. The rest of the lawn was a lunar landscape, mud and churned grass and the partially buried yellow rope that had been used to cordon the crowd.

In front of a row of hemlock trees that separated the yard from the neighbor's was a colorful collection of stuffed animals, flowers, candles and photos. A makeshift memorial to Ginny.

No one was around—investigators, construction workers, Islanders or gawkers. Christine exhaled the breath that she had been holding, letting the sadness wash over her at the destruction of the Whitmores' home and the tragedy of Ginny's death. The young woman had run over to the Whitmores' property from Clergy House after hearing about the demolition, clasped hands with other

Islanders in affirmation of their right to call the Island their home, a place where her family had lived for almost a hundred years.

Any sign of work by the investigators—chalking, measurements or evidence markings—had disappeared under the weight of machines and emergency vehicles. Christine crouched in the middle of the yard, the heels of her Oxfords sinking into the mud, and placed her right hand down on a mound of dirt in the area where Ginny had fallen.

The last thing Christine had said to Ginny as she kneeled beside her was: "Help is coming. Hang on." But Ginny hadn't received help. They had been too late. After gazing at the sky and the gulls flying overhead, Ginny's eyes had closed like blinds, like a shuttered window.

Christine pressed her hand into the soil and made a promise to Ginny to figure out what happened that day. How it went so wrong. And who was responsible for the truck tampering that caused the young woman's death.

As Christine pushed herself upright, brushing the soil from her hands, she spotted a wooden sign hammered into the ground by the memorial, partially hidden by the tree boughs. In large block letters was painted the word *SHAME*.

Christine wondered if the investigators had seen the sign. They were probably at the cemetery now, attending the funeral procession, observing the Islanders, scratching notes into their memo books. Did they check the demolition site, looking for clues from the tokens people had left? Would the perpetrator return to inspect his handiwork, to gloat at the misery he caused, to revel in the chaos that had halted the demolitions?

Or could the killer be horrified with his actions? The investigators were likely surveiling the site to see if the perpetrator visited the memorial to lay alms of flowers or candles. Ginny's death could have been accidental, if the intent was to break the machinery to stall the demolition. But if that was the case, why not puncture the excavator's tires or set its cab on fire? That would have stopped the razing at the get-go.

Yet the perpetrator cut the truck's emergency brake and brake line. He must have known that the truck driver would tap the brakes, unknowingly squeeze out the brake fluid. After ten or twenty seconds of driving, maybe a minute, the driver would lose control and plow into a tree, or the neighboring house, another vehicle, or a person, putting the driver and anyone else—fellow construction worker or Islander—at risk.

It was hard to believe a resident would risk one of their own. They were too tight-knit a community. Intermeshed. Maybe it wasn't an Islander after all.

And she was assuming that the perpetrator was male. Was that a generalization because the perpetrator had mechanical knowledge? Or a supposition based on facts regarding the typical perpetrator of violent crimes?

Christine walked over to the colorful mementos gathered to remember Ginny. She picked up a Winnie-the-Pooh teddy bear with a card attached to its paw with yellow yarn. Written in blue crayon were the words: Thanks for playing wit me. You were the best babeesiter. Love Chelsea.

Other tributes were spread on a blue-and-green striped picnic blanket: a clay angel, homemade beeswax candles, conch shells, a beaded necklace, a hand-painted silk scarf. A framed photograph of Ginny as a twelve-year-old, her arm around another girl, both leaning forward, laughing.

"Put that down!"

Christine whipped around, startled.

Nancy Hamilton emerged from the trees like a white phantom. Her shoulder-length hair was untidy, dry leaves and pine needles embedded in the gray-brown tresses. "This is a sacred place," she said. She repeated the phrase, whispering, as she paced, her actions frenetic, almost spinning each time she turned.

Christine placed the teddy bear against a clay vase of flowers. She stepped in Nancy's way. "Miss Hamilton, it's Policewoman Lane. Are you okay?"

Nancy stopped. She continued to whisper to herself, like a witch from *Macbeth*.

"Miss Hamilton, are you expected at the cemetery?"

Nancy clutched her ears. "No! No! No! No! I won't go! I won't go there! She doesn't belong in the ground. She doesn't belong there. With his family. He did this. He did this to her."

"Who did this?" Christine asked.

Nancy looped around Christine and continued her manic walking, muttering, "It's him. It's him. He did this. He killed her."

Christine tried to hold her by the shoulders, pause her, but Nancy slipped out of her grip.

"Who killed her?" Christine followed the distraught woman. "Who did this?"

Nancy whirled around abruptly and jabbed a finger at Christine. "He wanted to stop the demolition. He'd do anything to stay on the Island, with them," she spat out.

"Do you mean Daniel Rogers? Her father? He cut the brake lines of the dump truck?"

She nodded emphatically. "Him. Gary. Paddy. Samuel. All of them. They did this." Her arm gestured to the memorial.

She stepped toward Christine, eyes wide, chapped lips outlined with traces of coral lipstick. "It's because of Daniel. That's why they did it. Did you hear the great newsman on TV?" Her arms flung wide. In a deep, mocking voice she said, "Islanders will never leave. We belong here. They'll have to drag us kicking and screaming from our houses." Her arms fell to her side. In her regular voice, she said, "He made all the Islanders ready to fight, to kill for our homes. And someone did."

Nancy looked down at the picture of three-year-old Ginny on a tricycle. "The demolitions have stopped. Isn't that what we all wanted? He stopped it. We won. And my daughter is dead." She pulled on the ends of her hair with one hand. "She's gone, gone, gone. And no one can get her back." She turned and ran back through the hemlock trees into the neighbor's backyard, the folds of her dress fluttering behind her like wings.

Christine stood there, agape. Could Daniel Rogers or another Islander following his directive be responsible for Ginny's death? Was there a kernel of logic in Nancy's manic muttering? She should follow Nancy, make sure she got home, or find someone to take her to the gravesite. Ginny's mom needed a friend and possibly medical attention.

When no one answered the knock on Nancy Hamilton's door, Christine stepped inside, calling out for Nancy. The living room, with its couch layered in crocheted blankets and textile art on the walls, was empty. Five steps in was the small kitchen, the wooden table covered with casserole dishes and plates of dessert. The linoleum was scratched to the underpad in places, and the paint was peeling near the stove. Paintings and beaded fabric hung on the walls; a tangle of bells was strung around a hook on the pantry door. Artsy, Sergeant Bard would call it. Messy, and a bit worn, but bright and welcoming.

After checking the two small bedrooms and bathroom, Christine left to knock on the adjacent neighbor's doors; she wasn't surprised when no one answered. Islanders were still at the church or at the cemetery. She biked up and down the slab path that separated the facing houses, intermittently dismounting from her bike to search backyards. Over at the Eastern Channel, she walked the concrete pier that capped the east end of the Island. Swimming was prohibited here because of the heavy boat traffic and undercurrents. Would Nancy jump in? Was she suicidal? Christine turned away with relief when she did not spot a swirling white dress in the water's eddies.

Next, she checked Ward's Island Beach, her shoes filling with sand as she passed sunbathers and families wading in the shallows.

When Christine finally radioed Sergeant Bard, he told her Nancy had been spotted back at the church. He had arranged for a friend to accompany her to the gravesite, where she could spend a private moment with her daughter before Ginny's burial. A Harbor Police boat would pilot them to the mainland, and then a patrol car would drive them to the cemetery.

"Sergeant, she may need medical help," Christine said.

"I'll see if Annie Watts can take her to a doctor later. PW, it's time to report to the station."

As Christine biked back to Center Island for her shift, she considered Daniel Rogers as a suspect. He was a consummate professional—a respected news commentator. He had covered Martin Luther King's assassination and later the race riots in Washington and Chicago. His statements were thoughtful and conciliatory, asking people to connect as humans, to find similarities, not differences. Like Martin Luther King, he advocated nonviolence. Would Daniel risk his career, his livelihood, his fatherhood years, to stay on the Island?

Yet it was more than a house to these Islanders. It was their history, their geography. Giving up their homes was like abandoning their heritage, like giving away a grandmother. If they won their battle against Metro Council and were allowed to stay, would the end justify the means?

Christine met up with Fillingham at the Center Island Police Station, and they took report from Sergeant Bard before Morano, Ulster and Sergeant Bard left to catch the ferry to the mainland. Sergeant Bard handed Fillingham a list of homes to check for the hacksaw that had sawed through the truck's brake line. A bolt cutter had been used to snip the emergency brake line, and it would be hard to trace. But the police mechanic had been able to deduce the saw blade pattern from the striations on the broken brake line. So far, Island officers had not found a match from the sheds and toolboxes searched in the Algonquin and Ward's Island communities.

The partners walked out of the office, Fillingham scanning the list. He'd been quiet while Sergeant Bard gave report, quite different from the flirtatious young man she had observed at the hospital with

Julie. He hadn't spoken to her directly or met her glance. Obviously, he was unhappy with his partner assignment.

Christine shrugged. She was a good officer. If he had a problem, he could stew in his own resentment. And if he was so great, what was he doing on the Island anyway? Island patrol was staffed with problematic officers: Pilkington never left desk duty, Morano was a woman-hater and bully, Sarge and the other older officers were biding their time until they could drink themselves to death in retirement. No doubt Fillingham has irritated the brass in some way before being transferred here.

Christine chastised herself—she was being too harsh on her colleagues. If Fillingham asked her how she ended up on Island patrol, her answer would be her own stupidity. Her naivety was embarrassing—expecting her transfer from the Women's Bureau to be to a downtown station patrol car. At her first shift at 52 Division, she had lined up for morning inspection with the other constables, her silver buttons gleaming, her hair in a neat bun at her nape. Christine's shoulders were pulled back, eyes staring straight ahead as the staff sergeant examined the row of officers, checking hair lines, pant pleats, the shine of shoes. After the review, the men made their way out of the building to their patrol cars, everyone except Christine.

After a minute standing by herself, she approached the open door of the station's inspector. He was standing at his desk, inserting papers into an accordion file.

She lightly rapped on the wooden door frame.

"What is it?" he said, not looking up.

She stepped into the room. "Inspector, Policewoman Lane reporting for duty. I didn't receive my car assignment."

He looked up. "What?"

"I'm the new transfer from the Women's Bureau—PW Lane."

He made a sound between a laugh and a grunt. "You're not on patrol here, woman. You're on the Island."

"The Island? Toronto Island?"

"It's part of 52 Division." He glanced at his wristwatch. "And you're fifteen minutes late for shift."

Toronto Island patrol—staffed with drunks, cowards and officers so ineffectual that they didn't warrant a position at a city police station. What was the saying about Island officers: the lame, the blame, the incompetent and the troublemakers. A step down from the Women's Bureau, if you could believe it.

And that was how Christine had landed on Toronto Island.

"We're supposed to check the tool sheds at Centerville," Fillingham said, interrupting her thoughts. "See if there's a match."

He handed her the file, and Christine glanced through it as they walked in the direction of the amusement park. Included was a mimeographed copy of a hacksaw blade, sketched by the police mechanic to scale and then magnified, with a saw-tooth pattern of twelve identical triangular teeth per inch. A cross section of the blade showed a wave pattern of six teeth per wave. According to the report, the teeth in the middle were worn compared with the teeth at the blade ends. The subsequent pages in the file listed the houses on Algonquin and Ward's that had been checked, with twenty remaining. The last page in the file listed the other facilities to inspect: the four marinas on the Island, Centerville Amusement Park and the Parks and Recreation tool sheds.

Joyful screams of children sounded as the officers neared Centerville, the rumble of the roller coaster and tinkle of the carousel music a backdrop to the high-pitched voices.

Christine had walked through Centerville with Sergeant Bard, enjoying the entertaining stop on their patrol and the opportunity to get out of the police car. Sometimes they were asked by security to help with lost children—found ten minutes later with pink, candy-floss-stained mouths and tear tracks on their cheeks. One time they were called in for a rash of purse thefts; distracted mothers were easy targets. Most of the time they wandered the path between rides, smiling at the excited children, giving parents directions to washrooms and ticket sellers. Once a tourist asked her to pose in a photograph—he had never seen a policewoman before. Centerville was a loud, bustling place, and today it was a good antidote to thinking about Ginny Roger's white coffin, the button-toting Islanders and the vacant expression on Nancy Hamilton's face.

"Even if we find the saw," Fillingham said, looking straight ahead as they walked toward Centerville, "even if the perp didn't toss it in the garbage, it won't solve the case."

"Why not?"

"Islanders borrow stuff from each other all the time—sugar, bikes, tools."

"So the saw's owner may not be the perpetrator?"

He nodded. "And they never lock anything up—houses, sheds or bikes. Anyone who visited the Island had access."

"How about the marinas?" Christine said. "Their sheds would be locked, wouldn't they?"

He shrugged. "Depends. Let's see what the security is like in Centerville."

They passed under the arched wooden sign welcoming them to the amusement park. She glanced over at her partner. Fillingham might not be making eye contact, but at least he was sharing information. Hopefully, his petulance would wear off during their shift. They walked by the Bumble Bee ride, children orbiting up and down around a central motor. Donna would love that attraction. If Christine could pick up a few more paid duty shifts, maybe she could take her siblings here, make a day of it. Have her mom come too.

Fillingham walked ahead, and she followed him past the ticket booth and the swan boats in the lagoon. They stepped over the tracks of the train that motored tourists around the park and entered a shop built to resemble a village store from the 1800s. The manager emerged from a back office and told them that the ride mechanic, Hawk Johnson, was repairing equipment at the Antique Cars ride. He was the guy to ask about hand tools.

As the officers walked beside the split-rail wooden fence that surrounded the perimeter of the ride, an antique car with large, spoked wheels looped around a twin-rail track. A red-haired child clanged a pull-bell ferociously while her father turned the steering wheel and worked the pedals.

"That must be him." Christine pointed at the broad back of a man who was leaning into a car taken off the track near the ride's entrance. He straightened, tossing a wrench into a scratched metal toolbox. It was the man from Ginny's funeral, the one with the shiny black braids who had lit the sage grass and smudged the coffin.

Fillingham placed his foot on the lower rung of the wooden fence, leaned against it, and called, "Hawk Johnson!"

The mechanic looked over at the sound of his name, then wiped his hands on a rag hanging from his coveralls' pocket and headed over. He faced them on the inside of the fence.

"PC Fillingham, Toronto Police. Your first name is Hawk?"

The man paused. "It's 'Gekek,' but people call me Hawk," he said in a deep-timbred voice. He looked over at Christine.

"I'm PW Lane," Christine said. "We saw you this morning at Ginny Rogers' funeral."

He nodded.

"Do you know the family?" she asked. The Indigenous rite in Ginny's funeral was unusual, and Christine had wondered about Nancy's connection with the two men.

"Do you inventory your tools?" Fillingham said.

Christine frowned at Fillingham's impatience. Would he let the guy answer her question first?

Hawk's mouth twitched as he looked from Fillingham to Christine. He was tanned from working outside; the smooth skin on his arms was corded with thick muscles. Christine felt small compared to his barrel chest and broad shoulders; he hulked over Fillingham.

"I've known Nancy and Ginny for five years," Hawk said to Christine.

She nodded.

"Nancy is a friend," Hawk added.

"What type of friend?" Fillingham said.

Hawk frowned.

"Is she your girlfriend?" Fillingham pressed.

"No," he said.

"Was Ginny your girlfriend?" Fillingham said.

"No." His tone was annoyed. "Davy Morgan was her boyfriend." Looking at Christine, he added, "I don't have a girlfriend."

"What was your business with the family?" Fillingham asked.

Hawk's eyebrows raised. "Business?"

"Just answer the question," Fillingham said, crossing his arms. Christine looked at her partner. What was his problem? Johnson wasn't a suspect. Was Fillingham being aggressive because of Hawk's race?

Hawk stared down at the peak of Fillingham's hat. "And if I don't?"

This was becoming a dogfight, each male baring their canines.

"Mr. Johnson," Christine said. "We need your help."

Hawk's glance slowly went to Christine.

"I apologize if it sounds like we're giving you the third degree. We're gathering background information on Ginny Rogers—about her family, friends and acquaintances—to get a better picture of her life. To help us figure out who might want to harm her."

His face softened. "She had no enemies," Hawk said. "She took care of her mom. Had lots of friends." He glanced away, his eyes following a gaggle of ducks that had wandered out of the lagoon onto the path. "She liked working at Clergy House, but she also wanted to do her art and work with kids."

"How did you meet her?" Fillingham said again.

Hawk looked at Christine as he answered. "I used to work at a community center on Sherbourne. Building maintenance. Nancy was taking a beading class from an Indian woman, an elder, and we got to talking. Sometimes I saw her and Ginny at powwows." He shrugged. "I got to know them over the years. Been at their house for dinner a couple of times. I fixed her oven, helped with a leaking water pipe. That type of thing. Nancy asked me to do the smudging at the funeral to honor Ginny."

Fillingham said, "Is there a main tool shed in Centerville?"

Hawk paused for several seconds, as if to highlight that he didn't have to answer the question; he was choosing to. "There's two—one near the Ferris wheel and another one by the farm. Why?"

"Can you show us?" Christine said.

Hawk stepped over the fence with his long legs and headed toward the carousel ride, and the two officers followed. He stopped at a large brown wooden structure beside the Ferris wheel, unlocked the padlock and swung the double doors open.

Fillingham stepped into the shed and stood in front of the hand saws hanging on wall pegs.

"Is the shed always locked?" Christine said.

"Pretty much," Hawk said. "There're kids around."

"How many hacksaws are stored here?" Fillingham said.

Hawk thought for a moment. "Usually three."

Fillingham brought three hacksaws into the sunlight and placed them beside each other on the paved ground. Christine squatted down. Two of the saws were for cutting wood, not metal, their teeth large and in variating patterns. The metal saw looked new, the teeth uniformly pointy and sharp.

"We need to see the other shed." Fillingham handed the saws to Hawk, who rehung them.

Following Hawk through the competing aromas of popcorn, roasted peanuts and hot dogs, the trio passed the Log Flume and Bumper Cars rides and headed toward Far Enough Farm.

They followed Hawk into a barn, where he unlocked a storage cupboard and showed them the saws. Only one was for metal, its teeth tiny, probably twenty-four per inch. No match.

"Thank you for your time," Christine said. The man had been cooperative, despite her partner's antagonism. And he was probably grieving too, having known Ginny and her mom.

Fillingham drifted ahead and radioed Dispatch to say they were headed toward Algonquin Island to check out the tool kits and sheds of the residents.

"Did the poultice work?" Hawk asked Christine.

"What do you mean?" She turned to him as they walked past the fenced-in goats to the main pathway.

"I left it at the station for you. For this." He pointed at her cheekbone.

Christine's hand went up to her face. Were her bruises showing through the layers of makeup she had applied before the funeral?

"The yellow powder?" she said. The bag had come home with her with the plants and casseroles, but she hadn't read the instructions. She had assumed it was cornmeal for a baking recipe.

He nodded. "Mix it with two parts water; place it on your face for twenty minutes. It'll reduce the swelling, draw out the pain. Is it still sore?" He pointed to her face, taking a step toward her.

She side-stepped away. "No. I mean, it's better. Just a little sensitive."

She walked away from Hawk to catch up with Fillingham. Looking over her shoulder, she saw Hawk standing beside the Antique Car ride. She walked backward a few steps, facing him. "Thank you," she said. "I'll try it. We, uh, appreciate your help today."

He smiled, then turned back to the ride, whistling.

Christine recognized the tune. It was "Baby, I Need Your Lovin'."

Chapter 8

"Should we bike to the Algonquin Island Yacht Club?" Christine asked Fillingham the next day at the station. The other officers always drove, but Fillingham often biked and walked on patrol and had energy to expend.

"Sure. It's a nice day." It was three thirty, the beginning of their afternoon shift.

Fillingham raised his eyebrows at Christine's flower-bedecked bike but made no comment. He jumped on the shorter gray bike he had retrieved from the station's backyard and pedaled furiously away.

Christine let him draw ahead, following at a more leisurely pace along the path beside the lagoon, looping past the church. The arched front doors were closed, the yard cleared of the tables and chairs from yesterday's funeral reception. He waited for her at the foot of the Algonquin Island Bridge, which was the pedestrian access to the Algonquin Island community of a hundred houses. Yesterday, they had checked fifteen of the homes and sheds there for the handsaw. As she biked up the arced bridge with its cascading flower baskets, the family boats and small watercraft moored at the Algonquin Island Yacht Club came into view.

She gathered speed down the other side of the bridge and steered right to follow Fillingham to the marina's gate. He leaned his bike against the fence, then pushed the metal gate open. No lock. She wondered if they were slack regarding the security of their tool sheds, too.

The officers made their way to the main clubhouse, passing empty boat cradles, rows of masts on the ground like boxed pencils and a rusted boat engine. Flakes of white paint peeled off window frames, and wilted plants with brown leaves sat in clay flowerpots. The club had seen better days.

"Davy Morgan works here," Fillingham said as he opened the screen door to the building.

"Ginny's boyfriend?"

He turned to her. "He's a boat mechanic."

Christine hadn't seen him at the reception. It must be heartbreaking to lose your girlfriend, attend her funeral, see her in all those pictures and be expected to talk to people, accept their condolences.

"Morgan wouldn't have tampered with the truck, would he?" she asked as Fillingham walked up the stairs in front of her.

"Ginny's his girlfriend," he said. "By all accounts he loves her." He reached the second floor.

"Maybe she was an unintentional target. He works on the Island," she said, standing beside him. "The yacht club isn't doing well; he'll lose his job if the evictions continue."

"So will the Clergy House staff and many of the Parks and Recreation and ferry staff."

"Is he a local?"

He shook his head. "I don't think so. I think he's around because of Ginny."

They walked into a lounge with couches and a coffee table. To the right was a narrow hallway.

A door slammed downstairs.

A few seconds later, Fillingham greeted the club's manager as Paddy Jenkins reached the top of the stairs, a stack of mail in his hand.

Jenkins wore a blue golf shirt over khaki shorts, the Save Island Homes button pinned to the collar.

"Ah, it's our very own Island police," Jenkins said, tipping an imaginary cap to Christine. When he smiled, wrinkles fanned out around his eyes and mouth. His dun-colored hair was streaked with gray. He could be in his forties or fifties; his weathered face made it hard to guess.

"How's RCYC's pride and joy?" he asked Fillingham.

Fillingham smiled.

Jenkins twitched his thumb toward Fillingham. "He's one of the best racers in the harbor. Not just in the harbor, but the whole damn country."

"You sail?" Christine turned to her partner.

"The International Fourteen class," Fillingham said.

"He'll be an Olympian one day," Jenkins said. "Mark my words."

That made sense. Fillingham was fit, young, athletic—and rich, according to Sergeant Bard. Maybe he chose Island patrol to be near his yacht club.

"We're here to check the tool shed, Paddy," Fillingham said. "Your equipment under lock and key?

Jenkins shook his head. "Most members do minor boat repairs, so it's open all day. I lock the shed at night if I'm the last one here."

"Can we see the toolshed?" she said.

"Sure. Let me drop this stuff in the office." He entered the first room on the left in the hallway and tossed his handful of envelopes onto to the pile of papers and detritus on the overflowing desk. Through the open door, Christine could see a pennant with the marina's name thumb-tacked to the far wall. Beneath the pennant were wooden pegs hung with nets, ropes and life preservers.

Jenkins turned and caught Christine's gaze. "Needs a bit of spring cleaning," he said, then exited and closed the door with a click.

Outside, their footsteps crunched on the gravel yard until they reached the grassy area bordering the lagoon. The shed was a ramshackle structure built to resemble an old barn with a tin roof and peeling crimson sides.

Jenkins swung the door open and gestured inside with one arm.

"Can we look around for a few minutes?" Fillingham said.

"Sure."

"How's Davy Morgan holding up?" Christine asked as Fillingham stepped into the shed.

Jenkins shook his head. "Hasn't shown up for work since Ginny died."

"Does he live on the Island?" she said.

"Nah. Has a room down on Parliament. But he often stayed with Ginny over at her mom's."

"How long have they been together?"

"A year, year and a half. They were on and off for a while. Nancy didn't mind him, but Danny Rogers wouldn't give him the time of day."

"Why not?" she said.

He shrugged. "What father likes his daughter's boyfriend?"

"What's he like as an employee?" Fillingham said.

"Comes to work, does his job. Quiet. A bit surly. Knows his way around a boat engine, which is what I pay him for."

Jenkins left, and Christine and Fillingham examined the hacksaws they had found in the shed. Two of them were for cutting metal. One had larger teeth, and the other's blade looked new, the cutting teeth sharp.

Fillingham closed the shed door behind them. "There are probably ten saws lying around the club—in people's boats or storage units. This search is useless."

They walked back toward the yacht club entrance, side-stepping over a box of dumped nails and a rolled-up tarp filled with old sails.

"Place looks run-down," she said.

Fillingham shrugged. "It was always a second-rate yacht club. Not really a race club. Mostly for residents who want to tinker around the lake in the summer or teach their kids to sail." He paused. "A portion of the members don't sail; they hang out at the club, drinking, treat it like the local bar. We've been here a few times for drunk and disorderly calls."

"Is the club having money problems?"

He pushed the gate open. "I'm sure membership is down because of the demolitions and lease expirations."

Christine picked up her bike. "Is that the case for all the yacht clubs?"

He shook his head. "The Royal Canadian Yacht Club and Toronto Yacht Club draw members from the city, so the demolitions don't impact them." Fillingham hopped on his bike, and they rode beside each other.

"Next stop, RCYC," she said.

"I don't see the point," he said, frowning. "Islanders don't have access to RCYC grounds unless they are a member, and very few are. I know because I'm a member. The only pedestrian entry from Toronto Island is through the security gate. Members get boated in from the mainland to the dock on the north side of the clubhouse. Again, we have no stake in whether the demolitions happen. It doesn't affect us."

"RCYC is on the list Sergeant Bard gave us."

"Okay," he said after a minute, "but let me do the talking. We're not accusing anyone at the club of anything. Don't mention Ginny's death in association with RCYC at all." With this command, he pulled ahead and rode up the Algonquin Island Bridge.

Christine followed. She didn't expect a RCYC member to be the murderer. It wasn't logical, but their orders were to check the tool sheds of all the marinas. As police officers, they were supposed to be neutral investigators—not worried about the reputation of a local club or business.

She didn't want to seem combative. Or challenging. Fillingham was acting normal, looking at her when he spoke. She was mindful that she could be working with the woman-hating Morano.

As they headed back toward Center Island, Christine kept an eye out for Chippewa Bridge, which linked Toronto Island to the two small islands occupied by RCYC. After following Fillingham over it, they rode across a second bridge, then along a pathway shaded by a dozen weeping willows curved over a lagoon.

The path ended at a gate beside a wooden sentry box. Fillingham dismounted and opened the gate lock with a key he retrieved from his pocket.

"You come this way to your club?" Christine said.

"Sometimes—if I sail after day shift. That's why I have a bike. Comes in handy traveling between the police station and the club."

They left their bikes leaning against the sentry box and walked inside the property, past a boisterous group of teenagers playing volleyball and a trio of children heading out for sailing lessons. Arriving at a string of wooden buildings, Fillingham checked the individual door handles—all locked.

"Tools are in here," he said, gesturing to the sheds. "Let's go inside and find someone to open up."

On the way to the clubhouse that loomed in the distance, they passed a pool where children splashed in the shallow end while women in floppy hats and dry bathing suits reclined on loungers. Adjacent was a tennis court with players hitting balls in regulation whites. Christine followed Fillingham as he crossed the recessed kelly-green carpet of manicured grass used for lawn bowling.

The white limestone clubhouse rose in front of them like a grand southern plantation with a second-floor balcony that ran the full length of the building. Red and purple splashes of color from tall ceramic flowerpots and the landscaped gardens contrasted the white stone. Impressive. A team of full-time gardeners must maintain the place, she thought.

Fillingham ran up the tiered steps to the entrance and waved to patrons sitting at cast-iron tables on the porch, wine glasses or forks of buttered lobster in their grasp. Someone called "Geoffrey!" and Fillingham stopped at the table, hat under his arm, white-blond crew cut smoothed down.

Christine waited outside the double French door entrance. In her dark uniform, she could be one of the staff—a waitress or housekeeper. If she stood here any longer, someone was bound to ask her to refill a water glass or tuck a tip in her pocket. She turned her back to the tables and looked down the expanse of wooden porch out toward the lake. On the lawn, two black cannons aimed their nozzles at the harbor, probably placed there to protect members from outsiders—keep the riffraff away.

She gave herself a mental shake—she wasn't being fair. So what if RCYC members wanted to maintain the exclusivity of their club? Who wouldn't want to spend summer days sailing, playing tennis or swimming? Members paid for their luxuries via the exorbitant club fees. According to Sergeant Bard, the members were model citizens; the station never received calls about loud parties or public drunkenness. The group kept to themselves, rarely mingling with Islanders, other yacht clubs or tourists. So what if they were rich? They deserved her service and respect as much as any other citizen.

Fillingham pulled himself away from the people having a late lunch, and the officers went inside. A winding staircase bisected the lobby. Fillingham walked straight through the main room across a blue Persian rug.

Christine followed at a slower pace, viewing photographs of RCYC sailors at the Olympics, silver cups won in international races and wooden replicas of prize-winning sailboats. Every trophy, sailing flag and crew photograph emphasized the elite nature of the competitive sailing club.

She found Fillingham perched on a stool at the bar. *Oh no-, Christine thought, *not another drinker.*

He called the bartender over and ordered a club soda. Fillingham turned to her: "Do you want something?"

"The same, thanks," she said, snapping open her purse.

He looked at her wallet, shaking his head. "I'm a member. It's on my tab."

"I'll pay for my own drink," she said.

"They don't take cash," he said, as if instructing a child.

She blushed.

As the two men discussed a recent regatta, Christine sipped her soda from a heavy crystal water glass and surveyed the bar. A scattering of members sat at round tables. Well-groomed women in linen dresses and heels sipped gin and tonics, white-blonde or caramel hair sculpted into chignons or flipped into bobs. The men, in chinos and short-sleeved button-down shirts, appeared older than their wives. Ordinary-looking, yet somehow, with their tan and easy smiles, they radiated success.

"Any unusual activity in the past couple of weeks?" Fillingham asked the bartender. "Vandalism? Stolen items?"

The mustached bartender drummed his fingers on the counter as he thought. "Not that I can think of."

"Is Joe around?" Fillingham said.

"Check the boat shed."

They finished their drinks, and Christine followed Fillingham outside and back across the rolling green grass.

Two young women in white tennis skirts approached, squealing. "Geoffrey!"

Christine waited while one woman tried on his police hat as the other asked to see his baton. He jokingly pulled out his handcuffs, and more giggles ensued.

Finally, Christine stepped in front of him. "We have houses to check after this."

He said goodbye to the women, promising them a sail tomorrow before his shift and headed toward the trio of wooden buildings they had passed on their way in. "They can't help themselves," he told Christine.

"I can see that." She wondered how he fit policing into his social and sailing schedules.

"Joe!" yelled Fillingham, waving.

A tall man in white coveralls was painting the hull of an overturned canoe set on two wooden sawhorses. He placed his paintbrush down on the paint can, wiped his hands on his pant legs and came over to shake her partner's hand.

After a few pleasantries, Fillingham said, "Any thefts this past month?"

Joe said, "From the clubhouse?"

Fillingham shook his head, gesturing outside.

"Nothing that I heard of. Somebody broke into the toolshed." Joe pointed to the wooden structure behind him. "Must've been two weeks ago. Hank cleaned up the glass from the broken window when he came in the next morning."

Two weeks ago—right before the demolition.

"What did they take?" Fillingham said.

He shrugged. "They tossed things around. I chalked it up to teenagers who'd gotten into the liquor, maybe a member kid acting stupid."

Fillingham said, "Nothing is missing?"

"None of the power tools were taken."

"Would you have noticed if a hacksaw was stolen?" Christine said.

Joe crossed his arms. "Maybe not," he said. "Hand tools are hard to keep track of. We stamp or paint them with the RCYC initials, but members grab them to do minor boat repairs and never return them. We just restock."

"Do you mind?" Fillingham asked Joe, tipping his head toward the open tool shed. Joe shook his head and returned to his painting job.

Christine and Fillingham stepped inside the shed, its two open doors the size of the end wall. Horizontal wood planks boarded up the far window where the thief had entered. With the toe of his police boot, Fillingham poked a burlap bag that spilled a thick white coil of rope. Both officers searched the wooden drawers of the workbench and the hanging cabinets above. Most of the tools had the RCYC initials painted in yellow or stamped on the handle. Christine pulled a saw out of a wooden rack, and they both examined its blade. Without talking, she put it back.

They checked the two adjacent boat sheds as well. As Fillingham rummaged through a pile of boxes, Christine turned to look at the Georgian-style clubhouse she could see above the tennis courts, impossibly white against the blue sky, a shiny monument to taste and privilege.

Fillingham crouched in front of the cardboard box, rifling through its contents. With his blond hair, blue eyes, straight white teeth and tan, he was a quintessential club member, except for the uniform, which made him look like a chauffeur. Policing wasn't a typical career choice for this crowd. She wondered what had motivated him to join the force.

He straightened, brushing his hands together to remove dust. "That's it. Nothing here."

"No other sheds?"

He shook his head. "Members have storage units by their docks, but we don't have access to them. The units are privately rented or owned." A quick smile lit his face. "Do you want to see my boat?" Without waiting for her answer, he closed the shed doors and headed toward the water.

She followed him onto the floating wooden dock. She didn't enjoy boating or swimming, probably because she wasn't good at either. But it wouldn't kill her to know more about Fillingham, especially if they were going to be partners.

He ran down one of the side docks, and she slowed as the walkway wobbled with their weight, her hands extended for balance. Arriving at a white sailboat with the name *Calliope* in blue cursive letters, he jumped into its cockpit.

"Isn't she great?" he said.

Christine nodded from the dock. "She looks sleek."

He smiled. "She is one of the quickest International Fourteens in Ontario."

"Geoffrey!" a man's voice yelled.

They turned to see three young men walking toward them, their collective tread vibrating the boards under Christine's feet. All three sported short-sleeved shirts, shorts, deck shoes and tans that made their teeth look artificially white as they smiled at Fillingham.

They came up beside the boat and stood beside Christine. "Whoa," the stocky one with brown hair said, "look at you two in uniform."

She gave a small smile. The two blond men jumped lightly into the boat and shook Fillingham's hand.

"Geoff," the stocky one said, "figured you'd have a broad working for you."

Christine said, "I'm a police officer. We're on shift together."

He raised his eyebrows. "You're partners? Geoffrey, you dog. How d'you swing that?"

She glared at Fillingham, who shrugged and turned back to his conversation with his two buddies.

The stocky friend turned to Christine and placed a hand on his chest. "I'm Doug, by the way." He offered his arm. "Can I help you aboard?"

She shook her head. "We're working," she exclaimed, hoping Fillingham would take the hint.

"Come on," Doug said, touching her elbow. "You can be my partner." His hand slid down to her wrist.

Christine pulled her arm back, but Doug held on. She looked straight into his brown eyes. "Let go."

He faced her, leaning in to say softly, "Or what?"

From the corner of her eye, she saw Fillingham stop talking and move toward them. Christine pushed Doug's chest away with her free hand; he clasped her wrist tighter.

That was it. She placed her leg behind his and punched his chest hard with her free hand; he stumbled, releasing her wrist. Hooking his leg with her foot, she flipped him, and he sailed through the air in a pinwheel of arms and legs into the boat, landing on the padded bench and rolling onto the floor at Fillingham's feet.

The men looked at Doug, then back up at Christine.

Doug bounded up, shouting, "You bitch!"

The two blond men burst out laughing. Fillingham looked up at Christine, jaw slack.

Stupid, spoiled, moneyed brats. She turned and stomped down the dock. Heading back across the grass, she spotted the exit gate and realized she couldn't get out the locked door. After following the short fence for a few feet, she climbed it, scissoring her legs on top and landing in an inelegant squat on the other side. Grabbing her bike, she hopped on at a run and pedaled furiously over the bridges back to the main island.

She could hear the crunch of gravel stones behind her, so she pedaled quicker. Fillingham rode up alongside her, legs pumping, hat held in his fist as he clutched the handlebars.

"Lane, wait! Slow down!"

She ignored him.

He pulled ahead of her and craned his neck, looking back. "Can you stop for a minute? Stop, so we can talk."

She could deke around him or veer off the gravel path to ride along the grass—but what was the point? She was a policewoman; he was her shift partner. Chasing each other around Toronto Island was a waste of time; they should be searching for Ginny's killer.

She glided to a halt underneath a willow tree, panting.

He stopped beside her. "What the hell was that?" he said, laughter in his voice.

She glared at him. "I'm glad you find it so amusing." She sat back on her bike seat.

"Wait a sec," he said, laying his bike down. He approached her, hands in the air in surrender.

Christine waited.

He was laughing. "I mean, one minute Doug is on the dock, and the next"—he pantomimed throwing someone over his shoulder—"he somersaults into my boat." Fillingham laughed again. "And the best thing," he said, slapping his knee, "the best thing was the look on his face." He did an imitation of Doug's O-mouthed shock and wide eyes.

A smile twitched the corner of her mouth. It had felt great to throw Doug, like the old days on the wrestling team when she pinned a hotshot to the mat—a foul-mouthed one who had commented on her breasts or backside as they wrestled.

They began cycling parallel to each other. He said, "Seriously, Lane, where did you learn to do that?"

She answered, "I was on the high school wrestling team."

His bike wobbled. "Really?"

She pointed to the top of her head. "I was this height in grade nine. The gym teacher didn't know what to do with me. I was strong but too slow and uncoordinated for ball sports or running track. So I did shotput, javelin and wrestling."

Fillingham shook his head in wonder. "You had a girls' wrestling team at your school?"

"Boys."

His eyebrows raised. "They let you compete against boys?"

"I attended practices, but not the meets. The coach would line up team candidates, and only those who could win a point against me made first string."

Christine biked past him, heading back toward the police station. Arriving in the front yard of the station, she pulled the file folder from the front basket. "Want to split up the remaining houses to check for the handsaw?" She didn't feel like talking about wrestling or the scene back at the yacht club. Extracting two pieces of paper out of the file, she asked, "Ward's or Algonquin?"

He ignored the proffered papers. "Teach me," he said.

"Teach you what?" she said, arm extended.

"To wrestle." He gave her the high-wattage smile he had flashed the tennis players at the yacht club.

"No." She closed the file and headed toward the station entrance.

"Why not?" He followed her into the building.

She went into the little kitchenette in the back room and poured herself a glass of water. She took several big gulps. Fillingham regarded her expectantly.

She placed her glass on the small table with a clink. "I'm not wrestling my"—should she call him her partner?—"a fellow officer. It's not appropriate."

"Why? It'd be like basic training at the college."

She had a flashback of sparring with her karate instructor at the police college. PC Campbell had given her private sessions, leading to a sexual lesson that he had bragged about to the entire class later. Thinking about it made her cringe.

"I thought you were a sailor," she said to Fillingham.

"I am."

"Why wrestle?"

He shrugged and looked away. "I'm five-foot-seven and weigh one hundred and forty pounds, and I'm a cop."

How had he made the height and weight requirements during recruitment? "At least you have a gun," she said.

He crossed his arms. "How many times does a cop take his gun out of its holster, let alone use it? It's muscle and size that get people to cooperate. I'm fast, but I'm not big. I need technique."

"Most PWs aren't big. They learn to talk with people."

"It's different for a policeman."

Christine took another sip of water. A guy as small as Fillingham would have difficulty arresting the burlier suspects unless he knew how to put a hold on them, how to find their weak points. His small stature might have been the reason Fillingham gave Hawk such a hard time at Centerville—overcompensating with bark and bluster like a small, yappy dog.

If she was too tall and muscular for a woman, Fillingham was too short and light for a policeman. What a joke. They were like the Odd Couple from different sides of the track: Rosedale vs. Parkdale, Rich Man, Poor Man. Sergeant Bard had probably laughed his head off when he put them on the schedule together.

She had no desire to wrestle Fillingham, but she owed him. He had defended her in front of their sergeant. And got stuck with her as a partner for his effort. A long sigh of defeat escaped her lips.

"Whoo-hoo!" Fillingham hooted. He grabbed the checklist for Algonquin Island off the table. "Here's to being the next Buddy Rogers." He ran through the office and swung his body sideways up and over the counter. "See you later!" he yelled, and the door banged shut.

She shook her head. It was like being with her ten-year-old brother, Wayne. Fillingham was a grown-up child who raced boats, charmed women and wanted to learn how to beat up the local bully who had kicked sand in his face.

Maybe in return he could teach her how to boat—not his racing yacht, but she'd like to learn to paddle a canoe. If she was going to be stuck on this island for two years, she should learn to navigate the channels. And how to swim. She had barely pulled the truck driver to shore. Truthfully, her dog paddle couldn't be relied on to save anyone else, including herself.

Chapter 9

On her next shift on Toronto Island, Christine rode over to the cluster of one hundred and fifty cabins that made up the Ward's Island community and spent an hour knocking on doors, crosschecking the numbers posted on mailboxes and doors with the master list provided by Sergeant Bard. Fillingham was undertaking the same task on Algonquin Island.

It was dinnertime, and about half the families were home. With serious faces, residents opened the family toolbox or the door to their back shed. No one asked her why she was checking hand tools; the truck's severed brake lines seemed common knowledge. Christine carefully examined each hacksaw she came across, bringing it out into the sunlight to check the tooth pattern and wear. After each house, she made notes in her memo book and ticked off the address from the master list.

She confiscated one saw from a young family, the Lisbons. The blade looked slightly worn in the middle, although it looked like there were fourteen teeth per inch, not twelve. Christine recognized the family from the community meeting. The mother was a homemaker, busy with three children under the age of five. Her husband worked on the mainland in an appliance store.

They didn't fit the violent, revolutionary mold. The blade probably wasn't a match, but she would take it to the investigators. After giving Mrs. Lisbon a receipt for the saw, Christine placed it carefully in a paper evidence bag in case Identification needed to check for fingerprints. Six o'clock. Odds were the investigators had left for the day, but the community center was a two-minute bike ride away, so she might as well drop by.

Warm, stale air greeted her as she pushed open the community center door. Conversation halted between the two seated investigators.

"Investigator." She addressed Ron Allen, preferring him to the rodent-like Fenwick. "I have a handsaw that looks similar to the mechanic's sketch."

Allen took the paper bag from her and looked inside. "No match," he said.

"You can tell so quickly?" she said.

"Can't you?" he said as he handed her back the saw, then sat back down.

Christine took a step toward them. "Any leads in the case, Investigators?"

Allen looked at her, frowning. "We're following a few lines of inquiry."

"Such as?" She knew she should leave it alone, that she was crossing a line by asking a higher-ranked officer to dish to a junior officer. That wasn't how things were done. But she really wanted to know if they were closing in on the perpetrator.

Fenwick said, "Leave the police work to the professionals, PW."

Christine waited, then turned on her heel and headed back to the Lisbons to return the saw. The investigators were happy enough to allow Island police to check every local toolbox, shed and marina, but God forbid they share information. Like at the police college when some men refused to help the women train for the fitness test but were sure as heck eager to ask them about Ontario statutes ten minutes before the exam. At times like this, she sorely missed the camaraderie of the Women's Bureau.

Returning from the Lisbons, she braked her bike in front of the demolition site. A teenaged girl and her parents walked across the property to the memorial next to the *SHAME* sign. Tourists paused on the boardwalk to stare at the scarred footprint of the house.

Christine rolled her bike onto the beach in front of the Whitmores'. Grains of sand trickled into her heels as she gazed out over Lake Ontario. What a beautiful front-door view: the deepening lake colors, the angular formations of Canada geese overhead, the smudged chalk line of the United States on the far shore. No wonder the Whitmores, and all the Islanders, wanted to stay.

After setting her bike on the sand, Christine headed toward the waterline to retrace her steps from the demolition day, trying to slow down her memory of the kaleidoscope of events. She had run into the water after Kevin Lamprey pulled the driver out of the truck cab. Then a brick hit her, although she had no memory of that, her billy and purse drifting away. The next thing she remembered after the blackness was the quiet green ambiance as she floated, then the spike of fear as she choked on lake water until Fillingham pulled her upright.

A thick ribbon of curled seaweed floated in on the tide. Christine and Fillingham had been lucky they found the truck driver. The water was murky here, the lake bottom soft and knotted with underwater plants. A good place to hide something.

To conceal a saw.

If the perpetrator was local, he'd want to get rid of the incriminating tool immediately after sabotaging the truck; he wouldn't return it to a house or toolbox. Everyone knew about fingerprints. That's why criminals often threw knives and sometimes bodies into waterways, where evidence degraded quickly.

If the perpetrator threw the hacksaw in the water, here, in front of the Whitmores' property, it might never be discovered. Most people swam at Ward's Island Beach three hundred feet away, not in this weedy, mushy mess. Or headed to Manitou Beach on Center Island. The weapon in the Ginny Rogers' case, the evidence, could be thirty feet in front of her.

Christine looked down at her uniform. If she removed her jacket, belt, radio, hat, nylons, shoes and purse, she could go into the water wearing her blouse and skirt. Her blouse would be okay—she had two more and it was washable—but she only had the one skirt. Julie said the cleaners had a terrible time removing the bloodstains from Christine's uniform, and if you looked closely, there was a slightly darker spot on Christine's jacket from the largest stain. Hopefully, the lake water wouldn't ruin her skirt, because she would have to dry it herself before her shift tomorrow.

If only she could pretend her underwear and brassiere were a bikini and jump in with her undergarments, but with her luck, Morano or a photographer would come by, or a dog would abscond with her clothes. One option was to return to the station and change into civilian clothes; she had shorts and a t-shirt in her locker. She sighed; that would take too long.

After slipping off her shoes, she took a quick look around, then pulled off her pantyhose. Her bare legs felt so free. Nylons drove her crazy in the heat—hot and scratchy beneath her serge skirt. What she would give for lightweight summer pants like the men wore. All she had in her closet was the heavy-duty winter trousers that PWs wore for crossing guard duty.

After removing her jacket, she tied the tails of her blouse around her waist. By unzipping her skirt and rolling the waist, she was able to hike it up ten inches. After placing her clothes and file in her bike basket, she stored her purse and radio in the panniers. She quickly scanned for onlookers and then waded into the lake. The shallow water felt warm in the late-day sun, cooling as she ventured deeper. Hunching over, she examined the sandy bottom, trying not to disturb it with her steps. Organizing her search in a grid pattern, she checked a rectangular area of water, looking over her shoulder from time to time to locate herself by a beach landmark—a rock, wood stump or clump of wildflowers. She pressed her toes into the muck, wondering if her feet could tell the difference between the texture of a stone and the flat hardness of a wooden handle or steel blade.

After forty-five minutes, she had searched a block of water forty feet wide and ten feet long. What she needed to do was get into a bathing suit so that she could search the deeper waters. Odds were that the culprit would have flung the saw as far as he could, which would make the entry point about five to ten feet away from where Christine stood. She wondered if the diving team from the Harbor Police had checked the area for evidence. Somehow, she didn't think so.

Her skirt hem was sodden and her rolled-up sleeves damp. She wasn't the best swimmer, but she was partially wet already. In for a dime, in for a dollar, as her mom always said, usually about bingo. The water climbed up Christine's body like the mercury of a thermometer as she stepped farther into the lake. It crept past her breasts, shoulders and neck until she was submerged. Tilting her head down, breath held, she looked through the blurry green water. She moved forward, trying to anchor her feet in the soft sand to stop herself from floating to the surface. As a child, she had been heavy and muscular, with a tendency to sink in water, which was probably why she was never a strong swimmer, unlike her sister Donna, who bobbed in the local pool like a champagne cork.

Christine pushed to the surface for a breath and then placed her hands against her sides, toes pointed, to sink down to the bottom again. *Ow.* Her toes scraped against a rock. Something rolled under her arch and she hunkered down, scrabbling around the bottom until she found the object; she kicked to the surface with it held high in her hand.

An old plastic doll, one leg missing, one long-lashed eye in a permanent wink. What other junk was buried in the sand? She sighted her location by a big rock on the beach and moved eastward. Wind direction on the Island was usually westerly, which meant that the saw could have drifted down-current before settling.

She dog-paddled ten feet over and began the search process again, trying to sink her feet into the bottom of the deeper water, patting the lumpy sand with her soles.

There. She felt something. She had already pulled out three rocks, but this was longer. A stick, maybe? Her toes tapped along its hard, flat length. She kept her foot pressed down on the object, then squatted underwater, trying to reach the item with her fanned fingertips. It shifted; she pressed her foot firmly down. She grabbed a hold of the object with one hand and pulled it out of the water.

A hacksaw. With small metal teeth made for cutting metal. She held it by the straight edge of the blade, careful not to touch the handle in case it had prints. It looked like about twelve teeth per inch, but she couldn't be sure. She turned the saw over. The RCYC initials were stamped in yellow block letters on the wooden handle. The blade was well-used, the teeth smoothed down in the middle compared to the pointed teeth at the ends.

Christine thrashed toward shore, saw held high. She had found it! Evidence! Water streaming down her torso and legs, she staggered across the sand to the file folder in her bike basket and turned to the page with the mechanic's sketch. She placed the metal blade on the piece of paper beside the illustration, water drops dampening the page. They matched, as if the mechanic had placed the saw on the paper and drawn its outline. She had found it. The tool that had led to Ginny Rogers' death.

She must show the investigators immediately. Surveying her dripping clothes, ribbons of water trailing down her body from her wet hair, she knew she should go change. And that Dr. Jim would chastise her for getting her head wound wet. No doubt her makeup was smeared all over her face, revealing the yellowing, lumpy bruises underneath. But who cared what she looked like? She might have found the key evidence in a murder case.

She quickly shoved her bare feet into her shoes, water trickling into the heels. After depositing the saw in a paper evidence bag, she placed it in her front basket and rolled her bike onto the boardwalk, water squelching in her shoes at each step.

Excitement bubbled up in her chest as she approached the community center. She was going to help find Ginny's killer. Make restitution for her death.

She ran up the stairs to the community center and flung the door open. Thank God, the two men were still there. Ron Allen was pulling on his suit jacket. Fenwick stared as she walked toward them, her footprints leaving wet marks on the wooden floor.

"What happened to you?" Allen said.

"Fall off a dock?" Fenwick said. They both guffawed.

"No," she said. "I went in on purpose."

They laughed harder.

Christine said, "I have evidence in the Ginny Rogers' case."

Fenwick glanced at the paper bag in her left hand. "Again?" he said. He shoved papers into a briefcase.

"Yes," she said.

Allen sighed. "All right. Let's have a look." He motioned her closer.

She hid the bag behind her back. "Could you tell me how the case is going?"

He frowned. "Show me the saw so we can get out of here."

"I would like an update on the case," she repeated. "Island police know this community well, sir. The more we share information, the more likely we are to catch Ginny Rogers' murderer. Especially if the perpetrator is local."

"Show him the saw, PW," Fenwick said from behind Allen.

Christine tensed. It occurred to her they might wrestle the evidence from her. "I don't want to accidentally wipe any fingerprints."

There was a pause for several seconds. Allen stared at her, eyes cold.

"I'm eager to learn," she said, trying to mollify them. "To hear about your investigation techniques, how you create your suspect list. Any aspect of your job you'd like to share."

Allen and Fenwick locked glances. After a few seconds, Fenwick said, "We have no suspects."

She waited.

Allen added, "The Whitmores were in their house, packing. Daniel Rogers was in bed with his wife. Gary Owen walked the dog at midnight and went to bed with his wife. Paddy Jenkins slept at the marina, but there's no corroboration after 1:00 a.m. Samuel Fairmont worked at Clergy House until eleven and took a water taxi home to the mainland. Kevin Lamprey, John Williams and Reggie Farland were partying at a Yorkville bar and crashed at a friend's place on Cumberland Street. None of these alibis are foolproof. Any resident could have snuck out of bed to saw through the brake line. Anyone could have sailed or paddled a boat from the mainland and tampered with the equipment. So, no one. Everyone."

Allen pulled on gloves, and Christine handed him the bag.

"Where'd you find it?" he asked as he removed the saw from the bag.

"The water in front of 42 Lakeshore. About thirty-five feet from shore."

Fenwick approached to examine the blade. "Could be a match."

"Royal Canadian Yacht Club," Christine said, pointing to the initials on the handle. "Their tool shed was broken into a couple of days before the demolition."

Allen sleeved the saw in the evidence bag and placed it on the table.

Suddenly, Fenwick gripped her right wrist, hard. He stared at her as he squeezed, sliding down her hand to crunch her knuckles together, turning her wrist under. Tears rose in her eyes. God, he was going to break a bone. She leaned to maneuver out of his grip, but he moved with her, squeezing her fingers harder. He was too strong. She couldn't get out of his hold or angle herself to throw him off.

He smiled. "Don't ever fuck with our evidence." He squeezed harder, and a cry escaped her; she fell on one knee.

"There's four thousand of us, sixty of you," he said, looking down on her. "You're a smart girl. Do the math." He let go.

Blinking with tears, Christine pulled her injured hand to her chest.

The two men walked past her toward the door. "Clean up this mess," Fenwick said, pointing to the wet floor as he passed by.

Chapter 10

The next day, Christine and Fillingham met on the ferry en route to their afternoon shift.

"Why would a RCYC member damage the dump truck?" he asked for the third time since she'd told him about the club's imprint on the saw.

They leaned their elbows on the ferry's second-story railing, facing the Inner Harbor, the wind fluttering the hems of their uniform jackets, hats clenched in their armpits. Christine carried her dinner in a canvas drawstring bag. Her right wrist was wrapped in a tensor bandage, high enough to cover the mottled bruising on the back of her hand. She was trying not to think about Fenwick during the boat ride—his cold smile as he ground her fingers together and twisted her wrist—or whether he was in the community center right now.

"Maybe Tommy Thompson wants RCYC land for public use, which is what he's said about Ward's and Algonquin Island." She watched a tanker dock at the Redpath factory to the east.

"I've been a RCYC member all my life, and my father and grandfather before me. We have the land by Royal Warrant. We've never heard a rumor that we would have to leave." He turned to her, waiting until she looked at him. "An outsider must have stolen it from the shed."

"Is there overnight security?" she said.

"One guy, patrolling the entire club. Easy enough to get in when his back is turned."

She nodded, remembering how she had climbed the fence to leave. "The saw could be a red herring to put us off the trail of the real perpetrator."

"Exactly!" he said.

There'd be no convincing him that a RCYC member had anything to do with the demolition murder. Not that it was likely, but if forensics matched the striations on the brake line with the saw she had pulled from the lake, then club members had to be considered suspects too.

As they docked, Christine could see Sergeant Bard, Pilkington and Morano seated in the patrol car on a rectangle of grass. Christine and Fillingham walked over and listened to their sergeant give report. Two lost children had been found. A group of boisterous teenagers had been relieved of beer stowed in their picnic hampers. Clergy House was hosting a private function that evening and would be closed to the public. Hamlet, the horse from Far Enough Farm, had jumped the fence again and was munching grass near Gibraltar Point, farm hands in pursuit.

"I heard you found a saw in the lake by the Whitmores'," Sergeant Bard said to Christine.

"Is it a match?" she said.

"Don't know. Investigators aren't in. The lab takes a couple of days, anyway."

"Should we keep checking local sheds and toolboxes for the saw, Sergeant?" she said.

He shook his head. "We've finished the door-to-door, so let's wait to hear from Ident."

"Will the case be bumped up to Homicide?" she said.

Sergeant Bard shrugged. "If they got time. I heard the Yonge Street shopkeeper murder is keeping them busy."

Christine got in the passenger side, relieved at the investigators' absence.

At the station, she stowed her bologna sandwich in the fridge. "No dinner?" she asked Fillingham.

He shook his head. "I'll pick up something from Centerville or Clergy House."

Must be nice to have the money to buy meals. Christine thought of her lone bologna sandwich. There had been little food in the fridge this morning, which was her own fault. She was determined to use her wages to repay the loan for her mom's gambling debt, so the four of them lived on her mom's salary. The sooner she got her family free of George Ray's grasp, the better. Even if it meant she didn't get three square meals a day. Once they got out of debt, they could start saving money to move to a bigger apartment, put aside something for Donna's schooling and pay for baseball training for Wayne.

"Do you cook at home?" she said. She didn't know where he lived. With his parents? With those obnoxious RCYC buddies? On his own? Would it be prying to ask? She didn't want to push things, to seem inquisitive. He was acting normal today, no grudge, no chip on his shoulder regarding their partnership. Her encounter with Fenwick yesterday reinforced her conclusion that Fillingham wasn't so bad as a partner compared with other policemen. Even if he had family money to burn and flirted with every female under the age of thirty.

"I make a mean omelet, but that's it," he replied.

She filled the kettle with water, holding it with her good hand. "Tea before we head out?"

"I'm more of a coffee guy, but sure. Why not. What happened to your hand?"

"Just a sprain," she answered. "Slipped down the stairs."

"You seem accident-prone."

He sounded like her mother. Ever since the demolition, she'd been bugging Christine to return to the Women's Bureau or find a desk duty job at a police station.

"You're not trying to get out of wrestling me?" He hunched over and struck a pose, fists cocked in what he must think was a wrestling move.

She raised an eyebrow. "You caught me."

He shook his head. "You're not wriggling out of it, Sixteen. I'll give you a couple of days, but the match is on."

"Sixteen?"

"That's what we call you." His gaze went to the police badge on her hat. "Isn't that your number?"

"Yes." After a moment she said, "Shall I call you," she leaned forward to inspect his badge, "Three hundred and seventy-five?"

"Doesn't really roll off the tongue like Sixteen does, but sure."

"I think I'll stick to Fillingham."

He smiled. "Whatever floats your boat, Sixteen."

She shook her head, then grabbed the whistling teakettle off the stovetop and poured water into the teapot. Undoubtedly there were other names her peers were calling her behind her back, so Sixteen didn't seem so bad. Officers tended to give each other nicknames in policing: Pilky for Pilkington and CC for Ulster, the older officer who was fond of Canadian Club whisky. Fillingham's was Richie—short for Richie Rich, the comics character.

Placing a metal fan onto the kitchen counter, Fillingham aimed it at the square Formica table where they would have their tea. He unbuttoned his uniform jacket and hung it around the chair, then loosened his tie. Leaning back in his chair, he balanced on its back legs.

Christine shrugged out of her uniform tunic and hooked it around the back of her chair as well. If they were lucky, their tea wouldn't be interrupted by lost children calls or tourists dropping by the station for directions. Sitting down, she placed her palms on the table. "What do we know about the Ginny Rogers case?"

"Now we're the investigators?" he said, eyebrows raised. "I thought Allen and Fenwick were on the job."

She shrugged.

His chair banged to the ground. "Okay, Inspector Clouseau. What do we know?"

"The perpetrator hears about or sees the construction vehicles being ferried across to the Island between 11:00 p.m. and midnight on Wednesday, June 12th," she said. "He may have broken into the RCYC shed several days prior or already had it in his possession. He could be a RCYC member, an Islander or a mainlander like Kevin Lamprey. Between midnight and 8:00 a.m. the next day on the 13th, the truck's emergency brake is cut and the brake line sawed in two."

Fillingham said, "The emergency brake line would be relatively easy to snip with bolt cutters. Cutting the brake lines in a couple of places would take ten minutes. Not a lot of muscle is needed, just persistence with a hacksaw. Could be a woman, if she knew where to saw. Islanders are handy. Metro Council made it illegal for them to renovate, hoping their houses would fall apart and they would leave. So, most Islanders know how to fix things themselves."

"It could be a teenager," Christine said, "or more than one person." She sipped her tea, the steam dampening her face. "I want to know why they sabotaged the truck. Were they trying to halt the demolition, get an injunction? Was it revenge—by the Whitmores? Or another family who had been forced to leave? Someone from the empty house on Lakeshore?"

She looked out the small kitchen window, curtained against the bright sunshine. "The perpetrator must have realized that the truck would plow into something or someone. Islanders would know a crowd would gather at the site, as they have at other house razings. Could he have been so desperate to stop the demolition that he risked a tragedy? Or was that exactly what he wanted—to tarnish Metro Council by linking it to a death?"

Fillingham said, "So, the sabotage of the truck was a preventative strike or retaliation."

"What about Daniel Rogers?" she said. She thought about Nancy Hamilton's rambling accusations against her ex-husband.

"That would be a fall from grace." He paused, thinking about it. "He wasn't at the demolition, which is surprising—you'd think he'd be the first one they phoned. But if he's the culprit, he had to know Islanders would gather. Geez, it was his own daughter who got killed."

"Maybe he didn't think she would be there," she said. "She was supposed to be working at Clergy House. Samuel Fairmont let his staff run over after they heard the excavator." She paused. "Is Fairmont a suspect?"

"He would have to close his restaurant if the Islanders left," Fillingham replied. "No one is around from October to May except the residents. Without locals in the lean months, he'd go bankrupt. Fairmont can't survive on two months of summer tourist business." Fillingham banged his chair down on the floor. "Gary Owen comes to mind. He seems pretty fanatical."

She nodded. They should check Owen's background, see if the head of the residents' association had a record. Or was involved in civil disobedience.

"Many Island employees would lose their jobs if Islanders left," Fillingham said. "Not only from Clergy House, but it would impact ferry staff and water taxi owners too. The Parks and Rec staff would be halved, and the Algonquin Island Yacht Club would have to shutter its doors."

"Putting Paddy Jenkins and Davy Morgan in the unemployment line."

He nodded. "Hard to believe that Davy would do something to hurt Ginny. By all accounts, he loved her."

"Again, maybe he didn't know she would be there," she said.

He placed his empty mug on the table, then tipped back in his chair again. "Too many people. We have to narrow it down."

"Kevin Lamprey could have tampered with the truck and then showed up to the protest to see what happened," Christine said. She still wondered if one of his group had thrown the brick at her, and she felt a flicker of anger at Lamprey. Her cut was still sore, as was her cheekbone. "Except Sergeant Bard said they'd alibied."

"Who vouched for them? Their moms? Girlfriends? Or did they alibi each other?"

"Probably all the above. We should check Lamprey and his crew for priors like destruction of property or illegal squatting. See if they have a pattern." She took out her memo book and penned the key points they had mentioned. It was helpful to work with someone, throw ideas around.

"No women on the suspect list," Fillingham noted. "May Stellar has been lobbying to stop the evictions—she's a Toronto counselor and a lifelong Islander."

"Doesn't mean she'd kill to stay," she said, but she wrote the woman's name down in her notebook.

"The political route hasn't been effective." After a second, Fillingham laughed. "How about Mary Leonard?"

"Who's she?"

He leaned forward, and the chair legs landed with a thump. "She's seventy-five, if she's a day—lives on Ojibway Avenue. You must know the place: overgrown grass, lawn ornaments, hanging bird feeders. A rusty metal sculpture sits in the front yard beside a rotting canoe planted with wildflowers. A combination rainforest and junkyard."

"I know it."

He continued, "The backyard is the coup de grâce. She's got a totem pole—a real live Indian totem pole—and a flagpole. But she's not flying the new maple leaf flag or the Ontario coat of arms."

He paused for effect. "The flag has a marijuana leaf on it. And darned if she doesn't have a couple of plants tucked behind the lavender stalks and rosebushes."

Christine covered her mouth, laughing. "Did you arrest her?"

Fillingham shook his head. "Some Islanders smoke weed. You can smell it on rounds, especially in the evenings. If they are discreet, not causing trouble or selling, Sergeant Bard looks the other way. Plus, I challenge anyone to take Mary Leonard into custody and come out the winner."

The phone rang—the direct line given to Islanders. Fillingham went up front and answered the phone affixed to the office wall.

"Mrs. Clancy," she heard him say. All the officers knew the Islander who lived on Ward's. She called the station daily with her complaints, mostly about the tourists visiting her community.

As Christine washed their cups in the sink and placed them on the rack to dry, she heard Fillingham say, "Yes, people stepping on your marigolds would be upsetting." There was a pause as he listened. "We have something pressing right now, but we will be over later. Yes, we will remind people not to walk through gardens or look in windows. Bye for now."

Christine said, "Do you want me to deal with Mrs. Clancy and you can check with RCYC about the terms of their lease on Toronto Island?"

"Sure." His big smile reflected relief.

They locked the station and went their separate ways. Later in the afternoon, after Fillingham confirmed the permanence of RCYC's tenure on the Island and Mrs. Clancy had been mollified, they met up at Centerville and walked a circuit through the amusement park. After they returned to the station for dinner and let their food settle, they got on their bikes and patrolled Toronto Island end to end, from Hanlan Point in the west, to Manitou Beach in the center, to Ward's Island in the east. From there, Fillingham challenged her to a bike race back to the station, which he won, and they sat down at nine o'clock for a cup of tea.

"Tomorrow, I'm bringing coffee. Arabic," he said.

"That's fine. I drink both." She checked her watch. Two hours before shift change. The main task now was ushering tourists onto the last ferry to the mainland, since they were not permitted to stay overnight. This by-law prevented out-of-control beach parties as well as gave the locals a respite from visitors.

"We could split up to sweep people toward the ferries," Christine suggested.

"I'll check Manitou and Hanlan Beach," Fillingham said. "Can you take Ward's and Algonquin?"

"Sure."

Fillingham had chosen the more strenuous job—rounding up scores of tourists, picnickers and beachcombers and herding them toward the last ferry at eleven o'clock. There were fewer tourists on Algonquin and Ward's this time of night, just a few stragglers coming off Ward's Island Beach or finishing their dessert at Clergy House. She would check the empty house on Lakeshore Avenue a couple of doors down from the Whitmores'—the lease had expired and the tenants had moved out. Young people tended to congregate there overnight to continue their beach parties.

First, Christine headed to the phone booth at Ward's Island dock. She hadn't wanted to call home from the Center Island Police Station. Officers might think it weak or womanly. Besides, she didn't want anyone knowing her business.

Nine thirty. Normally, Donna and Wayne would be in bed. However, today was their last day of school—summer vacation had officially begun. Odds were they would be awake.

Wayne answered on the third ring.

He told her he had his shower already and brushed his teeth. Donna was in bed and Mom was reading in the living room.

"Can I talk to Mom for a sec?" she said.

Christine wondered if her mom thought she was checking up on her, making sure she was sober, that she hadn't gone to bingo. Of course, Phyllis could have a beer or two sometimes. But the deal was she couldn't drink more than that if she was alone with Donna and Wayne. And no more day-long benders, like she had with Eddie. Christine also asked her mom to go to bingo on Christine's days off. At ten years old, Wayne might be old enough to stay home by himself, but he wasn't responsible enough to supervise his younger sister. At the Women's Bureau, Christine had discovered children left alone while their parents were drinking, gambling, soliciting or shooting up drugs. Bad stuff sometimes happened to unsupervised children.

After chatting with her mom and bidding her goodnight, Christine biked up and down the Algonquin Island streets, enjoying the post-tourist lull when the Island returned to its residents. A strolling couple had to be reminded that the last ferry was at eleven. A lone photographer was taking a panoramic picture of the night cityscape, from the Redpath factory in the east to the Canada Malt silos to the west. After hustling him along, she biked the streets of Ward's Island in front of the compact cabins that were originally canvas tents before wooden floors and side walls lent them permanence.

Along Third Street, the air thick with the scent of honeysuckle and roses, a man's voice bellowed, "I don't give a rat's ass what you think!"

A woman responded, but the words were muffled. Christine pressed hard on her bike pedals and headed toward the house at the end of the lane. She saw a man kick a metal garbage can over and then thrash through the tiger lilies across the front lawn. He stomped down the road and around the corner, but not before she got a look at his lean frame, bearded face and furious expression. Gary Owen.

A woman in a furry mint-green housecoat exited the side door of the house, her mouth opened to yell. She caught sight of Christine, and her mouth clamped shut.

After introducing herself, Christine said, "Everything all right, ma'am?"

The woman clutched the lapels of her housecoat, silent.

"Are you hurt? Do you need assistance?"

She shook her head.

"Gary Owen, is he your husband? You're Mrs. Owen?"

She nodded assent.

"Did he hurt you?" Christine asked.

The woman shook her head again. She looked upset, eyes puffy, skin blotchy, but not bleeding or bruised.

"Do you want me to be here when he returns?" Christine said.

"No, but if you see him, you can give him a message from me." Her voice was low and angry.

"Okay," Christine said, her tone hesitant.

"Tell my husband he can go fuck himself, since he's fucked everything else on the Island." She stepped inside, slamming the door.

Christine's eyebrows raised. *Wow.*

There was no love lost between the Owens, that was certain. At least Mrs. Owen didn't seem in danger. As Christine pedaled away from the house, she wondered who Gary had been with. It was a small community; it didn't seem wise to have an affair with another resident.

Was Gary Owen a viable murder suspect? Tonight, he seemed volatile and out of control. Obviously, he had been making poor decisions as a husband. Was he capable of violence—to save Island homes?

At shift change, she'd ask the night patrol to check on Mrs. Owen, make sure she was okay. For now, Christine's last task was to check an abandoned house for squatters before heading back to the station. When she reached 50 Lakeshore, she hopped off her bike. It perplexed her that this empty home remained standing, while the Whitmores' cottage, which had housed a family, had been demolished.

Her flashlight illuminated the graffiti on the walls of the house, as well as cigarette butts, food wrappers and an empty pop bottle. The floor had been stripped of wood, revealing a stained concrete pad underneath. The place reminded Christine of the alleyway she and Gail once patrolled searching for a ten-year-old runaway. They'd been calling the boy's name, moving aside garbage cans and stacked wooden fruit boxes, when a homeless guy emerged from behind a bin and whacked Christine with a bat, thinking she was stealing his belongings. She jerked away at the last moment so that the bat tip hit her in the shoulder instead of her head, but it took her down to her knees. Thank God Gail had been there to wrest the bat out of the guy's grip.

"Hey, there!"

Christine screamed, her flashlight beam dancing over the ceiling. Not a little, "Oh," but an extended, "Aaaahhh!"

The large outline of a man framed the doorway. She targeted his face with her flashlight.

He put his hand up to block the beam. "It's me. Hawk Johnson. From Centerville. The mechanic."

She lowered her arm. "You gave me a scare," she said, coughing out an embarrassed laugh. She had sounded like the shrieking woman in a King Kong movie. Heading toward the door, she forced him to step back outside to let her exit. What was he doing on an abandoned property at ten thirty at night?

"Is there something I can help you with?" she said as they stood outside the house, her heart still pounding in her throat.

"You hungry?" he said.

"Hungry?"

"Are you?"

She *was* hungry. Her stomach felt flat beneath her skirt. She'd gobbled down her lone sandwich at the station, then watched Fillingham plow through his plate of sausage dog, onion rings and fries from the Carousel restaurant.

She nodded.

He motioned with two fingers. "Come with me."

"What for?" she asked.

"To eat."

"To eat? I'm on duty. I have to give report."

"Can't your buddy do it?" He meant Fillingham.

Both of them didn't need to be present at report. And it was always Fillingham who spoke anyway, as if no one would listen to a policewoman. "I guess so."

Hawk pointed to her radio on her belt.

She lifted it out of its case. "Dispatch, 52-25. PW Lane. I'm accompanying civilians to the ferry dock at Ward's Island. Requesting PC Fillingham give report at shift change."

"Request noted," Dispatch said.

"Dispatch, 52-25. PC Fillingham. Request confirmed. PW Lane, do you want me to hold the Center Island ferry?"

Christine looked at Hawk—his deep brown eyes fringed with dark lashes, his cheek dimpling on one side with his smile. She felt something twinge inside. "52-25. PW Lane," she said over the radio. "I'll take the ferry from Ward's. Over."

"I have to head over to the docks first," she said tersely to Hawk, turning her bike around. What was she doing, going out with this man, this stranger, at eleven o'clock at night?

"Want me to check the beach and let visitors know the last boat is leaving in twenty?"

"Sure." She wasn't sure if it was appropriate for Hawk to help her, but she had heard Islanders warning families of the ferry schedule so that they wouldn't be stranded on the Island or have to pay for a water taxi back to the city.

The last ferry blew its horn goodbye, stragglers onboard. She radioed for officers to check on Mrs. Owen and notified Dispatch she was off shift. She still had her radio on her hip, but there were extras at the station for the next shift, and she'd return it tomorrow.

Hawk waited for her a hundred feet from the docks. "Ready to go?" he said, straddling a rusty white bike, a large paper bag filling the front metal basket.

She retrieved her bike from behind the telephone booth.

"Nice ride," he said as they pedaled south.

"Courtesy of Mrs. Polotov," she said.

He nodded. "She makes a mean zucchini loaf."

"You know her?" she said.

"She lives a couple of houses down from me. I fix things for her—a leaking tap, a wonky shelf—so she feeds me."

If Mrs. Polotov let Hawk hang around her house, he couldn't be that bad. He wasn't an ax murderer or anything. Not that you could tell. Kenneth Leishman was nicknamed the Gentleman Bandit for the courteous way he stole thousands of dollars of people's money from Toronto banks.

Her stomach grumbled. It wasn't complicated. She was hungry and off-shift. She'd eat something with Hawk and then take a water taxi home. End of story.

They pedaled through the yellow circle of light that lit the dock area, past the community center toward the boardwalk that looked out onto Lake Ontario. Riding single file, they angled their heads to view the band of moonlight reflecting off the waves. She had never been on the Island after eleven o'clock, hadn't yet done an overnight shift. The voices of tourists had disappeared, replaced by an orchestra of cricket chirps and the lap of waves against the breakwall.

"Where are we going?" she asked, her voice sounding too loud as it carried over the water. She was trying not to think about being with this man, ignoring her rising alarm, the questions skittering in her head.

Hawk motioned forward with his arm, and they biked on.

The boardwalk ended; they rode across Center Island, past the shuttered ice cream stalls, hot dog stands and empty change rooms. A thick line of rocks broke the waves by the beach. A light breeze rustled through the trees, the dipping branches casting shadows across their path. Gliding the bike, she removed her belt with one hand and shrugged out of her uniform jacket, placing both in her front basket. She felt free and alone and yet connected to this man whose broad back she followed.

They continued along Lakeshore Avenue toward Hanlan's. Maybe he was taking her to a concession stand, the one that fed the bathers from Hanlan's Beach, although she was sure it was closed by now. Hawk continued westward toward the Island School attended by local children. She let him pull ahead, watching him disappear, then emerge in the circles of yellow lamplight that lit the road.

When he drew parallel to the school, he looked back over his shoulder at her, then veered right, taking the gravel trail that led to the lighthouse. She followed him, their tires crunching on the white stones. A light attached to a telegraph pole illuminated the limestone blocks of the Gibraltar Lighthouse, whitening it to pearl. As she pedaled past the decommissioned lighthouse, the path narrowed, a sudden veil of darkness enveloping her as the trees and shrubs closed her in.

Christine stopped. Hawk was ahead, bumping along the uneven ground. A marshy stench of decaying plants and algae filled the air. Ten years ago, a woman was killed nearby. She had been discovered in her high heels and dress in the bushes beside Lighthouse Pond, dumped there like an afterthought, like a discarded gum wrapper.

Christine shivered. Nobody knew where she was—including the Island officers now on duty, and her mom, who thought she was working overtime. If Christine called in a 10-1—officer needs assistance—on her radio, it would take Pilkington and Ulster ten minutes to get here and another ten minutes to find her. If Donna or Wayne did this, followed a stranger to a secluded place, Christine would give them heck. Ground them for a week.

Hawk stepped into a band of moonlight. He was holding up two fishing rods.

"We're fishing?" she squawked, her voice dry.

"Tonight's special: pan-fried trout, fresh from the pond. Here." He kicked a bag at his feet, which sounded a metallic ring. "Grab the frying pan. Watch your step."

The bag clanged as she picked it up and followed him into the bush. Twigs crunched underfoot, her oxfords sliding on the muddy patches. She held one arm in front of her to protect her face from the whip of branches, her eyes glued to his broad silhouette so she wouldn't lose him in the poorly lit shrubbery. She tried to place her feet in his footprints, but she still stumbled on tree roots and jutting rocks.

After a minute or two, the darkness opened up, and they were looking at a circle of inky black water: Trout Pond. She had never been here at night. During the day, she could see a sliver of Trout Pond through the bushes where the road curved toward Hanlan's Point. A bullfrog twanged like a plucked guitar string. A bird called out and its mate responded. A wan yellow light from the filtration plant illuminated the arched saplings, bulrushes and thorny bushes huddled around the pond, as if they were trying to stay warm.

Hawk followed a dirt path around the lake's perimeter until they arrived at two large boulders by a dug-out fire pit. He leaned the fishing poles against a boulder, and Christine placed the bag on the ground.

"Catch!" He tossed two items at her, which she fumbled against her chest.

"Wash the potatoes in the pond," he said. "I'll start the fire."

Before she could protest that fires were illegal outside picnic areas, he had headed into the bush to search for twigs.

By the time she had finished hand-scrubbing the potatoes, Hawk was arranging dry branches and underbrush in the pit. Within a few minutes, the fire was crackling, spitting sparks into the dark bowl of sky. He held the potatoes in one hand, pulled a Swiss army knife out of his pants pocket and stabbed the potatoes in quick succession. He wrapped them in foil and tucked the two shiny ovals into the base of the fire.

"Now for the main course," he said, smiling. He hooked bait on the lures dangling from the fishing lines and handed her a rod. She followed him to the edge of the pond.

"You fish before?" he asked.

"Not really."

"Hold the rod up behind your head, like you're going to throw it. Then give it a snap with your wrist," Hawk said, demonstrating with his rod.

Christine copied his actions, trying not to hook herself, wincing from the sharp pain in her injured wrist. Her stepfather had taken her family fishing once, but Wayne had held the rod. She dumped her line in the shallow water several feet away. Hawk took her rod, wound the reel, flicked his wrist and sent the line sailing to the middle of the pond. He handed her back her rod.

"What do we do now?" she said.

He smiled. "Fish."

They were quiet. Christine scanned the trees around the water, then stared into the impenetrable charcoal surface of the pond. She listened intently to the chirping, rustling, cheeping, and buzzing around her, trying to identify the source of each sound.

The silence between them lengthened.

She was fishing on Hanlan's Island in the middle of the night with a stranger. He could assault her. Her police radio sat in her bike basket by the lighthouse. She was a strong, experienced wrestler, but Hawk was an ox of a man—fifty pounds heavier and two inches taller. His arms were thick from working with machines. If he murdered her, no one would be the wiser. He could be Ginny's killer, for goodness' sake.

She looked at his profile in panic: his smooth forehead, straight nose and full lips. He swirled his line back and forth in the water, seemingly oblivious to her mounting fear.

Why would he tamper with the construction truck's brakes? He wouldn't lose his Centerville job if Islanders were evicted. The amusement park attracted tourists and mainland Torontonians more than locals. Maybe he didn't want to give up his house on Ward's Island—but it was a rental with two other Centerville employees; he could always get a place on the mainland for the season. Plus, he was a family friend. He seemed truly grieved by Ginny's death.

The fishing rod jumped out of her hand and clattered against a rock at her feet.

"Grab it!" Hawk said.

She lunged for the handle as it slid toward the water.

"Reel it in," he said.

She cranked the reel, her wrist complaining at the rapid movement. The fish flew out of the water, swinging toward her, its tail slapping her arm. She squealed, almost dropping the rod, embarrassed at her reaction.

Hawk grabbed her line, unhooked the fish with a twist of his wrist and tossed it into a pail of pond water beside him.

"I caught a fish," Christine said.

He laughed. "I see that." They fished for another thirty minutes, and Hawk caught two fish, much larger than hers. When they were done, he grabbed a fish from the pail, laid it on a flat rock and crushed its head with a rock. Christine grimaced. He cut off the head with his knife and slit the underbelly, then threw the head and guts into the water.

He grabbed a second fish. "Can you turn the potatoes? Tongs are in the bag with the pan."

After she rotated the potatoes, he set a metal grill over the fire pit. He placed the heavy iron pan on the grill with a thunk, waited for the pan to warm, then poured oil into it. He rustled something between his fingers.

"Garlic," he said as he peeled off the outer skin and dropped the crushed bulb into the pan. The oil sizzled, emitting a waft of warm, oniony fragrance. She never had food seasoned with fresh garlic before. Her stomach rumbled.

He retrieved the strips of filleted fish and lined them in the pan, sizzling. They sat down on the boulders as the fish cooked, watching a trail of smoke ascend. Christine hoped that the officers on duty didn't notice the fire during their rounds. She could never explain her presence with Hawk.

"Here," he said, offering a thermos.

She shook her head.

"It's water," he said.

She felt her face warm with mortification at her assumption. There wasn't a large Indigenous population in Toronto. During some of her shifts, she would see drunk or homeless men on Yonge Street. But of course, drink wasn't just a problem for native people. Look at her mom. And her sergeant.

Christine took the thermos and drank gratefully.

"Indians used to fish all around this island," he said.

"Really?"

He nodded. "For a thousand years. More. Different tribes would meet here to trade and hunt. Paddle down the rivers. We taught white people how to spear fish in the harbor."

"My stepbrother, Wayne, he's ten; he'd love to fish here."

"Is that who you live with?" he said.

She nodded. "My stepbrother and stepsister, who's eight. Then there's my mom, of course." She paused. "And you? What about your family?"

"They're back on a reserve near Sudbury," he said. "I have an uncle in town and a cousin in Belleville."

Hawk took a stick and rolled the potatoes out of the fire.

"Did Indians ever live on the Island?" she said. Many Algonquin Island streets featured tribal names: Seneca, Ojibway, Dacotah.

He shook his head. "Not all year long. Tribes visited the area seasonally—when the fishing and hunting were good. And used the land for healing and relaxing. Its Indian name is Menecing, which means 'of the island.' It's Anishinaabe territory."

"Is that what you are? Anish-i-naabe?"

He nodded. "Ojibway. From Whitefish Lake."

"Do...do you go back there?"

He got up to turn the fish in the pan. "When I can. It's deer season in the fall, so once I finish at Centerville I'll head home to hunt with my uncles."

When the fish was cooked, he seasoned it with salt and pepper, then slid a fillet onto her plate. He handed her a potato and cutlery. A waft of roasted garlic steamed her face.

"Sorry, no butter for the potatoes," he said. "But this should do." He poured the remaining garlic oil from the pan over her cut-open potato.

After he sat down, she took a hesitant bite of the seared fish. "This is delicious," she said, oil greasing her lips.

The potatoes had a fire-roasted taste, like they had been smoked. Within three minutes, she had cleared her plate. He pointed to the remaining fish in the pan. She nodded, and he split it between the two of them.

"You got a good appetite," he said.

She wiped her mouth on the back of her hand, embarrassed at her hunger. Why couldn't she eat daintily, like other women? "I know," she said. "I'm as tall as a man, heavy as a man; I eat like a man. The boys called me Ogre in grade school."

"You're definitely a woman," he said, his gaze level as he looked at her. The comment hung in the air between them.

He took her plate and cutlery and went pond-side to rinse the dishes. When he returned, he sat down on the rock across from her, leaning forward so that his braids hung down his chest.

"You look better," he said, scanning her face in the firelight.

She was embarrassed by a reminder of her injuries, her face evidence that she hadn't been able to control the crowd, to save Ginny.

"I tried the yellow paste you gave me," she said. "It reduced the swelling." Her skin had felt less itchy, too.

He nodded, smiling. The firelight flickered across his cheekbones, making his skin look like warm, polished stone.

"Do you braid your hair yourself?" she blurted out. She cringed. Was she discussing hair styles with him?

"Braids show unity of thought," he said, touching his temple lightly with his fingertips, then sliding his hand down a braid to the leather tie at the tip.

"It's beautiful." Rich, black, shiny. So different from the razor-cropped hair of policemen.

"You can touch it," he said.

She looked at him for a second, then leaned forward from her seat and ran her fingers down the length of one braid. Holding it in her palm, she felt its weighty, ropy beauty. He tugged the leather ties, and his long hair spread around his shoulders and over his chest, rippling with the red-white light from the fire.

She sank both hands into his hair, inhaling its grassy sweetness. Their faces were close. Touching his hair seemed more intimate than an embrace, than a kiss.

After a minute, he said, "Your turn."

Arms lifted, she pulled out the pins that secured her police hat to her head. He kneeled in front of her, took her hat and placed it carefully on a bed of twigs beside them. His thick fingers were gentle as he felt for the bobby pins that kept her chignon in place at her nape. Her hair spilled down, almost as long as his.

He whispered something as he ran his fingers through her tresses like a comb.

"What?" she asked, her eyes half-closed with the hypnotic rhythm of his stroking.

"*Zenibaanh*," he repeated, "like silk."

She lunged for him, pulling him to her, kissing him ferociously as she sank to her knees in front of him. At first, he pulled back, as if in surprise, then she felt his arms wrap around her waist, pulling her into his chest. She hooked her fingers in his hair as she kissed him, his scent wrapped around her.

A kingfisher called out in alarm from a branch close by. She paused. What was she doing? She pressed down on his arms. He released her, and she stood up quickly.

"Wait," he said, still kneeling, looking up at her.

"I'm sorry," she said.

He stood up, reaching for her hand. She stepped back.

"Christine, you've done nothing wrong. We've done nothing wrong," he said.

"It's Lane. PW Lane. This is a mistake."

"Why?'

"For many, many reasons."

"Give me one."

"You know why."

"No, I don't."

They stood facing each other in front of the fire, silent. It wasn't right, she thought, but people were unfair—afraid of anyone who wasn't exactly like them.

Hawk crossed his arms, his stance wide. "I want you to say it."

Did she need to tell him how it would be if a white woman dated a native? "I'm a police officer."

He cocked his head. "So?"

"You live on the Island; you work on the Island. You are part of the community I serve."

"So?"

"You could be a suspect for all I know."

He pointed his thumb at his chest. "You think I killed Ginny?"

She shook her head. "I'm sorry. I shouldn't have come. I shouldn't have...done that."

He took a step toward her. "I'm not sorry."

Leaning down, she retrieved her police hat and rammed it on her head, her hair still loose.

"Thanks for supper," she said, not looking at him. "It was delicious. I'll find my way back."

She turned, aiming blindly in the direction she hoped was the path to the lighthouse. Hands raised to bat away branches, she ran through the dark bush; she tripped on a rock, skinning her right knee and ripping a hole in her nylons. Immediately, she pushed herself up, wanting to put as much distance as possible between herself and Hawk.

Back on her bike, she pedaled to the Hanlan ferry dock as if a forest fire were chasing her. At the dock, she caught a water taxi with a couple from California who hadn't realized that the last ferry had left ninety minutes ago.

Christine sat by herself in the boat's stern, staring at the forested silhouette of Hanlan's Point, feeling Hawk's presence beyond the tree line. What had she done? The pulse in her neck throbbed, her breathing quick with fear, exhilaration, regret. She put her hands up to her face and smelled his sweetness, the meadow smell of his hair on her fingers, and she kept her hands pressed to her face until they docked.

Chapter 11

The bell on the station door jingled. Christine paused over the lost wallet report she was completing at her desk.

"Sarah!" she said in surprise.

Her friend stood inside the station in a floppy beach hat that framed her short brown curls, freckles sprinkled across her nose. Gail and Julie entered the station behind Sarah. Her three Women's Bureau colleagues, whom she had known since Police College, smiled at her.

"Hey," Fillingham said, addressing Julie as he approached the counter. Julie was sporting big white Jackie O sunglasses and a sarong over her bathing suit.

"Hi there, soldier," Julie said. "We need a hostage."

"Take me," he said, offering his wrists to shackle.

She pushed her glasses up into her white-blonde hair and looked at him with her wide brown eyes made to look bigger with eyeliner. "Tempting as that may be," Julie said, "our mission is to kidnap her." She pointed at Christine.

"I'm—I'm working," Christine stammered, standing up.

"You're off at three," Julie said.

"We have to give report," said Christine.

"She's grumpy today," Fillingham said in a fake whisper to the three friends.

Christine scowled at him. She'd gotten home at one thirty in the morning after fishing with Hawk and then had to wake up at five o'clock for day shift. She was tired, that was all.

"I can give report," he said. "You go." He waved her away with his hand.

Christine looked at Julie. "I told Donna and Wayne I'd be back at four after their camp."

"I called your mom," Sarah said. "She's home. The deal's done." She lifted the hinged section of the counter and came inside the office area. "Here." She shoved a straw bag into Christine's hands. "Go get changed. We brought you a bathing suit and towel." She turned Christine around by the shoulder and gave her a push toward the back room.

Christine went into the one washroom—there was no women's change room in the tiny station. Her friends' voices could be heard through the door, their high, tinkling laughter, followed by Fillingham's lower timbre.

She frowned as she pulled out a bikini top. It must belong to Sarah, who was closest to Christine's size but three inches shorter and slimmer. The bathing suit was navy, with red and white piping, giving it a nautical appearance. Christine didn't swim often. She owned a black one-piece, a bit stretched out of shape now. It was hard to find suits long enough in the torso. A bikini bottom normally sat at a woman's waist, which meant that this one would rest below her bellybutton, but at least it would cover her. The problem was the halter top. It barely squeezed over her breasts. She filled the bra cups to the brim, like a go-go dancer from the Zanzibar Tavern. Any sudden movement and she would spill out. There was no way she was going out in public like this. She pulled on her gray, police-issue gym shirt and shorts over the suit.

When she came out, Sarah said, "Geoffrey left to meet the next shift at the docks."

"Nice look, Lane," Julie said. "Would you like a winter coat as well?"

Christine lifted the countertop and walked underneath. "Some of us aren't screaming for attention."

"Take the catfight outside." Sarah pushed each friend toward the door. Out in the sunshine, she turned to Christine. "Which way?"

"If you want quiet, turn left to Ward's Island Beach. Go straight if you want a crowd."

Raising a manicured hand in the air, Julie said, "Give me loud and rowdy every time!" Her wedge sandals gave her a pronounced wiggle as she walked.

"You are loud and rowdy every time," Sarah told her.

"Okay, everyone," Christine said, feeling excitement bubble up. An afternoon on the beach with her friends was a perfect antidote to her sleepless night spent citing the reasons she couldn't date Hawk Johnson. "We're heading to Manitou Beach!"

Reaching the south end of the Island ten minutes later, the four women unrolled their towels onto the sand, Julie and Gail in front, Christine and Sarah behind. Christine pulled off her shorts but kept her shirt on. Gail wore shorts and a t-shirt, but that was Gail. Everything about her was sensible and blunt, from her haircut, to the way she dressed, to her advice.

Julie removed her sarong and rolled onto her stomach, her shoulders bare above her white and pink polka-dot bandeau top. "This is the life," she said, looking up at Christine. "Why didn't I think of transferring here?"

Christine said, "If you recall, I didn't mean to transfer to Toronto Island; 52 Division dumped me here because they didn't want a woman on their patrol."

"Downtown cops are unfriendly," Gail said, sitting cross-legged on her striped towel.

"They're not all bad," Sarah said.

"You're always defending them," said Gail, "because you married one."

Sarah shook her head, her short brown curls shaking. "Hans, Greg, the guys from the Youth Bureau, they're good people. We're all on the same team. We all serve and protect," she said, echoing the new motto of the force.

"You're such a social worker," Gail said.

"And you're such a hardass," Sarah returned.

"Wow, that didn't seem very counselor-like," Julie said, laughing. "Here," she handed a silver flask to Gail, "keep the peace."

Gail took a slug from the flask and wiped her mouth. A taste for whisky was one trait policewomen had acquired from their male peers. Sarah took a mouthful next and offered it to Christine, who shook her head.

"Miss Squeaky Clean doesn't want to imbibe in a public place?" Julie said. Drinking in public beaches and parks was illegal.

Christine frowned. That was exactly what worried her. It was different for her friends. This was their day off. For her, the Island was her place of work. Sergeant Bard or Morano might drive by, or she might see Mrs. Polotov, Daniel Rogers. Or Hawk.

Hawk. She had been trying to dismiss memories of him all day: fishing companionably side by side, eating beside the fire and the pressure of his mouth on hers. Her hand went to her lips, remembering the sensation of the kiss.

"We can't all flirt our way out of trouble," Christine said to Julie as she returned to the conversation.

"Oooh," Julie said, flicking sand onto Christine's outstretched legs. "Why don't you call Officer Fillingham on me?"

Great. Julie was infatuated with her partner. "Keep away from him," Christine said flatly.

Julie's eyes widened. "I'm sorry, when did you call dibs?"

Sarah pressed on Julie's arm with her bare foot. "We're supposed to be nice to Christine. She's recuperating, remember."

"He's the only Island officer who will work with me," Christine informed Julie.

"What a surprise," Julie said.

"Enough, Julie," Sarah said, her tone stern.

Christine could feel herself flush. Julie was getting under her skin. "I don't want another McMann," Christine said.

McMann was a court police officer who sometimes gave policewomen a lift to Five Division when a female suspect needed to be searched. Julie dated him once then dumped him. He wouldn't go away, hanging around the Women's Bureau, following Julie around, pleading with the PWs to put a good word in for him.

"You're so square," Julie said to Christine, then flopped onto her back.

They were all silent. Christine looked across the water to the Leslie Street Spit, following the maneuvers of the seagulls as they chased each other in diving loops. It was nice of her friends to come down on their day off, to force her to go to the beach. Aside from her family, her WB friends were her most important relationships. She hadn't kept in contact with anyone from high school, and her former colleagues from Records were older than her. She shouldn't let Julie or her tiredness make her cranky.

"Anybody know that guy?" Gail said, pointing to a boat motoring toward them a half mile away, sails down, the man at the helm waving.

Julie shaded her eyes, then quickly stood up. She walked a few steps closer to the water. "It's him," she called back.

"Who?" Gail said.

"Geoffrey."

Fillingham! What the heck was he doing?

The engine throttled lower as the boat slowed in shallower water. It wasn't Fillingham's racing scull; he must have borrowed another from his club or owned another boat.

"He wants us to come aboard!" Julie ran down the beach in her bikini, splashing into the gentle waves. She got waist deep and then started swimming, head held above the water to keep her makeup and hair dry.

The three remaining women stood up. Fillingham motioned for them to come aboard.

"Let's go," Sarah said.

Christine shook her head.

"You need to learn to have fun," Sarah said. "Grab her arm," she instructed Gail, and they half pulled, half dragged Christine down the beach into the water.

"What about our stuff?" Christine looked back at their towels and beach bags.

"We'll be back soon," Sarah said.

Gail swam ahead and reached the boat; Julie was already on board. Fillingham had cut the engine. He directed them to a metal rung in the stern to get in.

Christine ignored the hand Fillingham held out and pulled herself into the back of the boat. Water dripped down from her untied hair, her shirt clinging to her torso.

"Lane?" he said, scanning her body, "You're, you're..."

"An Amazon," Sarah said as she pulled herself into the boat and sat down on one of the padded benches on either side of the cockpit.

Julie stepped between Fillingham and Christine. Her polka-dot bikini, Cupid-bow lips and blonde bob made her look like a fair-haired Betty Boop. "Where we going, sailor?" she said.

It took him a few seconds to look at her.

Christine plunked down on the bench beside Gail.

"A tour around the Island, ladies?" he said. "Or across the lake?"

"Just the Island," Christine interjected, wanting to get this over with.

"Your wish is my command," he said, bowing to her, then to the other three. He started the engine.

As they chugged westward along the shoreline, Christine tried to relax. The light breeze was drying her hair, and the sun warmed the cushioned seats. The boat bumped gently as it motored through the waves. They passed stretches of sandy beach, juxtaposed between patches of rocks and shrubs, where couples and families picnicked and played in the water.

Fillingham stood at the helm in aviator glasses, the wind ruffling the top of his sun-lightened hair, occasionally ballooning his white golf shirt. He turned the tiller of the small motor, and they headed northward around Gibraltar Point.

"Is this the naked beach?" Julie yelled to him from her seat beside him.

"Up ahead," he said.

They puttered toward Hanlan's Point Beach. From a distance, the people standing in the water looked like beige animals with dark splotches. When they got closer, the boaters could see a scrawny man standing in two feet of water like a stork and a pair of large men strolling along the beach. All of them naked.

"Yuck," Gail said.

"I didn't say it was pretty," Fillingham yelled over the motor's drone. The boat eased away from the shore and headed toward the Western Gap between the Island and the mainland. "We'll take the scenic route," he said as he turned into a lagoon.

Christine pulled her hair into a ponytail so that it wouldn't whip in her face. They were in Blockhouse Bay. Over Julie's shoulder, Christine spied the new marina for Jewish sailors built because the RCYC didn't allow Blacks or Jews. In the pool beside the clubhouse, children cannon-balled into the deep end. She thought of Hawk. Did any of the marinas accept native people? She didn't think so, except perhaps the Algonquin Island Yacht Club, whose members were locals.

Fillingham maneuvered around a group of children learning to kayak. Seeing the Island from the water instead of land gave Christine a fresh perspective. Hanlan's Point seemed so green, so natural. For parts of the tour, she could imagine they were in an unpopulated wilderness.

"Trout Pond." Fillingham pointed to the small body of water visible through a narrow break in the foliage.

Christine felt the prickle of a blush, picturing herself kneeling in front of Hawk, kissing him as if she were ravenous, as if he were the last man on Earth. His attraction was almost hypnotic. What if she had stayed longer?

Across the pond loomed the white-brick wall of the water filtration plant. A flash of red appeared in the surrounding trees.

"What was that?" Christine asked, pointing at the shrubbery.

Fillingham shaded his eyes from the sun's glare. "I don't see anything." He turned to her. "It's a protected area—a sanctuary. No one is allowed back there, unless you're the horse on the lam from Far Enough Farm. He meanders over at night to nibble the clover." They all laughed.

As the boat motored slowly through the channels, they waved at the people ambling along the Island's paths. They entered the Inner Harbor, the waterway between the mainland and Toronto Island. Center Island, Olympic Island and then Algonquin Island passed by—the latter populated by homes that had been floated down from Hanlan's Island when the airport had displaced them. As the group passed the Ward's Island ferry docks, Christine spied kids playing tag on the field in front of the community center. It was the summer camp called Supervision. A photograph at the funeral depicted Ginny Rogers as a camp leader surrounded by laughing children in bathing suits.

A tall, gray-haired man was directing children to lift a banner in the air. It was Gary Owen. Christine recalled his voice the other night, his howl of rage and the way the house shook when he slammed the door. The campers moved along the length of the banner, then hoisted it up. In large black block letters was a message:

SAY NO

PIERRE TRUDEAU

SAVE OUR HOMES

It looked like the residents' association hoped that the newly elected prime minister would see their banner and intervene in their battle with Metro Council. The dispute over Toronto Island property continued. The demolitions hadn't been halted after Ginny's death, just delayed. There would be subsequent evictions.

Christine's shoulders tensed at the thought of more protests. More violence.

Fillingham steered them south through the choppy waters of the Eastern Gap and angled the boat toward Ward's Island Beach.

"Can we head back?" Christine yelled to Fillingham, pointing toward Manitou Beach. She had spent enough off-duty time with her partner.

"I want to stay," Julie said, crossing her arms, looking up at Fillingham.

"Can we sail her?" Gail said, pointing to the boom. Gail had been in the navy before joining the police force.

"Sure," Fillingham said. "You sail?"

Gail nodded, and they began discussing the sailboats they had crewed.

A discussion ensued about who would stay. They decided that Sarah and Christine would go back to Manitou Beach, and Fillingham would take Gail and Julie for a short sail.

Fillingham slowed down as he neared Center Island and then cut the engine. Sarah followed Christine to the boat's gunwale, and they slid into the water. Sarah turned and waved at the boat while Christine dog-paddled to shallower water. On shore, they shook the sand off their towels and lay down on their backs beside each other to dry off in the sun.

Christine exhaled, her arm flung over her eyes to block the sun. Sarah was right. She needed to get out and have fun. The warmth on her arms and legs felt soothing. The smell of the lake, the hardness of the sand underneath her, the cry of the cormorants and the chatter of children making sandcastles coalesced into a hypnotic hum. She was almost asleep when Sarah patted her elbow.

Christine lifted her arm and smiled at her friend.

"How are things going?" Sarah said. "You gave us quite a scare."

"Thanks for sending Julie to the hospital to check up on me."

Sarah touched Christine's arm again. "When we heard Dispatch say there was an officer down on Toronto Island, we were worried. Julie was frantic."

That was Julie: hot and cold. "I'm okay now," Christine said. "Bruises are fading, stitches removed, headaches are better." Her wrist still twinged when she rotated it, a gift from Fenwick, but she didn't want to talk about the investigators.

Sarah said, "It's so sad about that young woman's death."

Christine flashed to the image of Ginny lying on her back, pale face against the green grass. "Everyone knew her on the Island, knew her family. And she was young, barely out of high school."

Sarah said, "Kids are the worst."

Christine wondered if Sarah was thinking about the time the two of them had gone to the apartment of a heroin addict who had been jailed for prostitution. Another street walker had told them that the woman had a baby at home. After the building superintendent opened the door, Christine spied the six-month-old baby in a filthy pink dress on the couch, motionless, brown eyes staring at the ceiling. They thought she was dead. When Christine checked the baby's thin neck for a pulse, the infant's eyes had ever so slowly blinked; Christine had jumped back two feet.

"Ginny's mom is taking it hard," Christine said. "I'm not sure if she's doing drugs or drinking, but she walks around the Island like a ghost, mumbling about her daughter's killers."

"Who does she say did it?"

"She's accusing Ginny's dad—Daniel Rogers."

"The news guy?" Sarah said.

Christine nodded. "He has an alibi—in bed, sleeping with his second wife." She sighed. "Island officers don't have a clue who tampered with the equipment. The investigators keep their cards close to their chest, which is frustrating. It's like we are conducting two separate investigations, which isn't effective."

Christine looked around and cautiously peeled off her wet t-shirt, making sure her bikini top stayed on. After smoothing the shirt out to dry on Gail's towel, she and Sarah rolled onto their stomachs to let the sun dry their other side.

"What do you do on shift?" Sarah said, their heads facing each other on their towels.

Christine answered, "We patrol the amusement park and beaches, respond to calls about lost children, misplaced wallets. In the evenings, there may be an illegal fire to quench or people trying to camp overnight. The occasional drunk tourist or sailor has to be cautioned."

"Doesn't sound like you make many arrests."

Christine shook her head. "This assignment won't do anything for my monthly performance report."

"Hanlan's Beach give you problems?" Sarah said.

"Aside from the fright?" Christine said.

They both laughed.

"The only time I patrolled it was with this officer, Morano, once on afternoons," Christine said. "I could tell he didn't want to work with me. Station patrol is different than the Women's Bureau. At the WB, we get calls involving children, families, women. That's our purview. Sometimes, we work undercover with guys from the Youth Bureau or Morality, but policemen don't have to work with policewomen on a day-to-day basis."

"Island officers don't want to work with a woman?" Sarah said.

Christine replied, "Not really. When I worked with Morano, he barely spoke to me for the eight hours. Near the end of our shift, he tells me to get in the patrol car so we can round up the tourists to get them on the last ferry at eleven. So we head over to Hanlan's Point."

Christine turned on her side, facing Sarah. "He's driving fast—there's no cars allowed on the Island, except for police and the parks department. A few people are walking or biking along the path. He's beeping his horn, scattering people left and right. I'm afraid he's going to run someone over. I'm holding on for dear life, yelling at him to slow down, and suddenly he veers off the path into the dunes at Hanlan's Beach. We bounce over the sand toward the lake. It's dark; ten o'clock at night. I can see shadows diving out of the way of the vehicle and hear men's voices—screaming and swearing. Morano reaches down beside his seat and pulls out this long stick—but it's not a stick, it's a riding crop, like they use at the police stables."

"What did he do with it?" Sarah asked.

"People are wading in the water, back lit by the airport lights. As we drive closer, I can see they are mostly older men. They're naked. Morano aims the patrol car straight at them. As soon as they see the vehicle, they run, like they recognize him. Everyone is trying to escape across the sand to the shrubbery where they'd be safe. We drive alongside this bald guy, and Morano swats him across the shoulders with the crop. The man screams and falls in the sand. Then Morano chases down another man, and he smacks him twice on the rump. He drives up and down the beach, whipping people in the chest, shoulders, arm, back, and face, hollering, "'Queers to the dock! Queers to the dock!'"

Christine continued, "I'm yelling at him to stop. I want to jump out, but I'm afraid he'll run me over. Everyone's screaming, scrambling to get out of the way—a family with two young children dive into the scrub. Morano, he's laughing and hollering, totally excited. When the beach is clear, when everyone is hiding in the bushes or running along the path to the ferry, he guns it into the water and drives along the shoreline until he gets here." Christine pointed to the sand. "He stops near the Center Island pier, and I jump out of the car."

"What did you say?" Sarah said.

"I wanted to tell him he was a lunatic, but I was worried he would aim for me when I got out of the car. I told him I would round up more tourists by foot and took off to the bathroom, where I would be safe."

"What happened after that?"

"I tried to tell my sergeant after report, when Morano was already on the ferry, but Sergeant Bard said Morano was a queer-hater—like all Catholics. Had a temper. That's why Morano got transferred to the Island. I asked Sergeant Bard if Morano was a woman-hater too. Sergeant Bard said no, except if the woman was taking the job of a policeman. Then he didn't like her so much."

"Good thing you got paired with Fillingham."

Christine eased down on her stomach again. "Why don't you transfer to the Island, Sarah?" she said. "It would be great to work together again."

Sarah laughed. "And end up Morano's partner? Who knows how long you're going to be here? If any more houses get demolished, there'll be no community to police." She sat up, crossed her legs and pulled on her sun hat. "I don't know how long I'll be on the force, anyway."

Christine looked up, startled. "What do you mean?"

Sarah's brown eyes were warm as she smiled. "We're thinking about it."

"About what?"

Her smile widened. "Having a baby."

Christine scrabbled to a sitting position. "Why?" Her tone was plaintive.

Sarah laughed.

"I mean," Christine amended, "that's great!" She touched Sarah's knee. "Sorry. I'm happy for you and Robbie. You'll make great parents. But you have to quit the force if you're pregnant."

"That's the official policy, but I hear they might change it."

"I hope they do. You're the best PW I know."

"They revised the contract to allow policewomen to marry officers and continue working. We're hoping they change their mind about pregnancy, too."

Pregnant. Christine couldn't imagine having a baby. Her life was filled with caring for her siblings, worrying about her mom and taking extra shifts to pay off her mom's debt. She couldn't envision herself married, living separately from her family. Furthermore, she hadn't been on a date in ages—except for last night with Hawk. She remembered the tug of his fingers as they combed through her hair, the anchoring feel of his arms around her. For a moment, she was tempted to tell Sarah about Hawk, but what would be the point? They couldn't be together.

Sarah said, "How's your mom?"

Christine brushed sand off her towel, forcing the image of Hawk away. "The same. Still working at Records. Playing bingo when she can."

"Her drinking okay?"

Christine nodded. "Alcohol's not permitted at bingo, which helps."

"How are Donna and Wayne?"

Christine smiled. "Wayne is playing baseball every chance he gets. And Donna is the teacher's pet and a know-it-all. I'll be signing up for extra duty for the rest of my life to pay for her schooling."

The sailboat came into view with Julie and Fillingham at the tiller while Gail slackened the sail to slow them down. Christine and Sarah waved, and the women on the boat waved back. The engine cut and the sloop slowed to a stop. Gail joined Julie at the tiller and motioned her to step out of the boat. Julie continued talking with Fillingham, head tilted back in laughter, one hand on his forearm.

Gail turned Julie around by the shoulders and shuffled her to the edge of the transom. When Julie continued her conversation with Fillingham, Gail thwacked her in the back, sending Julie tumbling into the lake with a white spray. Gail calmly slipped in after her friend and began a leisurely front crawl toward the beach.

Julie surfaced, sputtering, and swam toward Christine and Sarah with short, angry strokes. She followed Gail out of the water, her mascara raccooned around her eyes, her blond hair flattened on her head.

Reining in her laughter, Christine said, "A good sail?"

Julie plopped down on her towel with an angry "Harrumph." Sarah handed her a tissue to wipe her smeared makeup.

Gail sat down on her towel next to Julie, an amused look on her face. Sarah motioned for Gail to offer Julie the remaining whisky to make amends for pushing her in the water.

Julie grabbed the flask from Gail's extended arm and tipped it back, emptying it.

After a few minutes, the four women lay down on their towels, adjusting their angle to match the sun's trajectory. Christine wanted to ask them to work a shift with her at the Mariposa Music Festival taking place on the Island in two weeks, but she didn't want to break the comfortable silence. The sun on her face, her friends by her side and the memory of Hawk's lips on her mouth—life was good.

Chapter 12

Fillingham was talking to a group of young women on the ferry. The trio sat on a bench, listening raptly to his storytelling, lipsticked mouths slightly ajar. At the punchline, their shoulders shook with laughter. Fillingham spotted Christine. She nodded, then turned away, not interested in joining his harem. It was enough that she had sailed with him and they were working together today. No need to chat on the ferry over to the station. And she was tired anyway. Yesterday was her day off, so she had signed up for a twelve-hour overtime shift at a Canada Day celebration so she could make an extra payment on her mom's debt.

Her eyes closed, and she let herself enjoy the breeze tickling her face as the boat chugged across the Inner Harbor.

A tap on her shoulder. It was Fillingham. "Tonight's the night." He rubbed his palms together.

"For what?"

He leaned closer. "Wrestling!"

She frowned. "You still want to do that?" Her hand had healed; she had no excuse.

"After what you did to Doug?" He laughed aloud, pantomiming throwing someone over his hip to the ground. "Absolutely!"

At the ferry dock, they took report from the day shift officers. Christine glanced over at Fillingham as they drove to the station. His aviator sunglasses made look like an advertisement for Air Canada. Why had she said she would teach him to wrestle? His eager, puppy-dog expression, contagious smile and amusement at Doug's tumble into the boat had sucked her in. A moment of camaraderie had clouded her judgment. Men said they wanted to learn, but when a woman pinned them to the mat, they changed their tune. No one wanted to be beaten by a girl. When the boys on the high school wrestling team were losing a practice match to her, they pinched the inside of her arm, pulled at her wrestling suit, hooked fingers into her eye—anything to regain the upper hand.

Except for Ron, the captain. He was respectful, treating her like an equal, like a competitor. In her senior year, she felt a shift between them, a tension. Their hands on each other were hot, pressing. He had a girlfriend—everyone knew that. Patty Sorenson draped herself on Ron's arm as they strolled down the hallway like the prom king and queen they would become. Ron's eye would slide over Christine as he gave a barely perceptible nod. But on the wrestling mat, within its circle, it was the two of them and their battle. Often, they were the last to leave the gym, the coach instructing Ron to shut the doors and turn off the lights when they were done.

She had liked Ron. He was nice to her. She would look out the window during class and daydream about him asking her to the prom, because Patty Sorenson was a blank pretty girl and Ron wanted more—a girl with substance, like Christine. In the stores, Christine let herself sift through racks of prom dresses, fingering their silky textures, wondering if she could convince her stepdad to give her money for a dress instead of his usual purchase of a forty-ouncer.

She had let Ron have sex with her on a mat in the girls' change room. It had been her first time. At the end of the next practice, she had sex with him again. In the hallway that week, she had boldly said hello to him, her eyes meeting his. A mottled blush stained Ron's shaved cheeks; his girlfriend blinked her long eyelashes with suspicion.

And that had been it. No more late-afternoon training sessions, no more laughter, tender fingers brushing her neck, pressing the length of her thigh. After two weeks of being avoided, Christine cornered him in the hall beside the gym and mustered the courage to ask him what was wrong.

"I can't do this," he said, his eyes drifting to the Canada Food Guide stapled to the bulletin board. "I have a girlfriend. Patty doesn't want me talking to you anymore."

"So it meant nothing?"

He looked at her. "Not nothing. Just..." His gaze drifted away. "Not something."

So now Fillingham wanted to wrestle. There was no risk of him becoming another Ron; she never dated policemen. But she didn't want a petulant partner plotting revenge because she humiliated him on the mat.

The shift was busy with calls from Centerville: two lost children and a boy who had broken his leg falling out of an antique car. The partners split up during their patrol of the amusement park; Christine scanned the ride areas for a six-foot-two, muscular man with braids, afraid of seeing Hawk but disappointed when he was not sighted.

By the time Christine and Fillingham ate their dinner, checked the houses of vacationing Islanders and pulled on the locked doors of the public school, the sun had set. There was only an hour and a half left in their shift.

Christine was finishing the incident report regarding the boy with the broken leg when Fillingham appeared in shorts and a t-shirt.

"Wrestling time!" He sounded like the announcer for *Hollywood Squares*. He pointed to the yard behind the station. "Get your gym clothes on. I borrowed mats from RCYC."

"It's too dark," she said.

"I have a floodlight. I'll bring a radio in case there's a call. Meet you outside in five." The door slammed.

Christine exhaled loudly. Wrestling Fillingham was wrong for so many reasons. Inappropriate. Unprofessional. Folly. Plus, she didn't like people touching her. She remembered the feel of Hawk's hands on her hips and felt her skin tingle. Okay, most of the time she didn't like it.

Reluctantly, she changed into her shorts and t-shirt and went outside, eyes blinking at the brightness of the orb of light illuminating four large black mats pushed together on the lawn.

Fillingham stood in the middle of the mat, hopping from one foot to another in his bare feet, occasionally throwing a punch. Spotting her, he ran over, vibrating with energy. "What's the regulation size of the mat?" he asked.

"The circle is twenty-eight feet in diameter," she said reluctantly.

"We're smaller, but that's okay." The mats looked like a dark rectangle of water underneath the light's glare. "Do I start like this?" He held his arms out front, weaving left and right.

"I don't want to do this," she said.

He stopped moving, his brow furrowed. "Why?"

"It won't end well."

"I won't get mad, like Doug, if that's what you're worried about. I want to learn."

She shook her head. "Wrestling is too...is too...."

"Too what?" He placed his hands on his lean hips.

"Too much contact." She wiped her palms on her shorts. "It's not right between two officers. Between you and me."

"We're wrestling, not fucking." The profanity hung in the air between them. After a few seconds, he added, "I need to learn how to do this."

"I can't."

He exhaled, his hands lowering to his sides. "I defended you."

"I know."

"Then do this." His voice sounded raspy. He cleared his throat. "What do you think will happen if we find the murderer and I'm not strong enough to tackle him to the ground, not big enough to cuff him?"

"I'll be there to help,"

"What if you're not here? I'm a hundred and forty pounds. I can outrun most perps, but I'm small. I need to defend myself against someone built like a tank."

"Someone like me, you mean." She was relieved to hear him snort a laugh, easing the tension.

"Yeah, someone like you." Then his face got serious. "You owe me."

She crossed her arms. "Are you going to throw that in my face forever? That you stuck up for me and then got stuck with me?"

"No. Wrestling lessons are the payback. Then we're done."

There was silence for several seconds. "Fine," she said in an exasperated tone.

"Great!" he said. His fists went up, and he bobbed back and forth, his earlier humor restored. "I'll throw in swimming lessons, free of charge."

"Swimming lessons?" she echoed.

"We work on an island, if you hadn't noticed. Lady, you need swimming lessons more than I need wrestling lessons."

She ignored his last remark. "First, we're wrestling, not boxing, so stop jumping around." He immediately stopped bouncing. "And it's holds in wrestling, not punches, so don't sock me in the face." She motioned him over to the middle of the mat, her back to the glaring light. "Let's start from the neutral position." She stood square to him, knees bent in a crouch with one leg slightly ahead of the other, bent arms in the air.

He copied her.

"Let's review the ground rules that my old coach played by. You touch me here," she gestured to her chest, "or here" she motioned to her crotch, "and I knee you there." She pointed to his shorts. "Are we clear?"

His eyes widened, but he nodded.

"Okay," she continued, "wrestling is about points: points for pinning opponents to the mat, one shoulder, two shoulders, for the takedown, or getting out of a pin. That's how you win the match, on points. But for us, let's focus on the wrestling moves you can use to control a suspect."

She shifted her stance, leaning forward, arms outstretched toward his legs.

"The goal is to get a suspect on the ground," she continued, "to cuff him. I'm going to go for one of your legs, get you off-kilter, and use my body to push you over. Let me show you in slow motion."

She showed him the one-leg takedown, then two-leg. He was a good sport, thumping down on the mat, then springing up to practice again.

"Now try it on me," she said. "You're at a disadvantage because I'm taller and heavier than you; usually competitors are in the same ten-pound weight range. But it's about leverage and speed as much as it's about—ooomph."

He lunged for her knee.

She braced herself while he pulled on her leg; she remained upright. "Good," she said, "you're fast. Try wrapping your arms around both my legs and using your shoulder to push me over. That's more successful with a bigger opponent."

He was able to get her down.

Christine clarified where to press on her leg, the pivot point, the weakest place. She showed him a reversal, where she wiggled her way out of a takedown and ended up on top.

They were both sweating in the damp, warm night. Fillingham couldn't get enough. He kept asking for her to throw him, then would pop up again from the mat and scurry after her, looping his hands around her waist or leg in an attempt to pull her down.

"Did you poke me?" she asked after he stepped in, then back.

"Did it work?"

"Do I look subdued?" she answered.

He lunged again, evading her hands that were trying to grasp his shoulders, and gave her another poke in her ribs.

"Stop that," she said.

He was smiling as he jogged away. "Why? Is it illegal?"

"No. Just annoy—"

He ran and threw himself around her waist. She stumbled back a few steps. As she slid him off her, his arm flayed out to poke her, and he jabbed her in the chest.

That was it. Men never listened. Or cared. Ron from high school. Her stepfather Eddie. The investigators. Fillingham. They were all the same. She pushed Fillingham down so he lay flat on his stomach, lifted him and slammed him on the mat. Then slammed him again. She placed her knee in the middle of his back, her entire weight on him, grabbed his hands and wrenched them behind him, holding them with one hand and part of her knee. With the other hand, she pressed his face into the mat. She went to lift his head and slam it down and paused, her fingers clutching his hair.

What was she doing?

A squeak came out of Fillingham. She released his head.

"Uncle," he said in a hoarse whisper.

Her total weight was on his ribcage, making it difficult for him to breathe. She stood up, stumbling back a few steps. What was wrong with her? She had totally lost control. She stared at her partner as he heaved for breath.

After a minute, he propped himself up on his elbows. Slowly, laboriously, he stood up. He straightened, his eyes going to hers. She tried to read his expression.

"So, no poking," he said. His mouth tweaked up at one corner.

Relief washed over her. "I'm so sorry—I don't know what came over me. A coach should never do that—"

The ring of the station telephone interrupted her apology.

Fillingham said, "I'll clean up." His voice was still raspy. "Get the phone."

She ran inside, still horrified at her behavior. "Toronto Island Police," she said, answering the phone. "PW Lane speaking."

"Teeny?" a small voice said.

"Donna! What's wrong?" Her hand went to her heart.

"I'm scared."

"Where are you?"

"At home."

"Where's Mommy?"

"Bingo."

Darn. Christine had asked her mom to stay home tonight because she had gone out to bingo the two previous nights. But Phyllis was on a winning streak and wanted to cash in on her luck.

"What happened?" Christine said.

"I had a nightmare."

"You're okay now, Donna. Go snuggle in with Wayne on the couch."

"He always kicks me," Donna said.

"I'll put you back in your bed when I get home. I'll be there in an hour and a half. Will you jump in with Wayne, for now?"

"Okay. I love you Teeny."

Christine smiled. "I love you too." She hung up.

"Who was that?"

Christine turned at Fillingham's voice. He was leaning against the counter.

The smile left her face. She didn't like anyone knowing her business, but she was in no position to be hoity-toity after almost suffocating him. "My little sister."

"Everything okay?"

"It's fine. She's only eight. A nightmare. My mom's out, so she's a little scared."

"She's much younger than you."

Christine moved toward the desk. "She's my stepsister. My dad died in the war."

"Where's your mom?"

She piled files neatly on top of each other on the desk, then placed the incident reports in the mail slot for pickup tomorrow. "Bingo," she finally said, not looking at him.

Inside the kitchenette, she retrieved her dinner container from the fridge and put it in a bag in her locker to take home. Fillingham poured himself a glass of water and drained the contents. After wiping his face with one hand, he said, "My dad's thing is poker. Or boozing with his club buddies."

She looked at him for a second, and then away. "My mom's been down that road too."

After a pause, he said, "Does she still drink?"

She put their dried dishes from the rack into the cupboard. "Sometimes. Keeps it to her days off, mostly."

"My dad's more of a seven-day-a-week guy." He looked at his watch. "Morano will be cursing us in Italian, wondering where we are. We better head to the ferry."

She picked up her bag with her uniform and headed to the patrol car, both partners still in their gym outfits. She kept thinking she should apologize again for her roughness, but she worried it would make it worse, remind him he had been beaten by a woman. He didn't seem to hold it against her—he was humming as they ferried back to the mainland. After waving a cheerful goodbye, he headed to his car parked in the nearby lot.

On the streetcar home, Christine chastised herself. Her behavior tonight had not only been unprofessional, but also alarming. What if she reacted the same way to a citizen or to anyone else who angered her? What happened today at wrestling practice could never happen again.

And what was she doing blabbing to Fillingham as if he were her best girlfriend? Soon, she'd be spilling the beans about her mother's gambling debt and her contract with the loan shark. Or asking him if it would be weird for a white girl to date an Indigenous man. He was not her confidant—he was her shift partner. She'd give him a couple more wrestling lessons, but she'd make sure that their conversation stuck to work topics—like how they planned to find Ginny Rogers' killer.

Chapter 13

"Very pretty," Christine said to the woman sitting behind her table of wares. Aside from beaded jewelry, the vendor was selling moccasins, fringed vests and purses painted with the bold outline of ravens, bears and coyotes.

Christine pledged to return on her break and buy a bracelet for Donna. Or maybe the beaded change purse. The overtime money that would be in Christine's next pay envelope allowed an indulgence.

PC Williams, her partner on patrol of the Mariposa Music Festival, yawned beside her, bored by the craft section filled with pottery, batik scarves and macramé plant hangers. "Hey," he said, "is that Joni Mitchell?"

Christine looked over at the main stage erected in the middle of Olympic Island, where the sounds of fiddles and foot-stomping vibrated the air. Two hundred people clapped to the beat, roaring in pleasure as a lean woman with long blonde hair strode across the stage with a guitar on her hip to join a group of young musicians.

PC Williams took off, following the flowing lines of people heading toward the stage whose backdrop was the cityscape across the Inner Harbor.

"Catch you later," Christine said to her partner's back.

Patrolling the Mariposa Festival on Toronto Island had turned out to be easy and more enjoyable than she had predicted. When Sergeant Bard had asked if she wanted overtime hours working the festival, she signed up for double shifts on the Saturday and Sunday. Policewomen were often requested to chaperone dance halls or supervise community events. They were needed at Mariposa in case female suspects had to be searched. Christine had called her Women's Bureau friends to see if anyone wanted the overtime. Julie was patrolling today with Sergeant Bard, no doubt charming him while finding time to flirt with a banjo player.

Leaving the craft area, Christine started her circuit of Olympic Island. She wasn't familiar with this northern part of Toronto Island—it was too unpopulated to merit a visit on her patrol. Connected to Center Island by a bridge, Olympic Island was an open, oval park bordered by trees, shrubs and wildflowers. There were no rides, restaurants or beaches—just a space for picnickers and the occasional theater production.

Today, musicians dotted the field, congregating on the smaller stages or on the grass, veterans teaching younger artists how to pick a banjo or the correct embouchure to play harmonica. Children shook tambourines and danced on stage, toddlers hopping in time to the beat of drums. Christine wandered past gathered groups: the family gospel singers practicing their hymns, a jazz group unpacking their drums, traditional Greek dancers lunching in their elaborately embroidered aprons and vests.

Maybe there was alcohol in some attendees' mugs, but nobody was stumbling, shouting profanities or engaging in tomfoolery. Occasionally, she smelled something musky, something earthy. When she searched for the culprit, the lake wind blew the scent away before she could identify its direction.

A young Indigenous woman with shiny braids and beaded tunic walked by. Christine thought of Hawk. Maybe she would see him at the festival. There was a small stage devoted to their performances. Perhaps he'd be at the powwow scheduled for later that afternoon, or maybe he would attend Joni Mitchell's solo performance tomorrow night.

Part of her yearned to see Hawk, but she was afraid. He probably would ignore her—she had practically accused him of being involved in Ginny Rogers' death before she ran away.

She shook her head. There was no point in thinking about Hawk, daydreaming about possibilities. She couldn't date him, couldn't be with him, even if they both wanted the relationship. They were too different. People would talk, especially policemen. They wouldn't think it was right for a PW to be seeing a native person. And Christine wouldn't let anything interfere with her job and her plans for promotion. Nothing could affect her family and her goal to pay down her mom's debt as quickly as possible.

Last year, a policewoman went out with a Black constable from Dispatch. Other officers got wind of it. The constable showed up for work one day with a swollen eye and a cast on his wrist.

Policing was a very traditional environment. Everyone—men, women, Blacks—had their place. Knew their role. It was enough that Christine wanted to patrol like the men, with the men. Dating an Indigenous man would be another reason for policemen to belittle her and block her advancement. And she could imagine what her mom would say about Hawk. Phyllis didn't trust Indians, Blacks or Asians, for that matter.

"Do you believe in community?" a voice called through a megaphone. Christine turned toward the familiar voice. It was Gary Owen, holding court behind a table filled with memorabilia from the Toronto Island community. She had been thinking about him since she saw him stomping out of his house the other night. Sergeant Bard said there was no love lost between the Owens—that Island police had been called to their house once before to mediate a conflict between the couple. When Christine called Records, she discovered Owen's trespassing charge from last year, an allegation later dropped by Metro Council. He and fifty other protestors had waged a sit-in at the council's office to protest Island evictions. To Christine, Gary Owen seemed erratic, with a hair-trigger temper simmering below the surface. But did that make him murderous?

She greeted Owen as she neared the table. He had been speaking with a group of young women, asking them to sign a petition to save Island homes. When the trio of women walked away with disinterested smiles, he turned to Christine. "Care to sign our petition to stop the government's rampant destruction of our one-hundred-year-old community?"

"I can't take sides, Mr. Owen," Christine said. Sergeant Bard had advised Island officers to refrain from commentary about the battle between residents and Metro Council, regardless of their personal feelings.

Owen grunted.

She examined the framed photographs depicting Island life: family baseball competitions, costumed characters marching to the beach for Gala Day celebrations, skaters on a frozen lagoon, families building sandcastles on the beach. There was an old school bell from the Island school and an oar from the boat of the famous rower Ned Hanlan. "Seems like a wonderful place to grow up," Christine said, reaching for a Center Island newspaper from 1946.

"You better believe it is," he said. "A historical place," he said louder, scanning the crowd to see if anyone was listening. A few people drifted across the grass toward them. Christine moved out of the way to let them examine the memorabilia.

"Are you enjoying the festival?" Gary Owen addressed a woman with two adolescent girls. "The Island's a beautiful place, wouldn't you all agree?" They nodded in unison, the teenagers' long hair rippling in various shades of sunlit brown. "Would you help us keep it this way?"

"Where's your partner?" a male voice said.

It was Sergeant Bard, his face shiny with the afternoon heat, and Julie.

Christine paused. "We agreed to split patrol and then meet up again in thirty minutes." That was a lie, but it was better than disclosing that her partner had run off in search of Joni Mitchell.

Pulling out a handkerchief, he quickly swiped his face. "All is well, PW Lane?"

"Yes, Sergeant, quite all right. Mostly musicians, fans, friends and families. Listening or playing music. A Catholic dance gives me more trouble."

"Later tonight, expect a few drunkards," he said. "A few disorderly. Head them toward the ferry docks. Watch out for any pot smoking, there's to be none of that. Send that type packing as well. The biggest issue for these festivals is the weather. Soon as it rains, everyone dashes for the ferries, resulting in a bit of elbowing, the occasional fisticuffs. But," he looked skyward, "looks like sunshine is the order of the day.

"There is one more concern." His finger tapped his bottom lip. "Last year, they didn't pay the police officers."

"What?" Christine and Julie said in unison.

"They're hippies," he said, shaking his head. "Disorganized." He raised a hand to stop their questions. "Never you ladies fear. I demanded half the money up front. We should be good."

Christine's frown remained on her face as she said goodbye to the pair and continued patrol on her own. She was working from seven in the morning to eleven at night, her whole weekend, so she could make an additional payment to George Ray. The Mariposa Planning Committee sure as heck better pay up.

Across the field, a group had settled under a maple tree to listen to two women, sisters it looked like, singing a cappella. No sign of PC Williams. She should head out to the main stage and see if he was still gaping at Joni Mitchell.

"Officer!"

Christine turned toward the voice. A tall man in a St. John's ambulance uniform jogged toward her, waving his arms.

She ran toward him. "PW Lane," she said. "How can I help?"

"Follow me," he said. They ran past a stage that was scheduled to host Howlin' Wolf that night. The medic pointed to a scrub bracketing the far side of the field.

Nancy Hamilton, Ginny's mom, was running barefoot in and out of the bushes, the soles of her feet black. One shoulder was bare where the dress strap had slid, revealing the top mound of her small breast. Nearing, Christine could hear Nancy talking to herself in an anxious string of words.

"She's been like this for an hour," the paramedic said. "Every time we get near, she disappears into the bushes, and we can't get her out."

"Miss Hamilton," Christine said, walking toward her. "It's PW Lane. Remember me?"

Nancy ran into the shrubbery, the twigs crunching under her toes.

"I heard it was her kid who died in the demolition," the paramedic said.

Christine nodded.

"If I can get close enough," the paramedic said, "I'll inject her with Haldol, calm her down."

"Let's see if we can talk her out first," Christine said. "I'll radio my sergeant; he'll find a neighbor to come be with her."

A flash of white in the bushes, and Nancy walked unsteadily out from behind an arch of entwined branches.

"Miss Hamilton—Nancy—can I help you?" Christine said.

Nancy stopped in front of her, red scratches on her arms and cheek, dirt smudged on her dress. "Did you see her?"

"Who?" Christine asked.

"Ginny." Her voice was calm.

Christine's stomach fell. "What, what do you mean?" she stammered.

"My daughter, Ginny. She was here a minute ago. And now I can't find her." Nancy's long, tapered fingers touched Christine's wrist. "Have you seen her?" Her brown eyes were big, guileless.

Christine glanced at the paramedic, then back at Nancy. "No, I haven't." After a few seconds, she added, "Do you want me to look with you?"

Brushing past Christine, Nancy yelled, "Daniel!" She broke into a ragged run.

Christine turned. Daniel Rogers and his family were walking toward them. He stared at Nancy, taking in her tangled hair, soiled dress and bare feet. Behind him, Daniel's wife Bianca stood still, their tow-headed son on her hip.

Nancy grabbed Daniel by both his wrists, staring into his eyes. "Have you seen her, our Ginny? She's lost somewhere close by, and I can't find her."

His face blanched.

Nancy patted his arm to comfort him. "Don't worry, Danny. We'll find her together."

Daniel's chest rose and fell quickly, breathing fast. He looked wild-eyed at the paramedic, then at Christine and back to Nancy.

"Here, sit down a moment," Nancy said.

He let her pull him down onto the lawn so that they were sitting beside each other. "We'll get her back," she said to him, one arm around his shoulders. "Don't worry."

He made a sound—a cough or a choke—then covered his face with both hands.

Daniel's wife watched the two of them, her face still, the toddler squirming in her arms.

"It's okay." Nancy rubbed Daniel's back. "We'll find her. She won't be gone long if both of us are looking."

After a minute, he leaned toward Nancy, easing down until his head lay in her lap, his hands still shielding his face. In a husky whisper he said, "I'm sorry. I'm sorry. I'm sorry," like a wind-up toy, as Nancy uttered reassurances.

Bianca Rogers watched them. Clutching her child close, she turned and strode across the field back toward the festival entrance.

The rumble of the police vehicle grew louder as it made its way over the bridge to Olympic Island. Sergeant Bard had arrived with Julie and Mrs. Polotov.

Daniel was sitting up now, shoulder to shoulder with Nancy, like Hansel and Gretel huddled together in the dark forest. Daniel stood up when the patrol car arrived, not meeting anyone's glance. He brushed the grass off his shorts, wiped his wet face with his forearm and then combed his hair flat with his fingers. Nancy remained seated, her face now blank as she stared straight ahead, upturned hands in her lap.

"Danny," Sergeant Bard said. "How about I give you and Nancy a ride back to your homes. Nancy, Mrs. Polotov is here to help you settle in."

Daniel approached Christine, eyes still averted. "Did you see which way Bianca went?"

Christine pointed westward. "They headed towards the children's area near the entrance."

He nodded his thanks and walked away, shoulders slightly hunched, face averted from the group.

Christine and Julie helped Nancy stand up. Nancy seemed deflated, the frantic hysteria of the past hour released like air from a balloon.

"Should I go with you, sir?" Christine asked as she helped Nancy into the back bench seat beside Mrs. Polotov.

"No, Constable, you and PW Spark stay here and mind the ship. I'll be back in thirty minutes."

Christine and Julie watched them drive away.

Christine took a big breath. "Do you smell that?" she asked Julie. The pungent, earthy smell of marijuana.

Julie inhaled. "What a surprise. Marijuana at a folk festival."

Christine said, "Sergeant Bard says there's no tolerance. It's a family event."

"All right, all right." Julie hooked her arm into Christine's. "Let's go find the culprit and lay down the law."

"Should I find PC Williams?"

Julie arched her eyebrows. "He doesn't look that helpful." She sniffed again. "The smell is coming from that direction."

She pointed to a patch of green at the eastern periphery of the field, well past any of the Mariposa activities, and they headed toward the dense thicket of small trees and wild grasses. Arriving at the copse, they couldn't see anyone, but the smell of marijuana was strong.

Christine pointed to a break in the bushes.

"If I get a run in my nylons," Julie said, "I'm making one of these hippies pay."

They stepped over rotting logs and eased branches out of the way, threading a path through the shrubbery. Thorns snagged their uniform, the cool faces of leaves wiped their skin, and then they were in a small clearing.

A thin, acned-scarred man stood beside a mustached man sitting on a rock. The air was acrid with marijuana smoke, although neither man was toking—they must have heard the women thrashing through the bushes and got rid of their stash.

Christine recognized the seated man as Davy Morgan—Ginny's boyfriend. He looked terrible—blood-shot eyes, recent growth of scraggly beard, lank, greasy dark hair.

Christine said. "PW Lane and PW Spark. Toronto Police. It's Davy, right, Davy Morgan?"

His brown eyes looked at her. She remembered when he had grabbed her sleeve and pleaded, "Help her." A flicker of pain crossed his face. He remembered her, too.

Turning to the tall man, Julie said, "Your name, sir?"

"Paul Massicotte," the man mumbled.

"What are you two gents doing?" Julie said.

"Nothing," Massicotte said. "Just relaxing."

"In the middle of shrubbery? During a music festival?" Julie said. Massicotte shrugged.

Davy stood up. "I got to go," he said, shifting his weight from one leg to another. He looked scrawny, his black jeans hanging on his lean hips.

Davy Morgan, Nancy Hamilton, Daniel Rogers. So much pain from Ginny's death.

Julie held her hand up to stop him. "Smells like marijuana." She leaned toward his t-shirt and inhaled loudly. "You smell like marijuana."

His face was expressionless.

Julie walked around the edges of the clearing, poking the toe of her Oxfords into the grass. Christine knew she was searching for contraband: roach ends, roach clips, rolling papers or other drug paraphernalia hastily tossed into the bushes.

"You gentlemen have a little business going?" she said over her shoulder.

Was Morgan using and dealing? Was Paul Massicotte? Christine scrutinized the two men as Julie searched the bushes, their shoulders hunched, faces averted.

"Go on," Christine said to the men. "I don't want to see you here in the bushes again. And if I were you, I'd give the rest of the festival a pass."

The two men ran past her before Christine had finished speaking.

Julie marched over and placed her hands on her narrow hips. "What was that? You didn't even search them."

"The shorter one was Ginny Rogers' boyfriend," Christine responded.

"Oh."

"He was there that day, when she got run over."

Julie sighed. "We could have made a drug collar, you know." Her hands fell to her side. "Who knew you were such a softie."

Christine scanned the foliage. "Let's do a quick search of the bushes."

"Why?" Julie said, exasperated. "My shin is already scratched. Didn't we find the culprits and send them on their merry way?"

"Maybe this is the local drug hangout," Christine said. "We should search the area, flush the users out."

"You got to be kidding me."

Christine didn't answer, and after several seconds Julie said, "Fine." She clumped through the scrub several feet ahead of

Christine. "But if I get a bee sting, I'm going ho—" She screamed and disappeared.

"Julie!" Christine called, elbowing her way through the branches, trying to see through the vertical columns of saplings and grasses.

"Stop!" Julie yelled from up ahead. "Don't come any farther. I fell over someone."

"What's going on, Julie?" Christine said.

"It's a guy. He's passed out or something. Hold on. He looks hurt." After a pause she added, "We need an ambulance."

Christine radioed in the request and then carefully stepped toward Julie's voice. About ten feet further in, she spotted Julie's police hat as her friend crouched in the long grass.

The man was face down between the trunks of two small maples, one leg bent, arms up around his ears. He had gray-brown hair, possibly in his forties or fifties.

"Is he alive?" Christine said.

"He's got a carotid pulse, but it's weak."

Christine crouched on the other side of the man. "Is he high or drunk?"

"There's blood on his face and his arm."

Christine pressed the grass away from the man's face. "I know him."

"Who is he?" Julie said.

"Paddy Jenkins. He manages the Algonquin Island Yacht Club. Where Davy Morgan works."

"Did Morgan do this to him?"

"I have no idea. Jenkins is his boss."

"Did Jenkins have enemies?" Julie said.

Christine shook her head. "Business is poor, that's all I know." A siren wailed. "Can you stay with him? I'll direct the paramedics in."

By the time they lifted Jenkins into the ambulance, he was regaining consciousness, emitting small groans, although his eyes were still closed.

Christine radioed Sergeant Bard about Jenkins and seeing Davy Morgan and his buddy Paul Massicotte nearby. "Stop finding trouble, PW Lane," he said over the radio for the entire police force to hear.

Of course, it was her fault that Nancy Hamilton was unstable, Jenkins was beaten unconscious, and Morgan was high. Just like it was her fault that someone tampered with the truck and Ginny Rogers got run over. "Dispatch, 52-25. PW Lane," Christine said. "Continuing patrol of Mariposa Festival. Over."

Christine was grumpy as they made their way back toward the crowd. Then Julie got her laughing, and they joined a group of children playing kazoos and whistles. Julie grew red in the face from blowing into the harmonica, which she swore she knew how to play. Christine missed this, having fun with a partner. She missed the Women's Bureau: the easy camaraderie, the teasing, the small acts of kindness.

They never did find PC Williams before he radioed off at the end of dayshift at three. Julie convinced Sergeant Bard to let her and Christine patrol together while the men paired up.

The two women ate barbequed hamburgers while strolling the grounds on their dinner break. The crowd was thickening; Murray McLauchlan was the headline act starting at eight, followed by five other bands. Julie left to find napkins to wipe their greasy fingers, and Christine paused at a smaller stage where Indigenous people in elaborately decorated tunics and headgear were dancing.

Christine neared the stage to watch the women dance in deerskin dresses decorated with shiny metal squares, their outfits flashing reflected light as they moved to the drumbeat. The applause at the end of their performance turned into cheers as two men in feathered headgear and intricately beaded clothing took the stage. As the drums started up again, the musicians called out to the male dancers, who began to move in time to the beat. The men danced, shaking their feathers as they kneeled, and skipped and moved their feet and body in quick combinations. Christine realized the men were not dancing together but were competing against each other, each quick rotation, each jump a challenge to the other. The tempo increased. The dancers whirled, spectators cheering and clapping, as the stage vibrated with the thump thump thump of the men's feet.

"Mama Pig!"

Christine turned.

Kevin Lamprey smiled at her. Clad in a tie-dye shirt, hair covered in a bandana, his scraggly beard had grown longer since the last time she had seen him.

"How's the head?" he said.

Christine frowned.

"Who's this guy?" Julie said. She passed Christine a serviette to wipe her hands as Kevin surveyed Julie from top to toe.

"Wow, Marilyn Monroe," he said to her.

"And you must be Jesus," Julie said.

Christine said, "A protester from the demolition."

Julie placed her hands on her hips. "Is this the joker who bricked you?"

Christine said, "Not sure."

"Hey!" His hands went up in surrender. "I'm a peaceful protester. I came over here to see how Mama Pig was recuperating." He smiled, his brown eyes dark and flat like a shark.

"It's Policewoman Lane."

"Okay, Mama Pig Lane, how you feeling? You're looking good." His eyes swept over to Julie. "You're both looking good."

"Something's wrong with you," Christine said and immediately regretted her remark. She was allowing him to get under her skin.

"Fix me," he said.

Julie stepped in front of him. "Enough chit-chat. Time to move along." She flicked her fingertips dismissively. Lamprey did not move. "We're not interested in what you have to say," Julie said. "Move on, or you'll escorted onto the ferry."

"Will you do that?" he said, looking at Christine. "Put me between the two of you and walk me onto the ferry?"

"How about I walk you into the lake?" Julie reached for her radio.

Lamprey backed away, hands in the air, smiling, then turned and disappeared into the crowd.

Christine shook her head. Good to know that Lamprey irritated all officers, not just her. And he kept appearing on the Island. Not only was he an attention-seeker, but also sly. They couldn't get any charges to stick after the demolition. Not for almost drowning the truck driver or the brick-throwing at Christine. After questioning, Lamprey had been released. Could he be the murderer? Christine wondered. He wouldn't care if an Islander got injured during the demolition; he would be ecstatic that the violence brought attention to his anti-government message. But the investigators stated Lamprey and his friends had an alibi for the night the truck was sabotaged.

She pondered possible suspects as they headed toward the food vendors. Julie was worried they would run out of ice cream and wanted to get their order in before their dinner break ended.

Vanilla ice cream in hand, Julie beelined to a table full of hand-dyed head scarfs while Christine headed over to the native craft table, finishing her soft cone before it melted down her hand. As she picked up a red-beaded purse, the table darkened into shadow.

Christine turned. One of the dancers, the taller one, white streaks of paint angled across his cheeks, stood resplendent in feather headdress and double bustle, the bright greens and blue and yellows of the beadwork and shoulder feathers making him a walking piece of art. He nodded at the female vendor, bowing slightly.

Christine moved over to make room for the dancer's shoulder epaulets and feather bustle.

"I'd pick the green one," he said to Christine.

Hawk. Christine stared at him, agape.

"I saw you watching the dancers earlier," he said.

Christine swallowed. "I didn't realize that was you on stage." She thought of the frenzied stomping, the quick kneel on the floor and back up to standing, the angled twirl blending colors as the dancers circled each other. "Your dance was so..." She grappled for a word to describe the formality, celebration and frenzy that was a powwow competition.

His head tilted, vibrating the short gray feathers attached to the beaded headband. "Passionate?" he said. Before she could respond, he added, "Or is that you I'm describing."

She felt the heat in her cheeks as she stared into his warm brown eyes, before her glance slid to his soft, smiling lips.

"Hello."

Hawk and Christine turned at the voice. It was Julie, one hand holding her ice cream, eyes glancing from Christine to Hawk and back.

Addressing Hawk, Julie said, "Aren't you hot in your, your—" Julie's finger went up and down, indicating his outfit.

"Regalia. It's a bit heavy, but not that hot."

"Do you guys know each other?" Julie asked, eyes wide with curiosity.

There was a long pause. Hawk looked at Christine to answer.

Christine gestured with her arm. "Um, yeah, he's—this is Hawk Johnson. He's a...."

"A suspect," Hawk said to Julie.

Julie's eyebrows raised.

"In Ginny Rogers' murder," he continued.

"I didn't say that." Christine's brow furrowed, her tone annoyed.

"You did," Hawk said.

Christine turned away to pay the vendor for Donna's gift, hoping that Hawk would go away. She could feel Julie's eyes on her.

"You seemed to enjoy the dancing," Hawk said to Christine. "You might want to watch the next performance."

Tucking the present away, she turned to face him. The headpiece increased his height to seven feet; his wide shoulders were draped with long yellow feathers attached to a beaded collar. He was regal and intimidating, and so damn attractive.

"It's the traditional chicken dance," he said.

She took a step away from the table, hoping that Julie would take the hint and start walking away too, but her friend continued to stare at the two of them as she licked her ice cream.

Christine shook her head. "We're working. Our dinner break is over."

"I thought you might know the chicken dance," he said.

"I don't."

"I think you do." He smiled, then walked away, feathers backlit by the sun so it looked like he was on fire.

Chapter 14

Fillingham's hand covered his mouth, smothering a laugh as he stood bare-chested in his navy-blue swim shorts, backlit by the yellow-white spotlight he had placed in the station's yard. He was lean but muscular, his leg, chest and arm muscles sculpted.

"What's so funny? Ow!" Christine stumbled over a tree root. She was in bare feet as she headed to the lagoon behind the police station for her swimming lesson.

"Is that what you're wearing?" He looked at her full-piece black bathing suit that started at her neck and ended in a skirt that covered the top of her thighs.

"Why? What's wrong?" She looked down at the swimsuit she had owned since high school.

"I would say you look like my grandmother, but my grandmother has better taste." He propped his hand underneath his chin as he pondered her. "Maybe my great-great-grandmother Fillingham, on my father's side."

"I didn't realize this was a fashion show." She turned back toward the station. People had laughed at her ill-fitting clothes and her size all her life. She didn't need to spend her dinner break getting humiliated. Enough.

"Stop. I'm kidding," he said.

She paused.

He added, "The more clothes you have on, the harder it is to swim. That's all."

Christine followed Fillingham across the backyard over to the stone edge of the lagoon. It was dark, except for the too-bright circle of light from the floodlight. The water looked opaque, almost oily. Across the lagoon, Christine could see the fence that bordered the south side of Far Enough Farm.

"How deep is it?" she said.

He shrugged. "Maybe six feet at the edge, ten in the middle."

"We just jump in?"

"Sure. It's a warm night. It'll cool us down."

"Isn't there a place with a beach, somewhere where we can walk into the water?" she said.

"We could walk over to the bank near the church and enter from there." He pointed eastward. "There's a dock beside a small patch of sand."

Fillingham continued along the stone edge of the lagoon, spotlight in hand, while Christine carefully stepped around the acorns and twigs on the grass.

"Here we are." He walked into the water from the small strip of beach and placed the floodlight on the dock so it lit the water's surface. From there he strode several steps and dived in, emerging mid-lagoon, treading water.

"Okay," he called to her, "your turn."

She walked in slowly, feeling like she was entering a pot of ink, her arms and legs being slowly dyed black. The water reached her chest, and she stopped.

"Swim over to me," Fillingham called out. His wet blond hair was slicked back on top where it was longer. "I'll check your stroke."

She counted to three and then dog-paddled over, frothing the water as her arms and legs churned to keep her afloat, her chin angled up to prevent water from getting in her mouth.

"Enough?" she panted.

"Show me your stroke," he said.

"I did."

His hands swirled back and forth as he treaded water. "That's how you swim?"

"Uh-huh," she grunted. "I—I'm going shallower; I'm sinking." She paddled toward land until she felt sand under her toes and stood up.

He swam toward her in three strokes of his front crawl. "That's not swimming, by the way."

"I can't help it. I always sink."

"You're Island police now. Lifeguards leave at six, and they're only here in the summer. If someone is drowning, they call us." He pointed a thumb at his hairless chest. "Do you know how many drowning people the Islanders save every year? If you live or work here, you have to be a competent swimmer."

"Can't people call the fire station?"

"Look how long it took them to get to the demolition."

"Harbor Police?" she said.

He shook his head. "Takes a while to get a boat out, and sometimes they're way out on Lake Ontario. They're checking capsized boats, rowdy sailors, contraband. They're not always around."

She frowned. "Fine. That's why I'm here. To improve my swimming skills."

"And this is how I'm paying you back for wrestling lessons."

She recalled Fillingham gasping for breath as her knee dug into his back. "You're not going to drown me, are you?"

He crossed his arms. "You can probably do that on your own."

She gave him a look. "Let's get this over with."

"Okay. The first lesson is about what you do before you jump in the water. Notify Dispatch you're going in to extract a struggling swimmer, give your exact location and ask for backup. Then take as many things off as you can—radio, belt, shoes, hat, jacket, purse. They'll weigh you down. You don't want to become a casualty yourself."

Christine thought of her ruined radio from her immersion in the lake during the demolition and her lost shoes and purse.

When she nodded, he continued. "Let's move deeper and practice treading water." He swam out several feet. "Treading allows you to conserve energy while you're waiting for a rescue, searching for a swimmer or you're tired. Move your hands back and forth as your legs circle inward."

Christine dog-paddled over and tried to follow his instructions. Hopeless. She would give a big kick, head popping above the water as her arms swirled, and then her body would gradually sink until the water lapped her chin and tightly closed mouth. Then she would give another big kick to raise her face out of the water, and the cycle repeated. Exhausting.

"Wider circles with your hands," he instructed. "Alternate, right hand, left hand, as your feet circle inwards." He watched her for a minute. She was panting with the effort of staying afloat.

"A bit better," he observed.

They took a break in the shallows, then he taught her the front crawl. She splashed toward him, trying to stay afloat for eight strokes before her legs, then torso sank and pulled her under. She improved when she straightened her legs, Fillingham reminding her to kick from the hip.

"Let's practice life-saving techniques from shore." He unhooked the ring buoy and rescue pole attached to a nearby tree. "If possible," he said from shore, "throw a drowning person a ring or reach with a pole. That way you can pull them to shore. If you go into the water to rescue them, people are so scared that they push you underwater and two lives are at risk."

He threw the ring to her and tugged her in. She practiced pulling him in with the reaching pole and ring, like she had done in police training in a swimming pool. Then he put the equipment away and reentered the water.

"If there's no safety equipment and you have to go in, bring a towel or short rope, something the struggling swimmer can hold on to as you pull him in. If the person is unconscious, or a small child, turn them on their back and hook your arms under their armpits." He motioned for her to float on her back, then he grabbed her under both arms. "Keep their face out of the water and back kick them to safety."

She was better at pulling Fillingham out of the water when he held on to a towel. Grabbing him underneath his arms and trying to swim with him resulted in both going under.

"You have to keep my face above water," he said as he stood up, sputtering. "That's twice you've tried to kill me."

She cringed, embarrassed to be reminded of her wrestling gaffe. "I'm persistent."

"But not effective," he said with a wide smile.

After the lesson, they sat on the edge of the dock, a comfortable distance apart, feet swirling in the water.

"Do you think Paddy Jenkins' assault has anything to do with Ginny Rogers' murder?" he asked.

Mariposa had taken place three days ago. At shift change, Sergeant Bard had told them that Jenkins did not see the person who hit him. The marina manager had no idea why he was assaulted. Wrong place, wrong time, he surmised. Furthermore, there was no bad blood between him and Davy Morgan, and he certainly didn't think Morgan was the culprit. Even though the boat mechanic hadn't shown up to work since the demolition, Jenkins was keeping his job available.

Fillingham said, "The investigators might know if Jenkins had enemies or had a problem with a club member."

Christine thought of Fenwick and Allen, how they had spoken to her when she presented them with the handsaws. "Or we could ask around ourselves," she said.

Fillingham shrugged. "Maybe another club member at the Queen City Yacht Club knows something. We can check it out tomorrow." He leaned his elbows back on the dock. "What's the deal with Daniel Rogers?"

"It surprised me when he lost control at the festival, although Nancy's search for Ginny was unnerving." She dried the ends of her hair with her towel. "It's sad to see the effect of Ginny's death on her parents." She paused. "I do wonder why Rogers kept apologizing to Nancy, like he'd done something wrong."

"His wife alibied for him, right, for the night of the demolition?"

Christine nodded. "We could interview Bianca Rogers, confirm his alibi. And ask Daniel about his apology."

"Couldn't hurt." Fillingham said, swirling his feet in the water.

"You know we found Davy Morgan and a friend in a fog of marijuana smoke," she said.

"What'd you do?"

She shrugged. "Morgan looked so ground-down, like Daniel and Nancy, I couldn't bring myself to arrest him. I sent him on his way and told him not to come back."

"Excitement follows you," Fillingham said.

"You sound like Sergeant Bard. Except he didn't use the word 'excitement.'" She paused. "Aside from those incidents, Mariposa was fun. The music acts were entertaining. Lots of variety. My mom, brother and sister came down on Sunday. The weather was great. You should have signed up."

"I never do extra shifts."

"Why?"

He shrugged. "I sail every chance I get. Or study."

"For what?"

"To be a Harbie," he said, smiling. Harbie was the Islanders' name for the Harbor Police.

That made sense. As an Island officer, Fillingham would have regular contact with the Harbor Police, whose application process was notoriously challenging. Maybe give him an inside edge on the competition.

"You're all work and no play, Fillingham," Christine teased.

He eased himself down on his back on the dock so that he was staring up at the constellation above him. "You're rubbing off on me, Sixteen."

Chapter 15

"Yawning already?"

Christine turned at the voice. Fillingham walked toward her seat at the back of the empty ferry as it chugged a path to Center Island.

"How are you going to stay awake all night?" he said.

She shook her head. "I'm not used to nights. At the Women's Bureau, it was mostly days and afternoons." Plus, she hadn't had a nap before work; Donna had wanted to play on the monkey bars in the park, then Christine helped make dinner and later corralled her siblings into bed. Before she knew it, it was time to put on her uniform and go to work.

He showed her the bag he was carrying. "Good thing I brought coffee."

"What smells so good?" she said.

"My cologne?" he said.

She made a face. Fillingham did smell like aftershave if you got close—an outdoorsy scent of trees.

"I picked up a roast beef dinner from Town and Country," he said. He glanced at her lunch bag. "I'll share if you like. I got lots."

"Thanks, I brought dinner." A peanut butter sandwich and a banana. Not much, but she didn't need him feeding her. She wasn't a charity case.

The ferry horn bellowed mournfully as they approached the dock.

Morano and Pilkington were waiting for them in the police vehicle, parked beside a short line of people waiting to take the last ferry back to the mainland.

"Fillingham," Morano acknowledged through the driver's open window. He ignored Christine. Pilkington sat in the passenger seat, looking out the front windshield.

Morano took out his memo book and reviewed the calls that the night shift would need to follow up: a noise complaint from Mrs. Clancy, teenagers who had started a fire on Manitou Beach, a group trying to tent overnight on Center Island.

"Any news about Paddy Jenkins?" Fillingham said.

"The guy saw nothing," Morano said.

"Were the investigators here today?" Christine said.

Morano ignored her.

"Any chatter about the Ginny Rogers homicide?" Fillingham said.

Morano shook his head.

The ferry blew its horn twice, a last call to board. Morano stepped out of the car, followed by Pilkington.

"Have a good night," Fillingham said and got into the driver's seat.

"Why do you do that?" she said after settling in the passenger side.

"Do what?" He started the engine.

"Ignore me when other officers are around."

Fillingham frowned as he steered the patrol car onto the pathway. "I don't ignore you."

"Morano speaks to you. You speak to Morano. I speak and no one responds."

"I hadn't noticed," he said.

They were quiet as the patrol car drove over the Center Island bridge. They veered left at the fountain, and the illuminated police sign came into view.

"You go along with them ignoring me," she said. "As if a woman isn't good enough for the job."

"Who said that?"

"Your behavior shows it," she answered.

"Aren't you being sensitive?" They entered the station driveway.

"You mean oversensitive. Like a woman."

"Yeah, kind of," he replied as he pulled on the emergency brake with a small smile to take away the sting of the remark.

Was it her partner's job to stick up for her? Male officers stuck together like rubber cement. Maybe she was expecting too much of Fillingham to break away from the pack. He had done that once and look where it got him. She was a policewoman among policemen; she was on her own. "Watch how this sensitive female shoves your face into the mat tonight," she said.

His eyebrows rose, but his smile remained.

They stored their dinners in the fridge—if that was the right name for the meal you had at three o'clock in the morning on night shift.

She checked the black leather station logbook for the day's incidents and complaints. Pilkington had returned Mrs. Clancy's initial call, but they would have to follow up on her second complaint. A lost child had been found wandering around Far Enough Farm. Incident reports had been completed and placed in the mail bag to be collected by the courier in the morning.

"Coffee?" Fillingham called from the kitchen.

"Sure," she said, hoping that he was making it and didn't expect her to serve him because she was a woman.

The coffee machine hummed into action, then started percolating. Christine inhaled the aroma. She needed to wake up, keep busy. Night shift had a lot of lag time. They only had a couple of hours of work, checking houses and buildings, locking up, patrolling for illegal campers. If Fillingham insisted on another wrestling lesson, that still left half of the shift to kill.

Some Island officers took a nap on the cot upstairs or lay down on a waiting-room bench. Fillingham wasn't like them; he would likely go for a run or swim. Maybe lift weights. Or study up for his Harbor Police application. She had brought several police newsletters and an old sergeants' exam Gail had found for her. Christine wanted to review the questions in case she ever wrote the exam herself.

"Dang," he called, "Morano used all the milk."

She walked into the kitchen and retrieved two mugs from the cupboard. "That's okay. I can drink it black with a little sugar."

Fillingham sat down at the square table with metal legs. "Word is that Jenkins has been hitting the bottle."

"Is that new?" She took a seat opposite him.

He shrugged. "He's always been a drinker, but in the last year or so, he's shown up at sailing events and board meetings three sheets to the wind."

"He's been home for the past few weeks, recuperating. You should talk to him. He likes you," she said.

Fillingham nodded.

She thought about the information Phyllis had given her. "My mom has a friend in Identification who said there weren't any good prints lifted from the saw. Water degrades evidence."

He nodded. "I checked out the Whitmores."

"You've been busy."

He smiled at her surprised tone. "I can't see them for this. Mom's on her own with two kids. Dad hightailed it to the States four years ago. She cleans rooms at a motel on the Lakeshore."

"How about the son? He's what, fifteen, sixteen years old?"

"I talked to the principal of his school. Kid's in the gifted program at Northern. On the baseball and volleyball teams."

"Doesn't mean he didn't saw through the brake lines to save his house."

Fillingham shook his head. "According to the mom, all the commotion with the machine delivery woke them up. When they realized it was demolition equipment, they stayed up all night, watching to see when the workers would start. Mrs. Whitmore was worried they'd plow through the house with the family still in it. They packed their belongings in boxes and suitcases as best they could 'til the wee hours of the morning. The kid wasn't out of her sight the entire night."

Christine sipped her coffee. She was totally awake now, and not because of the caffeine. She felt a spark of anticipation. They were going to do this. They were going to solve the case. Her partner was as keen as she was to find the murderer. And then Deputy Darlow would know that she was competent. Policewomen were competent.

"The city counselor who lives on Ward's Island, May Stellar, was in Ottawa, so scratch her off the list," Fillingham said.

"I called Records," she said. "Kevin Lamprey is on the books."

"That's no surprise," he said.

"For trespassing. Had another charge for break and enter, but that didn't go to court."

"No assaults?"

She shook her head. "What was Jenkins doing the night of the demolition?"

"Sarge said he stayed late doing paperwork at the club and fell asleep in his office."

"Any witnesses?" she asked.

"I'll go down to the club in the morning after shift and see if anybody remembers seeing him there." He took a sip of coffee. "I asked around to see if any members had a beef with Jenkins. There was some grousing about the state of the club, but not enough to cause someone to beat him unconscious."

"While you're there, check up on Davy Morgan."

"Is Morgan a suspect because he's a boat mechanic?" he said.

Christine shrugged. "He's young. Maybe more radical than we know, like Kevin Lamprey."

"The Indian from Centerville has mechanical skills and lives on the Island. We should check him out."

Christine remained silent. She had seen Hawk once since the Mariposa Festival, when she had stopped by to chat with Mrs. Polotov, who was watering her front garden. Four doors down, Hawk had emerged from the side of a house with his bike. Spotting the two women, he smiled and came over.

"Vera," he said, greeting Mrs. Polotov.

"Heading to work?" Mrs. Polotov asked him.

He nodded, staring at Christine.

She had passed his house every shift and didn't know it.

Mrs. Polotov glanced from Hawk to Christine. "PW Lane, do you know my neighbor, Hawk Johnson?"

Christine jumped in before Hawk could repeat his tale about being a suspect. "I saw him dancing at the music festival."

Mrs. Polotov smiled widely. "Isn't he wonderful?"

Hawk raised his eyebrows, looking inquiringly at Christine, who said nothing. After a moment, he addressed the older woman. "You don't fool me, Vera. I know it's my toolbox you're after."

"You do have a way with a wrench, Hawk. Which reminds me, could you look at a leaky bathroom faucet? The drip is keeping me up at night."

"Sure." He smiled. "I have time tomorrow before work."

"Your favorite?" she asked.

"I never say no to a butter tart." He turned to Christine. "I'll share mine with you if you like. You look like you have a good appetite."

Christine felt her face warm as she thought of their fishing date and how she had cleared her plate.

"Nonsense," Mrs. Polotov said. "There's always enough for my favorite officer."

Christine had left soon after to check the beach, making sure she didn't cross paths with Hawk, who was en route to Centerville.

Hawk couldn't be a suspect, Christine thought again as she sat opposite Fillingham at the station. He had no motive, and she couldn't see him intentionally sabotaging the equipment to harm an Islander.

After a moment, Fillingham said, "We could ask Nancy Hamilton if Davy Morgan stayed at their house that night."

Christine shook her head. "She's not a reliable witness in her present state. If Morgan stayed over, Ginny would be the only one to corroborate that. And again, he's not an Islander, so his motive isn't as compelling. The same goes for Hawk Johnson."

Fillingham got up and poured himself another cup of coffee. "We can do more investigating in the morning after our shift. I'd like to get a hold of the owner of the Yorkville dive where Kevin Lamprey, his girlfriend and his other buddies crashed that night. See if we can poke holes in that alibi."

"You're pretty keen," she said as he leaned against the kitchen counter, mug in hand. "Thinking a homicide collar is your ticket to better things?"

He drained his coffee cup. "Don't you?"

She thought about it. Would finding the killer land her in a downtown police station on patrol? Maybe, maybe not. But it would help her keep her job, which was her foremost goal. She thought of Deputy Darlow, his austere presence at her apartment door.

"Perhaps," she answered, "but I'd like to solve the case, for Ginny."

His expression was solemn. "She died in front of me, too." He set his mug in the sink. "Anyway," he turned back to her, "let's talk about tonight. My short-term goal is to get you in a half nelson."

She raised a skeptical eyebrow. "If I let you."

"No pity this lesson. I'm coming for you."

"Am I supposed to be afraid?"

"Absolutely. I've been practicing." He grabbed his uniform jacket off the back of the chair. "Let's split up," he said. "We can get the work done quickly and have more time for wrestling."

Christine pulled on her jacket too.

"I'll take Ward's and Manitou Beach," he said, "hustle out the tourists or illegal campers, chat with Mrs. Clancy if she's still up. Five families are away, so I'll secure their houses. You take Algonquin and Hanlan's Beach. And check the school while you're there."

"I know the drill," she said. Male officers always liked to tell PWs what to do.

"I'll lock up," he said, jingling the keys. "I'll meet you back here..." he looked up at the wall clock above the main desk, "at 2:00 a.m."

After pressing the switch to forward station calls to Dispatch, she followed Fillingham outside.

She rolled her bike from the shed and headed east along Cibola Avenue to the bridge to Algonquin Island. At the top of the bridge, she looked down at dark, silky water, the white hulls of the boats moored at the marina like cradles of sleeping children.

She glided down the bridge and turned right, bumping over the uneven concrete path. The gate to the Algonquin Island Yacht Club was wide open. *Geez.* What type of security was that? Noticing a yellow glow illuminating the yard, she dismounted and walked onto the property. Lights were on inside the club. She listened. No voices, gusts of laughter or clink of beer bottles sounded through the screened windows. Midweek, the marina usually closed by eleven. She'd go in and check if any members were still around.

Stacks of wooden struts used to store boats lined her path to the clubhouse. With Jenkins recuperating, it didn't look like anyone else was jumping in to organize the place; it was the same run-down club she and Fillingham had visited a month ago.

After climbing the outdoor stairs, she walked along the second-floor deck that bordered the length of the building, weaving between plastic patio tables and chairs. It would be nice to sit on this porch one afternoon, munching on sandwiches in the awning's shade, gazing at the incoming ferries and the eastern cityscape. However unkempt the club was, it had a remarkable view of the Inner Harbor.

The door at the far end of the deck was unlocked. Christine shook her head. After Ginny's death, Sergeant Bard had gone around and told the marinas, businesses and residents to lock up, be extra careful and report any suspicious behavior. Inside, the lounge was empty, the fluorescent light buzzing overhead, shining on the coffee table littered with dirty coffee cups and several empty beer bottles.

She turned right down the hallway, calling out, "PW Lane, Toronto Police. Is anyone here?"

Opening the office door, she peeked inside. *Wow. Messy.* She continued walking, checking a storage cupboard, the washroom and a room that was a combination library, trophy room and storage.

Returning to the office, she pushed the wooden door wide.

It was more disorganized than her previous visit, when Jenkins had tossed his mail onto the desk. Had it been vandalized? It had the feel of items being tossed—a sweater, book, photograph—and left where they had been thrown.

A rope had fallen off its hook on the wall and lay in a serpentine mound under several layers of orange life jackets. Items from Jenkins' desk, books and ledgers, had tumbled onto the floor, although it was still littered with papers, coffee mugs and binders.

Somebody had been looking for something. Or had upended the room on purpose. She would have to check to see if any of the boats, sheds or other club rooms had been disturbed.

Christine stepped over a stool and gravitated to the framed photograph on the wall of a sailor holding a silver trophy. It was Jenkins—a much younger version from maybe fifteen years ago. The sun hadn't yet leathered his skin, alcohol had not pouched his face. In another photograph, his arms encircled two other men in front of the freshly painted shed.

From the corner, Christine viewed the room. Was this a fight scene, a targeted search or a vandalization? Could Jenkins have been assaulted here, in his office, then dumped on Olympic Island? The Mariposa Festival was over two weeks ago, in mid-July. Had no one been in the office since then? The lack of black dust residue indicated that the investigators hadn't fingerprinted the room. And Sergeant Bard had said nothing about a break-in at the club.

More lines of inquiry to follow. She surveyed the room, trying to assess if something had been stolen or if there was a pattern to the chaos.

At Jenkins' desk, she examined the papers and folders fanned across its length: contract agreements for dock repairs, delivery bills, a work schedule for the kitchen. Christine picked up a pencil, eraser-end down, and moved papers aside with it. More bills. Electrical. Water. Underneath an inch of papers, she spied an empty whiskey flask. Yes, Jenkins was a drinker. If he was anything like her mother had been, he had bottles stashed in the filing cabinet, behind a bookshelf, in the bottom desk drawer—hedges for the terrible moment when he drank a bottle dry and craved more. Christine had found a bottle hidden in Donna's diaper bag when Donna was a toddler. That was when her mom was still married to Eddie, who didn't feel the need to hide his forty-pounder from its anchor point on the kitchen counter.

With her pocket handkerchief, Christine opened a rectangular ledger and examined the columns of numbers, the black-inked deposits and red-inked withdrawals. Crimson red dominated the pages. Although she hadn't taken accounting in high school, clearly the club was having money troubles. She pushed the ledger aside, and a blue ticket edged out from under the bottom of an empty coffee mug.

A bookie bet. Like the tickets her mom used to hide in a can in the cupboard above the fridge, when she was still betting, before Christine threatened to leave and take Donna and Wayne with her. Before she found out how much her mother owed her bookie.

Christine pulled the ticket out from under the mug. A horse race at Woodbine, dated a month ago. Horse No. 2 to Place. She'd have to check how it did. Probably not well, Christine hazarded.

It wasn't surprising that Jenkins was a gambler; that often coincided with being a boozer. Maybe his personal finances were as problematic as the yacht club's. Maybe the marina looked like a dump because he used club money at the racetrack. When he couldn't pay his debts, he got a beating.

After a last glance around the office, she left to check the rest of the property, calling out as she passed rooms, turning off lights as she went, but only the frogs and crickets answered back through the open screened windows. The shed and outdoor storage bins were locked. A few boats had their interior lights on—several owners lived on their craft during the summer—but all was quiet at the docks.

Mounting her bike again, Christine toured the roads of Algonquin Island, Omaha, Ojibway, Seneca, all named after Indigenous tribes, intended as a tribute to those who used to hunt and fish on the Island, like Hawk had said.

At the northern shore of Algonquin Island, she stopped and peered left then right, checking for pitched tents or small bonfires. This spot, with its panoramic view of the cityscape across the dark band of moonlit water, was a popular vista with tourists. All clear. She told Dispatch she was heading out to secure the Island School.

As she neared the Algonquin bridge, her radio crackled with Fillingham's voice: "Dispatch, 52-25. PC Fillingham. I'm escorting visitors to the Center Island ferry dock. Waiting for a water taxi. Over."

She couldn't wait to tell Fillingham what she had found at the yacht club: the bookie ticket, whisky bottle, accounting ledger, the disordered room. It was a piece of the puzzle. If Jenkins' beating was due to his financial problems, then Jenkins desperately needed to retain local club members. Houses couldn't be demolished; Islanders couldn't be evicted. He needed their club fees to survive.

Maybe this was sufficient motivation for Jenkins, someone who knew his way around simple machinery, to tamper with the truck. He could owe money to some bad guys, like Christine's mom did. His desperation made him a prime suspect.

Pushing hard on the pedals, Christine headed toward Gibraltar Point and the Island School. Toronto Island was quiet at midnight on a Wednesday; the tourists were gone, and the school's overnight science program was on summer hiatus. The parks and recreation staff had ferried home, and the locals were tucked in bed. All that remained were the buzz of insects, the rustle of leaves and the occasional squawk of birds resettling on branches.

It was as if she had the entire Island to herself—the flora and fauna, the waves crashing against the breakwall, the trees, the wind that had loosened strands of her hair from its bun. She smiled as she biked. It was a slice of paradise, like Sergeant Bard had said. She couldn't believe that the other officers patrolled by car, as if biking were belittling, something a man, a police officer, wouldn't deign to do. Thank God she had Fillingham as a partner: the almost-Olympian, the guy who ran everywhere, who wanted to be outdoors as much as possible.

Christine glided along the concrete slab pathway. Nearing the Island School, she cocked her head. You could sometimes hear people partying on the small stretches of beach that faced out onto Lake Ontario, their voices carrying across the water, the volume enhanced proportionally with the amount of alcohol imbibed.

Silence. Most visitors hung around Manitou Beach on Center Island, where there were washrooms and change rooms, and Fillingham had already taken care of any stragglers there. She'd head down to Hanlan's Point Beach, the Naked Beach as everyone called it, after securing the school. Hopefully, most of the beachcombers had made their way onto the last ferry. She felt embarrassed flushing naked men out of the bush as if they were a bevy of quail, although she would use a flashlight to round them up, not a police vehicle like Morano. Sergeant Bard said the queers never gave police a hard time; they scuttled away like beetles when approached, half of them hiding wedding rings in their pockets.

In her experience, there were worse things than queer men: twelve-year-old prostitutes, teenagers high on dope teetering on balconies, bleeding wives cowering behind drunk husbands. Christine didn't want to witness men grappling with each other naked in the sand, just like she didn't want to discover a man and woman together, but she could deal with it.

After dismounting, she leaned her bike against the school's clapboard siding. Across the road, swarms of gnats hovered under the streetlamp that lit the stone tower lighthouse, which was no longer functional. One hundred years ago, the lighthouse had anchored the southwestern tip of the Island, warning sailors away from the rocky, shallow shore with its whale-oil lantern. Mounds of earth had been dumped on Hanlan's Point, infilling the marshy spots, so now the lighthouse stood five hundred yards inland. Christine peered past the tower into the ink-black blot of trees flanking Trout Lake, remembering the two large rocks placed companionably around a fire pit. Was Hawk fishing right now?

She was tempted to plow through the scratchy branches and find her way to his warm presence, to his attentive gaze, to the soft push of his lips against hers.

Shaking her head, she dismissed her fantasy. She and Hawk were going nowhere. Flashlight in hand, she quickly climbed the stairs to a classroom door, pulled its handle to see if it was locked, descended the stairs and ran up the steps to the adjacent classroom. Each classroom featured an additional external exit that channeled students into the middle courtyard furnished with picnic tables for fair-weather eating and a vegetable garden. She had to run up and down the stairs of twelve classrooms, as well as check that the two main doors were secured. It was labor-intensive, and she doubted Morano or Ulster ever did it, but Sergeant Bard had warned that unlocked doors invited summer squatters, people who lived off the garden produce, hid on the beach during the day when the janitor was inside cleaning and sneaked back into the building at night. Last summer, Sergeant Bard had spent two weeks searching before successfully nabbing a squatter. The vagrant had peeled back the screen from a window, climbed in and then nailed the screen flat so no one was the wiser.

At the sixth classroom, she checked her watch in the circle of a security light—twelve thirty. She slowed her pace. No need to get sweaty before the wrestling lesson at two o'clock. She had an hour and a half to finish checking the school, clear out Hanlan's Point Beach and bike ride back to the station. More than enough time.

When all the door handles had been rattled and the property circumnavigated to ensure that no one was loitering, she made her way back to her bike. Pedaling west, she passed snaked pathways leading to the rolling sand dunes of Hanlan's Point. To her right, shrubbery hid Trout Pond.

She could smell the pond, that musky bulrush smell of water teeming with frogs, water lilies and minnows. When she was with Hawk, the pond had been both quiet yet noisy, bird chirps, rustling reeds and insect drones a backdrop to the serenity of the still water. Wayne would love to fish there. The day her stepfather Eddie took the family fishing on Lake Simcoe was one of the few positive memories she had of him. Wayne, five at the time, had been enthralled by the lures and the reel and having to sit silent, waiting for the pull of the fishing line.

Christine braked. The grass on this side of Trout Lake was mowed so that only a thin border of shrubs blocked the pond from her view. She could find a spot for Wayne to night fish, away from Hawk's fishing site. She wouldn't go back there, of course. Her brother would get a kick out of staying up late and catching trout in the dark.

After setting her bike down, she approached the bushes bordering the pond. The top of the cylinder-shaped filtration plant emerged above the tree line. As she stepped into the scratchy foliage, she inhaled deeply to check for the scent of burning wood. Was that why she was there? To see if Hawk was frying trout over an open fire. Was she scouting a fishing locale for Wayne, or was she checking on Hawk?

Suddenly, something dark covered her face. She inhaled in panic, smelling a sweet, antiseptic scent. She tried to touch her face, pull at the covering, but after a few quick breaths, everything went black.

Chapter 16

Christine woke with a start. She was lying on her side on something hard. Was she in her bed? Her eyes were open, but it was still dark. She blinked, and her eyelashes brushed against a cloth covering her eyes. She tried to speak, to call out, but could only grunt. Her mouth was taped shut.

Fear spiked through her. What was going on? She tried to sit up, head woozy, but her movements were abruptly checked, and she fell back down. Her wrists were tied in front of her, and her ankles were bound too. When she stretched out, she discovered her wrists were tied by a short cord to her ankles, limiting her movement. Trussed like a pig to market.

She breathed quickly through her nose—nauseated, panicking.

Calm down. She had to stay calm. If she threw up, she'd choke on her own vomit. That thought frightened her even more.

Stop it. Breathe. She made herself breathe in and out through her nose slowly five times, loudly, trying to hear her exhales over the pounding rush of her heart. Swallowing, she pushed down the saliva pooling in her mouth.

She was a policewoman. She needed to figure out what was going on.

The air was cool, breezy; it was still nighttime. She listened intently to the call of a bird, the chirping of crickets, the buzz of a horsefly. She couldn't say for sure, but she felt she was still on Toronto

Island—she caught the sulfur smell of marshy water. Near Trout Pond? Longhouse Pond? A lagoon?

She shifted her bound arms, feeling the sharp edge of stones underneath her limbs. The back of her arms, legs and back felt wet and sore, like they had been burned or scraped.

Wait.

What was she wearing? Where were her clothes? Panicking, she tucked her knees into her stomach so that she had enough rope slack to push herself upright. Her forearms rested against the bare skin of her legs. Where was her uniform skirt? She cinched in her arms, elbows touching the skin of her stomach. Her eyes blinked tears underneath its blindfold. What had happened to her? What was happening?

Thank God. Her arm brushed the cotton of her underwear, then the nylon of her bra. She wasn't naked. She concentrated on her body. Had they hurt her? Had she been raped?

No. She was okay. Her head was killing her, pounding, like the headaches she suffered after the demolition. The skin on her back, legs and arms stung, but otherwise, she was all right, nothing broken. She could shift a little under her bindings, but not a lot. She could lift her tied hands, but when she pulled them toward her face, the cord halted her movement, jackknifing her knees.

Someone had knocked her out, removed her police uniform, tied her up and covered her eyes and mouth. Why? And where had he put her? She wriggled over the stones, ignoring the sting from her legs, until her wrists and feet pulled into the air. Her wrists were not only corded to her ankles; they were also attached to a longer rope that was pulled taut. She wriggled the other way to give the rope slack and felt something hard poke into her back. It was a step or ledge, made of stone, its edge unfinished. She grabbed the rope between her arms and pulled herself up on the step. Her hip butted against hard material. She leaned her shoulders back, and her head whacked something with a dull thud that sounded like wood. A door? Was she at someone's house? The water filtration plant? The Island School?

She banged her head against the wood several times, although each rap sent a dizzying flush through her head. She couldn't pass out.

She listened for a response, a movement in the building. The knocks had echoed, like no one was home, like the building was empty, unfurnished.

She had to get the tape off her mouth so she could call for help. But she could only pull the tape if her hands were free, and right now they were corded near her feet. Inching back to the step, she leaned awkwardly against it so that the cord draped over the edge of the stone. She moved her arms back and forth, using the rough lip like a saw blade against the binding. It was hard work, and she couldn't tell if she was making progress, but she continued through her dizziness, trying to bite down on panic and focus on the fraying spot on the cord.

After five minutes, she paused, exhausted, her breath heaving in and out through her nostrils. This was going to take all night. She counted ten breaths and started sawing again. A mosquito buzzed around her ear; she swung her head away and nausea rolled through her.

Fillingham! She paused her work. Fillingham would look for her when she didn't show up at two o'clock for their wrestling lesson. He might call her over the radio before then; if there was no response, certainly he would come looking. And if she was roped to a building door, a parks and recreation shed, the school, or a house, certainly someone else, if not Fillingham, would find her.

Unless *he* came back.

She froze. What if her attacker had dumped her here temporarily but intended to return? To rape or kidnap her or something worse. Frantically, she rubbed the cord against the step, emitting soft moans as she sawed back and forth.

Please don't come back, she thought. *Please don't touch me. Don't kill me.* She had Donna, Wayne and Mom to think about. To take care of. They needed her.

She tried to slow down, set a methodical pace as she wondered if he was watching her, enjoying her frenzy, her attempt at escape.

A crunch of stones sounded nearby—she froze. It wasn't the patrol car—no engine rumble. Someone was coming. Walking? Riding a bike? Was it her attacker? She swallowed a whimper. No. She didn't want to die. Her mind scrambled, trying to devise a plan. Maybe if she faked she was dead, he would leave her alone. Or if he approached to check on her, she could head-butt him, knock him out.

She scooted over to the place where she had woken up, lying down in the same curled fetal position on her side, facing outward from the door. Trying to control her trembling, she purposefully relaxed her limbs, shoulders and neck to imitate the slack pose of unconsciousness. She was listening so hard, her head ached.

Bang!—then the crunch of stones, loud, close by, a pattern of left foot, right foot. Faster, the person was running toward her. Her heart was beating in her throat; she closed her eyes, trying to keep her breathing shallow and even, although she felt like screaming in terror.

No. This can't be it. It can't end like this. Donna, Wayne, Mom. I love you.

She smelled him before he reached her, a spruce-tree odor with a hint of citrus which she recognized from wrestling. Fillingham!

"Lane!" he said.

She lifted her head up at the same time his fingers felt for the carotid artery on her neck.

"Thank God!" he said. "You're alive! Lane. Christine. It's me, Fillingham. I'm going to sit you up, lean you against the step. Can you do that?"

She nodded, swallowing her rising sniffles, trying to check the sobs of relief that were building in her chest. He gently sat her up by the shoulders.

"I'm going to take the covering off your eyes." Christine blinked rapidly in the yellow light, squinting as she spied the school down the pathway to her right. She was sitting in a sepia circle of light on the step of the Gibraltar Lighthouse, tied to a metal ring on the arched wooden door.

She frantically scanned for her attacker, worried that he would get Fillingham when her partner's back was turned and she was still tied up.

He touched her bare shoulder gently for a second, then let go. "You're safe now. Hold on. I'm going to take the tape off your mouth." He pulled it off quickly, like you would a bandage. Her face stung.

He pulled his police knife out of its sheath, carefully cutting away the rope binding her hands. She shook them out, rotating her wrists as he squatted at her feet, sawing away at her ankle bindings. Looking along the length of her body, she had no hat, no uniform, no nylons, no shoes. Her purse, utility belt and radio were gone.

Her ankles pulled away from each other as the rope severed. He sheathed his knife and pulled his radio out. "I'll call you an ambulance."

"No!" she yelled in a loud croak.

The radio paused halfway to his mouth. "You're hurt." His gaze traveled the length of her body.

Christine looked down at her underwear and bra, acutely aware of her partial nakedness, and crossed her arms.

"Do you need, I mean, did he...?" he stuttered.

She knew what he was trying to ask. When she worked at the Women's Bureau, she had posed the same question to dozens of women who had been assaulted.

She shook her head. "I'm okay. He didn't do anything." She touched her head. "He knocked me out somehow, covered my face so I didn't see him. I guess he dragged me to the lighthouse when I was unconscious."

"Let me check you out." He pulled a flashlight off his belt and kneeled beside her. "Can you move your arms and legs?"

"Yes. I think they're scratched, but okay. It's my head that hurts."

He stood up and gently touched her hair, sectioning off parts, his fingers touching the front, side, then back of her scalp.

"The stitched cut from the demolition is here at the hairline, right?" he said.

"Yes." She was trying not to nod because that increased the pounding in her head.

"Okay, I can't see a new abrasion or swelling. Did he hit you with something?"

"I don't know. One minute I'm walking by the pond, the next second everything went black."

"What pond?" he said as his light beam moved over her limbs, finding the long, vertical scratches down her calves and the back of her thighs, the scrape on her back that she could feel but not see. After he examined the abrasions on her arms, the light settled on the smeared blood on her knuckles from sawing the rope against the step.

"Here." He unbuttoned his long-sleeve blue police shirt. "Put this on."

It was too small, and she'd get blood all over it, but she put it on anyway, holding it together in front as she sat on the step, knees together, grateful for the coverage.

He squatted in front of her in his white undershirt. "Some of those abrasions are deep. And you've had a head injury. You need medical attention." He pulled his radio out from its holster.

Christine punched the radio out of his hand, sending it tumbling onto the stones.

"What the hell!" he said.

He moved to retrieve it; she clutched his left wrist with both hands, pinning him in a squat.

"You can't call it in!" she said.

"Why?"

She swallowed, trying to formulate the words that would stop him.

"You were assaulted," he said. "A Harbor Police boat can take you to the mainland and a waiting ambulance."

"NO!"

"Lane. You're not making any sense." He kneeled in front of her. "You're in shock. You need help. We got to call for backup—search for whoever did this to you."

She gripped his wrist. "Nobody can know about this."

"I don't understand. Why?"

She eased the pressure on his hand, but still held on. "I'll get fired."

He pulled back, his expression quizzical. "Why would they fire you?"

"Deputy Darlow came to my apartment."

"When?" he said.

"After the demolition. He wanted to discuss the *Telegram* photo." Fillingham waited.

"He said that if I got hurt again," she explained, "then it's clear that the job is too much for me. That I'm not cut out for policing."

Fillingham shook his head. "The brass wouldn't fire you for getting beat up. For saving someone from drowning. It's not your fault. I'll tell them that." He pulled away from her loosened grasp, stood up and took a step toward the radio.

She launched herself at his back, flattening him on the stone pathway, stars exploding in front of her from the sudden movement.

He grunted as she landed on him like a crab, splaying him underneath her.

"Are you nuts?" he said, trying to get a knee under himself to push her off.

"I can't let you call it in," she said, her voice breaking. "I can't lose my job. I have to pay back my mom's loan."

He stopped scrabbling and angled his head to look up at her.

She tried to control the tremble in her voice. "If I can't pay the loan shark, I'm worried they'll hurt my mom, like they did Paddy Jenkins."

She released his shoulders, and he turned to look at her. "What are you talking about?"

"My mom got into debt from betting on horses. So she took out a loan from a guy named George Ray. He works for a gambling syndicate with roots in Montreal."

"How much?"

"Originally, a thousand dollars, but it's ballooned with their steep interest rates."

"What?"

She slid off him, aware that she was in her underwear, and clutched the shirt to cover herself.

Fillingham turned over onto his backside and propped himself against the stone step. "How did she get so in debt?"

She sat on the step beside him. "She and my stepfather used to drink, bet on the races. Illegal bets. They got in over their heads, couldn't pay their losses. My stepfather took off, leaving my mom on the hook for it all."

"Can't you get a loan from the credit union to cover it?"

"What would I say when they asked me what it was for? And what collateral do I have?" After a pause, she added, "I make a payment every two weeks, almost all my paycheck. I add extra if I've done overtime shifts."

Fillingham looked away, shaking his head. "There's something going on here. This attack doesn't feel random. It doesn't feel like the perp jumped the nearest woman for kicks or a dare. It feels planned, like he's sending a message. I don't know if we should cover it up."

"Please," Christine whispered, a tear leaking out of the corner of her eye. Her job, her life, her family's life, was in Fillingham's hands.

"If I don't call it in," he said, "I'm complicit. I'm withholding information, interfering with an investigation."

She remained silent. He was right. The *Police Act* demanded that all officers perform ethically in their role to serve and protect. He could be disciplined. Or lose his job.

"Why did the attacker choose you?" he said, changing the subject.

She exhaled with relief. "I don't know."

"What were you doing?"

She cleared her throat. "I had secured the school and was heading to Hanlan's Beach. I got off my bike to check Trout Pond."

"Why?"

She thought of Hawk. She wished she had seen him, that she had found him in his fishing spot; then she would have stayed safe. Unless, could it be that Hawk saw her spying on him, and he was the one who jumped her? Tied her up because she wouldn't go out with him?

"What were you doing there?" Fillingham prompted.

She blinked. She was so confused. "I was looking for a spot where I could take my younger brother night fishing. I'd heard Trout Pond was good. I walked a couple of steps into the shrubbery on the northwest side of the pond, then everything went dark."

"What could you see from where you were standing before you blacked out?"

She shook her head. "Not much. Just the top of the water sanitation plant. It was dark, and I hadn't reached the water. The shrubs blocked my view front and back."

"You got hit? Or was it like a bag over your head?"

She pondered. "It was like a black curtain went up in front of my face. I smelled something sweet, but acetone, like nail polish remover. Then I woke up here, my wrists and ankles bound, eyes and mouth covered."

He propped his hand under his chin. "Why did he attack you and then drag you here to the lighthouse? And why did he take your uniform? He didn't rape or kill you. What was his point?"

Christine had no answer. She was so glad to be alive, relatively unhurt, that her attacker's motivation for tying her to the lighthouse wasn't important. She wanted to get dressed, go home, hug her family and climb into bed with the cover over her head.

"You're not any woman out at night; you're a policewoman on patrol. Your uniform was removed. You were tied to a historical building. He wanted you to be found—humiliated. Who would do that?"

"Lamprey," they both said at the same time. Christine could see Kevin Lamprey, a self-confessed agitator, enemy of the government, enjoying her degradation, getting excited by her fear. Was he watching them now? Would he look for the story in the morning news?

"Okay, one suspect noted," he said. "Anyone else have a beef with you?"

"The police investigators," she said, trying for a joke. Fillingham raised an eyebrow. She thought of Fenwick and swallowed the lump in her throat. If the investigators had discovered that she and Fillingham were investigating Ginny Rogers' murder, was this their message to back off? She remembered Fenwick's pressure on her wrist, the magenta bruising that blossomed on her hand. She shivered.

"You're shaking," he said. "Enough talking. Let's get you back to the station. Where's your bike?"

She blinked, trying to remember where she had left it, but she was so overwhelmed with relief that he wasn't going to call Dispatch that she found it hard to think.

"Your bike?" he said again.

"I left it on the grass, near the pond," she said, pointing north.

He looked over his shoulder, then back at her. "I don't want to leave you here to look for it or go back and get the patrol car. Do you think you can ride my bike back to the station? I could hold on and steady you."

She nodded.

Fillingham jogged down the path to retrieve his bike. At first she was wobbly, like a child learning how to ride, and the abrasions on her leg made her grimace as her legs pumped up and down. Her partner held on to the handlebars and seat to steady her. After she got the hang of it, he jogged beside her.

As they passed the school, she wondered who had done this to her? Kevin Lamprey? Hawk? The investigators? Someone who disliked female cops?

"There may be a silver lining," he said as he ran beside her, his breath even.

The bike wobbled. "To my attack?" she said incredulously.

He grabbed her handlebars to stabilize her. "It could be him."

"Who?"

"The murderer."

She stopped pedaling, the bike coasting as she stared at him.

"He knows we've been asking questions," Fillingham said. "We must be getting close. He's trying to scare us—get us to back off and shut down our investigation."

"If that's true," she said, "then he's after you too."

Chapter 17

Biting down on a cry, Christine closed her eyes as Fillingham daubed the scrapes on her arms with hydrogen peroxide. She sat beside the kitchen table at the station in her police-issue shorts and t-shirt, arms raised.

"Arms aren't as bad as your legs," he said as he stood beside her, swabbing. "He must have pulled you by the wrists, then later switched to your feet."

She tried to block the image of her assailant removing her clothes, dragging her heavy body along in the dark. A single tear leaked out the edge of one eye and traveled down her cheek. She was trying to keep it together, accept that she was safe, that her partner had found her, but her body kept shivering, spasms she tried to control by tensing her muscles.

"I see grass stains and dirt in your cuts, so he dragged you over the lawn, as well as along the road." He squatted down, examining her calves. "Your leg ran over something with an edge—probably a sharp rock on the gravel path. The gash on your right leg is deep—it might need stitches."

He cleaned her wounds and covered the deeper abrasions with gauze. After putting the first-aid kit away, he sat down opposite her at the table. "You need a doctor," he said, "for the deeper cuts. And to check your head."

"I'm okay," she said, exhaling, trying to relax her shoulder muscles, the pain of her salved cuts diminishing.

"Do you have a doctor?"

She shook her head. When Medicare started last year, she took Donna and Wayne for checkups, but Christine hadn't seen a doctor herself yet. She could go to a hospital emergency, but she didn't want staff asking questions about her injuries or have a paper record of her visit. Deputy Darlow couldn't know she was assaulted. Again.

Fillingham stood in front of her. "If you don't close the cut, it might get infected. People died of small wounds all the time in the Middle Ages."

She frowned. "How do you think I'm going to explain my injuries—headache, loss of consciousness, abrasions, the rope burn on my wrists and ankles? A doctor is going to know that I didn't walk into a door." She had responded to numerous calls where women had accidentally fallen downstairs, tripped on rugs or walked into the corner of a cupboard. Emergency room doctors heard every excuse.

Ding.

The doorbell chime. They must have forgotten to lock the station door. They looked at each other, eyes wide. It was four in the morning.

"I'll go," Fillingham said. "It's probably a wayward tourist." He stood up, sporting a fresh shirt, and headed to the reception area. His right hand hovered over his gun holster.

Christine listened through the half-open door between the kitchen and the office, prepared to respond if she heard anything awry. A low rumble of conversation sounded between Fillingham and a woman, the words indiscernible.

Fillingham returned to the kitchen, followed by Mrs. Owen, Gary Owen's wife.

"Mrs. Owen wants to have a word with you privately," Fillingham said, his eyebrow raised to show he did not know what it was about. "Here, Mrs. Owen, have a seat."

Christine sat across from the Islander at the square Formica table, trying to hide her bandages, edging her elbows into her sides, tucking her legs under her chair.

Fillingham disappeared into the front office. Mrs. Owen, in a housedress, looked down at the table, her hair pressed flat on one side from sleeping.

"How can I help you?" Christine said, trying to sound normal, act normal.

The older woman did not raise her eyes. "I woke up half an hour ago, and my husband wasn't home."

"Okay," said Christine with a question in her voice. Was this visit about her husband's alleged extramarital affairs? She remembered Mrs. Owen's angry face, the slammed door, the expletives.

"It's happened before," Mrs. Owen said.

"Are you worried that he's missing? That something has happened to him?" Christine asked.

Mrs. Owen shook her head. Her triangular face was freckled with sun and age spots, as if she spent a lot of time in her garden. Purple circles pouched under her eyes. Her hard brown stare met Christine's. "It happened before," she said, "the night before the demolition."

The investigators had checked Gary Owen's alibi; he had been with his wife all night. Now she was declaring that this wasn't the case.

Mrs. Owen slipped off the chair and walked through to the office. Fillingham came back into the kitchen. "I'm going to drive Mrs. Owen home. I'll lock the door behind me. Don't open it for anyone." He took his gun out of his holster and placed it on the table in front of Christine. "I'll be back in ten minutes." The door dinged as they let themselves out.

She sat at the table, hand beside the gun, thinking about her attacker, what he had done to her, what he could have done to her, wondering if he was out there right now, circling the station. The fingertips of her right hand trembled on the Formica, and she grabbed it with her left hand to stop the vibration.

Think of something else—Ginny's investigation. She reviewed the lists of suspects: Kevin Lamprey and his buddies, Paddy Jenkins,

Hawk Johnson (he wasn't really a suspect), Daniel Rogers, Gary Owen. They should check Davy Morgan and Samuel Fairmont, who owned Clergy House. She thought of the next steps they needed to take with each suspect, who they needed to interview, the people they needed to call.

The door chimed, and Christine's shoulders tensed, her hand hovering over the gun.

"Just me," Fillingham called out.

He came into the kitchen and put the gun back in his holster. Hands on hips, he announced, "In an hour, I'm going to call a doctor friend of mine and tell him to meet us at RCYC at seven." His hand went up before she could protest. "He's discreet. He won't say anything. Okay?"

She gave a reluctant nod.

"We have a couple of hours to kill before then," Fillingham said. "I'm sure you're sleepy, but I don't think you should lie down with a head injury until you get the doctor's say-so. Want some dinner?"

"No. No food."

"Coffee?" he said. "Tea?"

"Tea would be great." She was still trembling, spasms in her hands and shoulders, her teeth occasionally chattering. In this cottage-station by the lagoon, she felt bunkered in with Fillingham, the outside world shadowy and menacing around them. Her attacker was out there somewhere. And so was the murderer. And her partner thought they might be the same person.

On her second cup of tea, she was able to tell him about Mrs. Owen's confession and the bookie ticket and accounting ledger in Paddy Jenkins' office. After that they kept busy, Fillingham chattering as he did the dishes, swept the floor and restocked office supplies from the second floor while she sorted through old files piled on the kitchen table.

Christine greeted with relief the yellow-pink light of dawn edging the windows. Morning. That night, that terrible experience of being tied up and blindfolded, was over. She got up and pulled the curtains back, ignoring the soreness of her scrapes, as she opened the drapes on every window in the station.

Fillingham grabbed the keys from the desk drawer. "I'm going to drive you over to RCYC for breakfast. I'll go meet the next shift at the ferry, give report and then meet you back at the club. Dr. Whitney should be there by then."

She sat down on a bench in the waiting room. "Don't say anything to Sergeant Bard during report. Nothing happened last night."

He stood in front of her. "I told you I wouldn't."

At the RCYC clubhouse, Fillingham ushered her to a table near the kitchen door. The club was deserted, except for the restaurant staff and a gardener watering the flowers out front.

"The kitchen's not open yet," he said, "but I can get them to rustle up something for us. I'll be back in twenty minutes. You okay?"

She nodded. It was morning; she was ensconced at a linen-covered table at the Royal Canadian Yacht Club, the bastion of privilege, surrounded by the hum of a vacuum cleaner and the scurry of wait staff placing vases of fresh hydrangeas on tables. She felt safe, or as safe as she could be.

She asked a waitress for access to a phone. When Phyllis answered, Christine told her she was working overtime and wouldn't see her before her mom left for work.

"You okay, Teeny?" her mom asked. She hardly ever used Christine's pet name. Sometimes Phyllis had a sixth sense when something was amiss.

"I'm fine," Christine lied. "A bit tired."

"Keep safe," her mom added and rang off.

Christine gingerly sat back down at the table, keeping her back, legs and arms away from the chair.

True to his word, Fillingham returned in the allotted time with two plates full of food. "Ta-da!"

Bacon, eggs, toast and fruit salad. Her stomach turned, but she accepted the dish and gratefully nodded to the waitress with the carafe of fresh coffee.

She nibbled on a piece of toast as Fillingham chatted away about the history of Olympic racing at the club, describing his upcoming race where he hoped to place in the top five in the province. She nodded in the conversation lulls. Did the guy ever get tired? He looked freshly scrubbed in his clean shirt, his uniform pants still holding a razor-edge crease. A slight smudge under his eyes was the only evidence he'd been awake for thirty-six hours.

He was being nice, talking to get her mind off the attack and distract her from her worry.

She placed her half-eaten slice of toast on her plate. "I can't do this," she said, interrupting him.

He paused mid-sentence.

"Thank you." She reached across the table and touched his shirt sleeve. "You've gone above and beyond the duty of a partner."

He frowned.

"I'm going to call Dispatch and tell them about the attack." She stood up, grabbing for the chair as she stumbled.

He stood up too. "What are you doing, Lane? The perpetrator's long gone."

"What we should have done when you found me at the lighthouse."

"I don't understand," he said, coming around the table to face her. "I thought we had a deal."

She gestured. "You're a good police officer, Fillingham. A solid partner. You're going to be a heck of a Harbor Police officer one day. Your job can't be in jeopardy because of me."

He barked out a laugh, his hand pressed against his chest. He continued to laugh, harder, looking at her, then up to the ceiling as he howled so loud that a waitress peeked her head in from the adjoining room.

"What's so funny?" Christine said, trying to speak over his voice.

"Excuse me." He grabbed a white linen serviette from the table and wiped his eyes then loudly blew his nose.

He sat back down. She followed suit, sitting on the edge of her chair.

"You're hilarious," he said. "PW Christine Lane gives up her job, her future, her family's future," his thumb pointed to his chest, "for a guy!"

She frowned. "That's not what I'm doing."

"I wonder what your mom will say if you get fired and can't keep up with her debt payments. What do you think the loan shark will do to her? Go for the kneecaps or something more personal?"

"Stop!" she said.

"Donna, is that your sister's name? She's going to enjoy living in poverty as she grows up. Maybe an older guy will come around to take care of her, offer her little gifts, things you can't afford to give her."

"Shut up!" she screamed, ending in a sob.

"Are you crying?" he said. His lower lip pouted out. "Boo-hoo. Poor me. I'm going to run on a sword and take my family with me."

It was too much. Last night. Today. This argument. She had failed. At her job. As a partner. With her family. Everything. Her face scrunched up and her shoulders rounded as she cried.

"You think you're so different," he said over her sniffling. "*I don't need men,*" he mimicked in a falsetto.

Her hands covered her face, but through her fingers she could see Fillingham's sneer.

He continued in a trebly voice. "I'm as good as these male buffoons I work with. In fact, I'm better." In his normal tone, he added, "You're like all the other sniveling women you despise—the prostitutes, housewives, policewomen—who give up everything for a pimp, husband or boyfriend."

She shook her head, unable to speak.

"Go ahead, babe," he said. "Throw yourself off a cliff. No skin off my nose. There's always another one like you to take your place."

Her hands fell from her face and clenched in her lap. "I know what you're doing," she whispered hoarsely.

"What am I doing?" His arms went up in the air. "Telling the truth. Think your mom is going to stop drinking if you lose your job and there's no food on the table because all her wages go to the loan shark? Will your brother hang around with the right crowd if he can get a wad of bills from purse-snatching or selling weed?"

"No," she said, her voice louder. "I won't let you do this."

He stood up. "You begged me not to call in your assault, and I chose not to. Who are you to alter my decision? You're not my mother. You're not in charge of my life."

"I'm not trying to be in charge of it."

"I've had a lifetime of people telling me what to do, what fork to use at the dinner table, what debutante to date, what job is appropriate. My dad can write the book on that. Do you think he wanted me, Geoffrey Fillingham III, to be a cop? It's worse than being a blue-collar thug or a Catholic. After all the money and education he threw at me. And I did it! I got on the force without his help. Without his permission. So I can make my own mind up. No input from my father or from you. You do what you like, but I'm not calling it in."

Someone cleared his throat. A tall man stood twenty feet away. His silver-gray styled hair deepened to a gunmetal gray at the back. Dressed in chinos and a short-sleeve linen shirt, he was holding a black leather medical bag. He must have arrived by water taxi and entered the club through the back door.

Christine quickly wiped her wet face with her palms.

"Alex!" Fillingham exclaimed as he walked over to shake the man's hand. Christine wondered how long he had been in the room, how much he had heard.

The doctor looked over at her. "Dr. Whitney, but please call me Alex. At your service."

"PW Lane," she said, her voice tremulous. "Thank you for coming, but it wasn't necessary."

He smiled. "Geoffrey said you'd say that." He bowed slightly. "Please, follow me."

The two officers trailed the doctor as he weaved past the tables into a hallway and then turned left into a small, tidy room. It featured a patient table, metal cupboards, sink and a counter lined with glass containers filled with cotton swabs and bandages.

"Alex is the doctor for the RCYC competitive sailing teams," Fillingham said as he took a seat in one of the black leather chairs pressed against the wall.

"You don't have to stay," Christine said, her tone abrupt.

"And miss all the fun?" Fillingham said.

She burned with hatred for him. For the things he had said to her.

"I'll hold your hand," he said, smiling.

She glared at him.

Alex motioned for her to sit up on the table. "Your charm is wearing off, Geoffrey."

"She's like bulletproof metal," Fillingham said. "Check her right calf. There's a puncture."

Alex asked her to lie down on her stomach. He gently removed the bandages from the back of her legs. Christine waited for him to say something about the bright red gouges, how she got so scraped up, but he did not comment.

"Looks clean," was all he said. "You did a good job disinfecting, Geoff. The wound needs three stitches, five at the most." He went over to his bag and took out a spool of thread and a small vial. "PW Lane," he said, after placing his materials on a tray, "do you have another name I can call you? It seems a tad formal for early on a Wednesday morning."

"My first name is Christine," she said, turning her head to the side so that she could see him.

"Can I call you Christine? Or is there another name you prefer?"

He walked toward her with a syringe to freeze her calf. "I'm sorry, I didn't catch that. Did you say your sister calls you Tina?"

"Teeny," she said.

The doctor turned and met Fillingham's glance. They simultaneously burst into laughter.

"I'm sorry," the doctor said, smiling. "I didn't expect that."

"She had trouble pronouncing my name as a toddler." She glared at Fillingham. "Only my family calls me that."

God, she must be tired, blurting out her nickname. While Alex injected her with freezing, she let her forehead rest on the table. The constant sting was making her nauseous, her thoughts jumbled with fatigue.

She could feel a tug on her skin as he sewed her up, but no more pain.

She sensed Fillingham beside her. "Nice straight line," he said to Alex. "Very tidy."

"Thank you," the doctor replied. "I have honed my technique from years of patching sails."

The doctor finished suturing and rebandaged her legs, back and arms with fresh gauze. She sat up on the table.

"Take acetaminophen for the pain," Alex said. He handed her a small tin of pills. "It will help you get to sleep. Geoffrey mentioned your head. Let's have a quick look."

He checked her out—her head, pupils, blood pressure and heart rate.

"I can't see any contusions. How long were you unconscious for?"

Christine shrugged. "I don't know. Half an hour? Longer?"

"What do you remember?"

She told him about the black veil over her face, the sweet, antiseptic smell.

He brought her over a bottle. "Did it smell like this?" He unscrewed the lid.

She inhaled. "Sort of. The same alcohol smell, but there was a sweetness to it. Not flowery, but sugary."

Alex opened the cabinet beneath the sink and brought out another bottle. He poured a small amount of the clear liquid on a cotton ball and held it up to her nose.

"Yes," she said, nodding. "Yes, that's it!"

"Chloroform," Alex said, looking at Fillingham and then back to Christine. "Someone wanted you out cold."

The partners were silent. Christine remembered the hazy feeling of being moved, then waking up, that spike of fear when she couldn't see or speak.

"How easy is that to get?" Fillingham asked Alex.

"It's used in science labs, so it's around. You can make your own with bleach and alcohol."

The police officers pondered that.

Alex said, "Chloroform will make you nauseous, leave you with a nasty headache. The side effects diminish over time." He gestured to the door. "Christine needs to go home and rest. Recuperate. As do you, Geoffrey. Saving the world from crime can wait another day."

The club's water taxi motored them back to the city-side ferry docks. Despite her protests and her proclamation that she didn't need or want his help, Fillingham drove her home from the ferry terminal in his MG convertible. They were silent the entire drive. When he parked in front of her low-rise, she got out of the car, slammed the door and walked to her apartment door, her steps unsteady.

The car roared away, and she paused at the entrance to her building, forehead pressed against the door. She was so glad to be home, to be off the Island, away from Fillingham and whoever had dragged her to the lighthouse. She was safe. For now.

Chapter 18

"Sixteen, you got to get down here!" Fillingham said over the phone.

Standing in the kitchen, Christine squinted at the stove clock, her eyes sandy with sleep; it was 3:12 p.m. She had crawled into bed this morning after Fillingham dropped her off and then woken with a start at noon, frozen, reliving the moment of being bound and blinkered in front of the lighthouse. It took an hour to calm herself. After drinking warm milk and taking another round of pain medication, her body and mind eventually relaxed back into sleep before the incessant ringing of the phone woke her.

She leaned against the fridge with the wall phone in her hand. "Where are you?" The events of last night cascaded in her mind like playing cards: Trout Pond, waking up tied to the Gibraltar Lighthouse, her rescue by Fillingham, Dr. Whitney.

"Hanlan's Point!" he exclaimed. "I've traced your route to the place where you were attacked by Trout Pond. I found it!" His voice was gleeful.

"Found what?" She stood taller.

"Pot plants!"

"What? Where?" she said.

"North side of Trout Pond. Get in gear, Lane, and get down here."

"I'll be there as soon as I can." The strangling fear that had haunted her sleep dissipated. They were homing in on the perpetrator. They would find him, arrest him, before he could do further harm.

"Meet you at the ferry docks," Fillingham said and hung up.

Hurriedly, she retrieved saltines and peanut butter and left them for her siblings to snack on when they returned from the free summer camp they were attending. Her mom must have made them a bagged lunch before she left for her day shift.

Christine's hot anger at Fillingham had also waned after a night of cycling between fury at her partner's comments and intense gratitude for his silence. She wasn't quite ready to forgive him for his insults, but her job was safe, as was her family, so she would have to swallow her resentment and press on.

She dressed in lightweight pants and a long-sleeve shirt to cover her injuries. Her stitches were sore, and her abrasions felt raw, but her head was clear. The chloroform had left no residual effects—nothing like being hit by a brick.

Before she left the apartment, she made a phone call.

"Centerville Management," said a male voice.

"This is Policewoman Christine Lane, Toronto Police. Is Hawk Johnson working today?"

"I sure hope he's working. He better have caught the bus from Belleville, cause he's due on shift in ten minutes."

"He's been out of town?" Relief washed over her. He wasn't at Trout Pond last night. He couldn't have attacked her.

"He went to see a cousin or something," the man added.

"He wasn't in Toronto yesterday?"

"Lady, I'm not his babysitter."

"Please answer the question."

"As far as I know, he had three days off. He left Monday to see family and was coming back today. But you'll have to ask him yourself."

She rang off, feeling better than she had all morning. Hawk wasn't her attacker. And she still had her job and paycheck.

After taking taxi fare from the emergency tin, she headed to the Island. The Hanlan's Point ferry was a smaller craft than the Center Island boat, the latter usually crammed with hundreds of visitors heading to Centerville or Manitou Beach. The Sam McBride had a different clientele: Europeans who preferred nude bathing, teenagers who intended to bike the Island end to end, and queers—mostly men, but also women, in pairs or on their own, with striped towels slung around their necks and picnic baskets clutched in their grip.

Christine shouldered her way to the front of the ferry so she would be the first to disembark. A few people frowned as she nudged in front of them. Halfway through the fifteen-minute ferry ride, she heard her name called.

She turned. Mike Stanton stood behind her in his white sailor uniform.

"Hello, Captain," she said.

"Could I have a word?" he said. He touched her arm, and she winced as he pressed her abrasions.

"Is there a problem with the vessel?" she said, her voice low.

He shook his head. She threaded her way back through the passengers and followed him up the stairs to the third-story cabin. The first mate was at the wheel. Mike took over steering, and the other sailor left. Christine stood off to one side and waited.

Mike said, "I was with him."

"Who?" she asked.

"Gary."

She blinked. "Gary Owen?"

He turned to her for a second, his blue eyes searing. "The night of June 12th to the morning of June 13th."

The time when the demolition equipment arrived and the brake lines were severed.

The engine geared down as the vessel approached its berth. Mike expertly throttled into reverse, and the boat softly nudged the tires padding the dock. They watched the ferry workers secure the boat lines to the dock cleats.

"Wanda Owen wants to make trouble," Mike said, "but Gary didn't mess with the truck. I met him at midnight near his house. And he was with me until seven in the morning."

So Owen liked to be with men, like some of the ferry passengers heading to Hanlan's Point Beach. She was surprised but not shocked. A handful of adolescent boys hung around Jarvis and Gerrard Street selling their services to men. Christine wondered if Wanda Owen knew the "other woman" was a man.

Looking at Mike's thick biceps, facial hair and gruff demeanor, she wondered if Sergeant Bard and the other poker buddies knew about his preference. Probably not.

"I appreciate your honesty," she said. "I will keep it as confidential as I can."

Christine disembarked and spotted Fillingham thirty yards away, holding on to the handlebars of their bikes. He must have picked them up from the police station. When she reached him, she recounted Mike Stanton's confession to her on the ferry.

"We're narrowing the suspect list," he said. "At least for Ginny Rogers' murder."

Pedaling, they passed a straggling line of dispersed ferry riders as they headed to the junction of Lakeshore Avenue and the path to the lighthouse. Fillingham dismounted and gestured toward the limestone tower. "The perpetrator dragged you along the grass from Trout Pond to Lakeshore Avenue, then along the gravel path to the lighthouse. By the deepness of your abrasions, I would say he was on the road for a while, so let's head back this way from the lighthouse and retrace his steps." He pointed back in the direction of the ferry docks.

Last night, her attacker had dragged her, unconscious, right past where she now stood. She shivered as she thought of her half-naked self—so vulnerable and powerless. Dr. Whitney said the attacker would have to readminister the chloroform to keep her out cold, and she pictured a man bending over her supine body with a chloroformed cloth.

"Show me where you walked to the pond," Fillingham said, interrupting her reverie.

After a minute or two of riding on the road, she angled her handlebars to the right and bumped across the grassy field, heading toward the thick layer of bush that encircled the pond.

They set down their bikes. "Show me," he said, pointing into the thicket.

Her shoulders hunched as she took a few steps into the shrubbery, then paused. She reminded herself that it was daytime, that her partner was right behind her, but she sensed the attacker's presence, watching, ready to pounce again.

She jerked when Fillingham placed a hand on her shoulder from behind. "Lead me in," he said, "so I won't lose you."

Comforted by his proximity, she slowly forged ahead into the shrubbery. Fifteen feet in, she stopped. "I think he got me here."

Fillingham stepped beside her, crunching down on the ferns and wild grasses growing between the bushes. He pulled a yellow ribbon out of his pocket and tied it around the forked branch of a dogwood tree to mark the location.

"Okay," he said, turning, "Follow me. Watch out for the branches."

She was glad she had worn pants and long sleeves, though it was hot. Saplings poked her legs, and branches snapped against her arms and chest as she followed her partner through the underbrush. Although she didn't hold on to him, her gaze did not stray from his back.

After a minute of tromping, he stopped at a small clearing. Christine squeezed in beside him and regarded the ten pots of marijuana seedlings and the twenty mature plants growing in the soil.

"Someone knocked me out so I wouldn't find this?" she said.

He shrugged. "It's the obvious reason."

"Does this," she gestured to the plants, "have anything to do with Ginny's murder?"

"I don't know."

"So the pot grower doesn't want the demolition to go forward because..."

"Maybe the Islanders are his customer base," he said. "Maybe he lives on the Island and doesn't want his side business affected."

"It's not a big crop. Too large for personal use, but this is no fifty-thousand-dollar bust. Would someone kill for thirty marijuana plants?"

"I don't know," he replied. "Are the plants connected to your attack? Probably? Is it related to Ginny Rogers' homicide? Who knows?"

They checked the area for another hour, crunching through the underbrush surrounding the north side of the pond. Finally, they exited the shrubbery, itchy and hot.

Fillingham swiped his brow. "Have you eaten?"

She shook her head.

"You look ashen. Dr. Whitney will have my boater's license if he sees you like this." He led them back to the bikes.

"Where are we going?" she said.

"RCYC."

Christine looked down at the dirt smudges and green stains on her white shirt. "I'm not dressed for it."

"We'll eat on the back patio or grab a picnic table near the volleyball courts."

She shook her head. "I feel out of place." She paused. "I...I can't do it today."

He regarded her for a few seconds. "Okay. The kitchen can make us a picnic hamper, and we'll eat dinner at Center Island."

She reluctantly agreed, and within forty minutes they were sitting cross-legged on a red-and-white-striped blanket eating smoked salmon sandwiches and munching on a cheese plate embellished with grapes, figs and crackers.

"Who smokes marijuana on the Island?" she said.

"Mary Leonard," he responded with a smile.

"It could be the old woman's," she said, thinking about the marijuana flag flying in Mary's backyard.

"I don't think she feels the need to hide her habit," he replied. "Last month, I caught an Islander on Third Street strolling with a reefer between his fingers. A university student who rents out a cottage on Ward's."

Christine said, "Remember, Julie and I found Davy Morgan and his buddy Paul Massicotte in a cloud of marijuana smoke at Mariposa, although we didn't find any weed on them."

"Don't forget the American boats moored on Blockhouse Bay," he added. "Every weekend there's a party. Mostly booze, but I smell weed from time to time."

They paused, pondering the possibilities.

She brushed the crumbs from her hands and looked at him sitting cross-legged on the blanket. "I have to tell you something."

"You sound serious, Sixteen." A small smile lifted the corner of his mouth.

"Maybe I should have told you before," she said, "but it's not a big deal. He's alibied."

"Who?" He took a bite of his sandwich.

"Hawk Johnson."

Fillingham swallowed quickly. "The Indian?"

"He fishes Trout Pond. At night."

He lowered his sandwich. "How do you know that?"

"I went with him."

He stared at her, eyes wide.

"It just happened," she responded. "That's why I was at Trout Pond last night. I was searching for a fishing spot to take my brother."

"Hawk's your attacker," Fillingham said.

She shook her head. "He can't be. First, what's his motivation? Second, he was in Belleville visiting a cousin."

"Is this joker your boyfriend? Is that why you're defending him?"

"Of course not. His boss said he was out of town last night."

"Based on what? Hawk's say-so? What do you bet that the marijuana belongs to the Indian?" Fillingham leaned over the basket and pulled out a wax-paper bundle.

"Just because he fishes at the pond doesn't mean he's the grower. Tourists, boaters and other Islanders fish there."

"It's too coincidental—the fishing spot, the attack, the marijuana plants. All at Trout Pond." He shook his head. "I don't trust him. Or any Indian. You shouldn't either. They have different morals than us."

"What do you mean?"

"For one, they don't know how to treat white women."

"And you do?" she said.

He ignored her comment. He bit into the lemon square he had unwrapped. "Anything else you're keeping back?"

She hesitated.

He lowered the dessert to his lap. "Spit it out, Lane. We won't be able to find your attacker or Ginny Rogers' killer if you withhold information."

She poured herself a glass of freshly squeezed lemonade from the pitcher. "It's not information, really. I wonder if someone on the force noticed we were asking questions about Ginny's homicide."

"Who noticed?" he asked.

She took a sip. "The investigators."

"Gordon and Fenwick?" he said.

She nodded.

"What's the theory?" he said. "We're overstepping, so they knock you out, drag you half a mile and tie you up like a dog?" He sounded skeptical.

That was exactly her thought. "They don't want anyone messing with their investigation." She paused. "Fenwick didn't like me asking questions, challenging him."

"They probably told you to go powder your nose. That's not the same as rendering you unconscious."

"You're not a PW. You don't understand. Some policemen hate female cops. They'll do anything to keep the brotherhood male." She paused. Was she sounding hysterical? "Fenwick threatened me," she said.

"How?"

"Remember my bandaged hand, the bruising, my sore wrist? That's a present from Fenwick. Removing my uniform and tying me up in my underwear sounds exactly like his style."

"Shit!" He ran his fingers through the top of his short, white-blond hair. "Too many players, too many motives, too many crimes. And we haven't even discussed how Kevin Lamprey fits into all this. Is your attack connected to the demolition murder? Who knows? And what the hell has marijuana to do with any of it?" He took a long swig from his glass.

They finished their dinner and hid the basket under a picnic table to pick up later.

"We've got an hour of sunlight left," Fillingham said. "Let's borrow a canoe and search for other crop sites."

"You think there's more?"

"If there is, it means the person is dealing, not just using. That's more incentive to protect it."

They biked to the Island School, where Fillingham found a way inside the locked boathouse and borrowed a canoe. Holding it above their shoulders, they carried it to a patch of sand on the edge of Lighthouse Pond.

They paddled into the bulrushes on the perimeter of Trout Pond, examining the greenery for telltale starburst leaves.

"Marijuana doesn't root in water," she said. "I don't think we'll find anything in the marshy areas."

He steered them across Lighthouse Pond to the cement buttress bordering the water filtration plant. When the concrete ended in shrubbery and rocks in front of a wooded area, he said, "Let's beach it here and have a look around. Watch you don't get your bandages wet."

Christine hopped out of the canoe onto a flat patch of land and helped Fillingham wedge the boat behind two trees so it was hidden from view.

"What's here?" she said, peering through the vertical lines of birch and poplar bark.

"Not much. It's a protected area—a nature reserve. No picnic tables or tourist access. Turtles, herons, chipmunks—that's about it."

He took a step into the forest, pine needles and twigs crunching underneath. "Let's see if our enterprising gardener has been here."

It was slow going as they stepped through the underbrush, Fillingham in the lead. After ten minutes of trudging, he called out, "What's this? Corn?"

She came up behind him and stopped. In the clearing were thirty rows of corn plants, cob ears sprouting under the floppy leaves.

Kneeling beside a stalk, she said, "Not only corn." Between the thick, leafy stems were shorter marijuana plants, their star-shaped leaves frosted with small white flowers.

Fillingham wandered down the muddy central pathway that divided the crop in half. "Geez, there must be three, four hundred plants growing underneath the corn. That's quite the production. What do you think it's worth?"

"Thousands?" She shrugged. "More?"

They walked around the crop, mapping out the perimeter of its growth.

The light was dimming. "We should head out while we can still see our way back to the canoe," he said. "Then we need to figure out what the heck we're going to do about our treasure trove discovery."

Chapter 19

"You guys dating?" Morano stood behind the counter at the police station, frowning, his thick eyebrows almost meeting as he stared at Christine and Fillingham in their stained civilian clothes.

"Jealous?" Fillingham said.

"Of Richie Rich and Sasquatch?" He snorted.

Christine glared at him as she headed to the washroom to scrub off the dirt and sweat before changing into her uniform for duty. She had brought an old uniform from home that was darned in several spots and was shiny from repeated cleaning (it would never pass muster at roll call at a mainland police station), but it was the best she had until her new uniform arrived—one that she had to pay for herself given her assailant had absconded with her new one and she wasn't due for a replacement until next year.

Fillingham changed and drove the other two officers to the ferry. When her partner returned, Christine offered him a mug of coffee. He took a few sips, standing in the middle of the kitchen.

"If we take the patrol car to Hanlan's Point," he said, "the perp might hear us and stay clear. Let's bike to the filtration plant and reach the marijuana crop by foot."

"Are we going to stake out the clearing all night?" she asked. "How about our routine tasks? Sergeant Bard will notice if they are missing in the logbook."

"We can do those later in the shift. There's not much to do on nights. We've got to get this guy. He could be the key to everything."

Hidden by the rabbit-ear leaves of the corn plants, they sat on a log on the northern perimeter of the crop, looking southward toward the lake. Closing her eyes, Christine inventoried the night sounds: the chirp of crickets, receding and approaching buzz of mosquitoes, the hurried flap of a bird's wing, the whoosh of wind and stirring of dry leaves. Occasionally, she heard the scurry of a small animal through the underbrush. She reached into her pocket for the butterscotch candies Julie had bought her and handed one to her partner.

"Wow, Sixteen has a sweet tooth," Fillingham whispered as he unpeeled the candy wrapper. Later, he added, "By the way, Sergeant Bard asked for a policewoman to be transferred to the Island. He thought it would be a good idea with all the families and children around."

Christine shook her head at this revelation—after all of her boss's histrionics about being saddled with a policewoman.

One hour eased into the next. She wasn't afraid, as she had been last night following the attack. Fillingham was by her side, and she felt nestled in by nature, soothed by the sounds of the forest. Sometimes one of them would stretch and shift positions on the log. She had to will herself not to scratch the abrasions underneath her pantyhose. Her legs were so itchy and sore. When she felt herself getting sleepy, the insect drone fluttering her eyelids, she forced herself to remember kneeling beside Ginny, the supplication in the young woman's eyes before they closed.

Fillingham elbowed her. She sat up, listening. Twigs snapped as something moved through the underbrush, heavier than a squirrel or the coyote that had streaked by earlier.

Her hand went to retrieve the billy from her purse. It was him. He was coming. The drug grower—probably her attacker. And maybe Ginny's killer.

Fillingham sat tense beside her. A tall, dark shape entered the clearing and halted at the perimeter. A corn stalk rustled, then crunched.

"Wait." Fillingham stood up. He shook his head, then chuckled.

She stood up beside him. The shadowy blob raised its head as it chewed, and she could make out the long neck, the pointed ears.

Hamlet—the horse from Far Enough Farm. He had escaped his fenced yard to chew on corn ears. She snorted a laugh. "I wonder if he's tried the marijuana?"

The horse was reluctant to move until Fillingham pulled off an ear of corn and led him away from the clearing.

When he returned, she asked him, "What's our plan? In a couple of hours, we have to leave to finish our house checks and then give report to the next duty officers. Are we coming back here after our shift when the sun is up? Odds are the grower tends to his plants in daylight when he can see what he's doing."

"I'd like to return." He yawned widely. "However, we need to sleep and eat. We're this close"—she could just make out his two fingers a half inch apart—"to discovering how this all connects."

They sat back down on the log. She whispered, "We don't know how often the plants need to be tended. The grower may come back today or next week. The growth cycle for marijuana is six months. These plants won't be ready for harvest until the fall." She paused. "Do you think we should tell Sergeant Bard about the plants? Or inform the investigators?"

He waited a couple of seconds before answering. "We're doing all the work, taking all the risks. You've taken the brunt of it. As soon as we open our mouths, Allen and Fenwick will take over. And when the perpetrators are found, the investigators will receive the glory. After all of our persistence and investigating."

"I want to keep my job," she said. "And get Ginny's killer, and the guy who knocked me out."

He turned to look at her, his face a light smudge in the forest shadows. "You and I are committed to doing that more than anyone else." When she remained silent, he said, "Let's watch the clearing for another hour. That leaves two hours for housekeeping and our normal patrol. At shift change in the morning, we go home, sleep a couple hours, check other leads and return in the afternoon to stake out the clearing. The problem is that tomorrow begins Gala Day weekend, which means it will be a busy overnight shift for us."

"What's Gala Day?" she said.

"The annual reunion for Islanders that takes place every August long weekend. Hundreds of people show up. They have music, performances, games, sports competitions, a bonfire."

"Maybe they'll be finished by the time we come on nights."

He shook his head. "The celebrations go on into the early morning hours. We help with water taxis, lost children, crowd control. And check that the permitted fires have been safely extinguished. It'll be busy."

They waited in silence for another hour amidst the gnats and calls from a red-winged blackbird, then got to their feet, stretched and biked back to the station.

As she climbed into the patrol car to head to the dock for shift change, Christine found a twine of sweetgrass on her seat.

Hawk.

She tucked the six-inch braid in her sleeve before Fillingham got in the driver's side. Hawk was back. He wanted to see her. At the ferry dock, she said, "Go give report to Sergeant Bard. I'm going to check a few things."

He looked at her. "What things?"

She paused.

"Lane," he said, his tone warning.

No more secrets. She took a breath. "I'm going to interview Hawk Johnson."

"Wait. I'll come with you."

They got out of the car. Fillingham spoke briefly to Sergeant Bard and Ulster, and the two older officers drove away in the police vehicle.

Christine glanced at the ferry loading locals who were heading to the city for their day jobs. She wanted Fillingham on that boat.

"It's better if I see him alone," she said.

"No way. This guy could be your attacker. Or a drug trafficker. Let's extend it further—does he have an alibi for Ginny's murder?"

"He was sleeping in the house he rents on Ward's Island with his two buddies."

"Maybe he's using you for cover—takes you fishing, flatters you, asks a few questions about the investigation, hoping that no one remembers that he's a mechanic and could cut the brake line blind-folded."

She thought of Hawk's hands in her hair, tugging out her hairpins. Was that all a lie?

"Why is it so unbelievable that someone would go out with me?" she said. "Hawk must be a liar and a criminal. What other motivation could there be?"

She stomped off toward Centerville, Fillingham trailing behind her as she found the manager and got him to radio for Hawk. Hawk smiled at her when he came into the store, the smile fading when he saw Fillingham scowling beside her.

She suggested they sit outside at a picnic table by the train ride. Hawk sat on one side, the police officers on the other.

"You were looking for me?" Hawk said to Christine. He was wearing denim work coveralls over a white t-shirt.

She couldn't let him charm her. "We have a few questions."

"Where were you this past Wednesday night?" Fillingham said.

Hawk waited a few seconds, then replied, "At my cousin's."

"Where's that?" Fillingham said.

"Belleville," Hawk replied.

"Do you have proof of that?" Fillingham said.

Hawk said, "Call him."

"Hard proof. Like a gas station fill-up bill, grocery receipt, train ticket."

"I might have the bus ticket." He pulled his wallet from his pants pocket and sifted through its contents with two fingers. He placed a ticket stub on the picnic table.

Fillingham examined it.

A wave of relief flooded Christine. Hawk had returned to Toronto Thursday morning, after her attack, as the manager had said. It wasn't Hawk. He hadn't chloroformed her and dragged her across the Island.

"What happened Wednesday night?" Hawk asked.

"Someone attacked me when I was on patrol," she said.

"Are you okay?" Hawk reached across the wooden tabletop and touched her uniform sleeve. She nodded but pulled her arm away.

Fillingham chided her, "Lane. That information is confidential to the investigation." He turned to Hawk. "You fish on Trout Pond?"

"Yes." Hawk looked over at Christine and smiled, his teeth white in his tanned face. She knew he was thinking of their fishing date, kneeling on the sand, kissing. His smile widened, cognizant that she was thinking about it too.

"Do you do anything else in that area?" Fillingham said.

"Like what?" Hawk said, looking over at him.

"Something not as legal."

Hawk frowned. "If you have something to ask, ask it. Did I attack Policewoman Lane? No. Did I hurt Ginny? No. What do you think I've done this time?"

"Have you ever fished the north side of Trout Pond?"

"Is this about the marijuana?" Hawk said calmly.

Fillingham gasped. "You know about that?"

Hawk scratched the side of his face. "Been there the last two summers."

"Is it yours?" Fillingham said.

Hawk paused several seconds, a small smile on his lips. "No."

"Do you have anything to prove that?"

Hawk said, "Do you have anything to prove it's mine?" There was a pause. "There's more on the small island," he added.

"Which island?" she said.

"The one in Lighthouse Pond," Hawk answered, looking at her. "By the filtration plant."

"Do you know who planted it?" she asked.

He shook his head. "Never seen anyone."

"Ever?" Fillingham said incredulously.

Hawk shrugged. "I'm only down that way once every week or two, mostly late at night to fish."

"Have you found any other illegal crops on the Island?" she said.

Hawk shook his head.

Good, Christine thought. He wasn't the one who planted the crop in the nature sanctuary with the corn.

"Why didn't you tell the police?" Fillingham said.

"The plants don't bother me," Hawk answered.

"Do you think they belong to an Islander?" she said.

He shrugged. "Maybe. Some Islanders are into that."

"Are you into that?" Fillingham said.

"My tribe uses plants for ceremonial use, as you saw at Ginny's funeral," he responded.

"I take that as a yes," Fillingham said.

"We use sage, cedar, sweetgrass and tobacco," Hawk said. His broad shoulders spanned half the length of the picnic bench, his thick arms taking up most of the tabletop space. Fillingham looked like a child, or a porter in his uniform, as he sat across from the larger man.

"I'm not a drug dealer, woman beater or murderer," Hawk said slowly. "But thanks for asking."

The two men glared at each other.

"I think we're finished here," Christine said. No one moved. "PC Fillingham, why don't you hold the seven thirty ferry. I'll meet you in a minute. We have a lot to do today, remember."

Fillingham looked over at her, then at Hawk. He got up, his hand briefly touching his gun holster, then headed out toward the ferry.

"Fun guy to work with," Hawk said.

"He's not that bad," she said. "I got hurt on shift with him. And Ginny's death. He's keen to get the perpetrators."

"He reminds me of the two hot shots working out of the community center."

"Investigators Allen and Fenwick?" she said.

"Them's the ones."

"They interviewed you?"

"An Indian is always a suspect." He was smiling, but his eyes were cold.

Fenwick and Hawk. That would be a battle. "Did they interview you more than once?" she asked. She wondered if Hawk got the same treatment that she did at Weasel's hand.

He shook his head.

What were the investigators' thoughts—of Hawk, or any other person they had interviewed? If only they would share information, combine forces with Island patrol, rather than have two police teams running parallel investigations.

She checked her watch. "I better go. We've been up all night." She stepped out of the bench, and they walked toward the amusement park exit.

"Are you okay?" he said.

She nodded. "Just scraped up." She pointed to the bandages on her calves.

He frowned as he looked at her legs. "You didn't think it was me, did you?"

"I was hoping it wasn't."

He chuckled. "Because you like me." He said it as a statement, rather than a question. "I like you too."

She shook her head, looking down. "We can't, there's nothing—"

He stopped and took her hand. "If you're in trouble, come to me for help. I'm the third house down from Mrs. Polotov's with the three long windows in front."

His hand felt warm. She allowed herself to give his fingers a brief squeeze. "I'd better run. Fillingham might let the ferry leave without me."

She got home in time to help her siblings pack their bathing suits and towels for summer camp. Phyllis had already left for work. Christine was glad that the campers went swimming every afternoon. She didn't want her siblings to end up like her, barely able to stay afloat. Although, after her last swimming lesson, Fillingham said that she was thrashing less and her kick had improved, so she was more buoyant.

Christine walked Donna and Wayne to the community center. A wave of exhaustion washed over her as she climbed the stairs back up to her apartment. In the last three days, she had slept for only six hours. At least the empty apartment would be quiet. Tucked in bed, she reached over and set her alarm for one o'clock. She was meeting Fillingham downtown for lunch at two thirty to review their plan.

Her room was hot and stuffy in the July heat, but she fell immediately into a dreamless sleep. Four hours later, her alarm buzzed. It took two minutes before she was awake enough to swat it off, her skin layered with sweat, the sheets twisted at the bottom of the bed. A cool shower would wake her, rinse her off, but she grimaced at the thought of the spray on her abrasions and the time it would take to resalve and rebandage her cuts. A wipe-down with a washcloth would have to suffice.

One day soon, when this was all over, she would let herself sleep all day. She would wake up in time for dinner—and cook something decadent, like pork sausages from the St. Lawrence Market and pancakes with real maple syrup, not the corn syrup her mom usually bought. And, because Donna would love it, she would add a dollop of real whipped cream and a maraschino cherry on each pancake and eat until she was stuffed. After dinner, she would watch *The Wayne and Shuster Show* with her siblings and not move all evening.

She met Fillingham at a restaurant on Front Street close to the ferry docks. It felt weird waiting for him in a booth, as if they were on a date. Her eyes on the door, she spied her partner entering. He was wearing light denim jeans and a short-sleeved button-down shirt in sky blue, looking every inch the private club sailor with his short blond hair and tanned arms. When he saw her, his face lit up. He had news. She had news too. She smiled as she waved him over. Things were coming to a head.

The waitress arrived immediately with a carafe of coffee. Fillingham ordered a hamburger and fries while she chose an omelet. She wasn't that hungry, maybe due to lack of sleep or her mounting excitement. They were going to find the culprits—the drug growers, her attacker and Ginny's killer.

When the waitress left, Christine asked, "What's up?"

"Daniel Rogers was working the night of your assault. I spoke with him this morning at the CBC building. He signed out at midnight and headed to an apartment that he rents with a coworker. The coworker corroborates Rogers came home at 12:30 a.m. and went straight to bed."

"We should still talk to Bianca Rogers to confirm Daniel's alibi for the night of the demolition." She paused. "How is Rogers doing?"

"Trying to keep busy with work and family."

"You don't see him as a credible suspect?" she said.

"Tampering with brakes is not his style. His angle is political—work the crowd and show the Islanders' humanity. His strategy is persuasion, not armed revolution."

"Any pro-marijuana speeches in his broadcasts?"

Fillingham shook his head. "I doubt it. CBC is liberal but not anti-law. But I'll check. What did you dig up?" he said.

"Paddy Jenkins is in big trouble. He has a ten-thousand-dollar gambling debt. And get this—he secured a second mortgage on the yacht club and has missed the last two payments."

"How'd you dig that up?"

"I saw a bank statement on his desk, so I knew which bank to contact and his account number. And," she paused, "I asked the bartender at Sammy's on Yonge Street to get me the information. He's the guy I give my loan payment to. Works for George Ray."

"And he told you?"

She rubbed the edge of the fabric placemat. "For twenty-five bucks."

"Geez." He pulled out his wallet and handed her a twenty and a five-dollar bill.

"We should split the cost."

He shook his head. "Don't worry. The force will reimburse us when we solve the case."

"Samuel Fairmont, who owns Clergy House, has a mortgage at the same bank."

"Anything unusual?" he said.

She shook her head. "Moderate mortgage on the restaurant. He lowered his monthly payments last year, since business was dipping, but that's about it. He pays consistently."

Their meals arrived, and she tucked into her omelet and toast, her appetite appearing for the first time in days.

Fillingham forked some fries. "Let's recap. Three crimes committed: illegal drug production, assault of a police officer and homicide. Crimes A, B and C. We don't have many clues for the marijuana grower other than he must be trafficking and may be an Islander. That would make the most sense. He could be the perp for your assault; you got too close to the goods. Or not. We don't know if the same perpetrator planted in the two locations. We know your assailant is not Hawk, Daniel Rogers or Paddy Jenkins, who is still recovering from his beating. Kevin Lamprey is a contender, but we can't locate him."

"Don't forget the investigators," she said.

He gave her a level look. "That would be hard to prove and career suicide."

"And for Ginny Rogers' murder," she said, "Gary Owen has an alibi now. Rogers, Jenkins and Lamprey are still suspects. We're stuck in the same conversational loop. We have key suspects, but almost anyone on the Island could have committed one or more of the three crimes."

"And is Crime A related to Crime B, related to Crime C?" he said.

"What do we do now?" She took another sip of her coffee.

"We ambush him." He smiled and took a huge bite of his hamburger.

Chapter 20

"Ow," Christine said as she tripped over a root. She was following Fillingham as he threaded his way through the shadowy forest to their canoe.

She was hot, tired, hungry and out of patience. They had sat silently by the marijuana and corn crops for five hours, watching the sunset through the glimmering tree leaves while her stomach growled and her bladder pressed against her waistband. Adding to the soreness of her abrasions, a determined horsefly had bitten her several times on the ankle.

And now they had to head to the police station, clean up, sign in for night shift, monitor any lingering Gala Day celebrations and return to stake out the forest all over again. At a break in the trees, she stumbled down a small hill and almost landed in the lagoon water. To her left, the lights from the water filtration plant shone onto Lighthouse Pond, the outline of the white building with its russet roof mirrored in the water.

Christine inhaled the cool night breeze, glad to be out of the claustrophobic forest.

Fillingham stepped out from the bush carrying their canoe overhead, then slid it into the water. She retrieved the oars from behind a tree, and they got into the boat.

As they paddled, he pointed to a rocky outcrop in the middle of the pond with an oar. "Let's check it out."

"It's hard to see anything this time of night," Christine protested. She was not keen on another trek through rough terrain. They weren't using flashlights in the dark to prevent alerting people to their presence, but it meant they stumbled through the forest.

"It will take only a minute. Let's see if Hawk was telling the truth about plants growing there."

She sighed her acquiescence and dug her paddle into the water as Fillingham steered the canoe toward the small island outcrop. It felt good to move her limbs, get the circulation going. She enjoyed paddling, keeping her shoulders stacked as Fillingham had demonstrated, bending at the waist to get her torso into the motion—much more than she enjoyed swimming.

"You ever paddle before?" Fillingham asked.

"You mean competitively?"

"Yeah. We could use you on the RCYC women's team."

"No." Once, her stepfather Eddie had driven the five of them to a lake north of the city, where they had rented a canoe. Mom didn't want to paddle, so Christine did. They didn't have lifejackets, since that cost extra, and none of them knew how to swim well. Before they got to the boat rental, Eddie had already imbibed a couple of beers in the car en route, the glass empties rattling around on the back seat floor as they drove. Eddie was the last one to get into the canoe, and they almost capsized when he stood up. Thank goodness the attendant had one foot on the boat to steady it. Her family had zigzagged their way around the lake, Christine and her stepfather paddling, the boat riding low in the water because of the weight of five people. She mentally ticked down the minutes until Eddie would announce he'd had enough, and they could return to the dock. If they overturned, she would have to save her siblings and her mom, and Christine wasn't a strong swimmer. She wasn't sure if her stepfather could swim—she had been too afraid to ask him during the boat ride.

"I can't paddle for your club," Christine reminded Fillingham, coming back to the present. "I'm not a member."

He shrugged. "If you're skilled, they'll waive the fee, especially for female athletes. RCYC likes to win. You're too old for our women's team, but maybe the master class."

"I don't have time to practice and compete," she said impatiently. "I have a job, a family, debts to pay. And we have three crimes to solve."

"Fine. Whoa. Slow down. Lift your paddle out," he said as the island loomed in front of them.

A line of water dribbled onto her pants and into her shoe as she placed her paddle across her knees. He steered the canoe parallel to a rocky outcrop.

"Is there a sandy area to land?" she said.

He shook his head. "I'll get us as close as we can—it's pretty craggy. You get out first, then I'll tie the canoe to a boulder."

He swirled his paddle while the canoe hovered beside a flat rock, keeping the boat stationary with flicks of his paddle. She sidled over to the boat's gunwale, lifted her leg and planted one foot on the large stone.

Something flashed by.

"Hey!" Fillingham shouted. He sprang to his feet, and the canoe rocked.

Christine yelped, half in and half out of the canoe, clutching the rail.

Her partner sat back down and hauled her into the boat by her shirt collar.

"Ow!" she said, falling against the center yoke.

"It's him!" he yelled. The canoe lurched forward with choppy jerks as he plunged his paddle in and out of the water.

Christine sat up and stared. A black-hooded figure in a canoe was darting across Lighthouse Pond with swift, sure strokes, heading toward the road.

"Paddle!" Fillingham roared from the stern.

She grabbed her oar and dug it deep into the pond, trying to push them quickly across the water.

The man neared the small beach at the tip of Lighthouse Pond. He gave one last thrust, stood up and ran along the gunwales to the bow, where he leaped out of the canoe and landed in a crouch on the sand. His black-clad figure disappeared from view.

"Faster! Faster!" Fillingham bellowed.

She exhaled loudly in bursts as she plunged the last couple of strokes to shore.

"Lean left," he yelled. She barely had time to move as Fillingham stepped onto her seat, put one foot on the boat rail and launched himself after the suspect.

Their canoe ground against the sand, anchored by Christine's weight. She jumped out and quickly hauled it up on shore and headed to the road, head swiveling to locate her partner and the suspect. Had they gone to the lighthouse? Trout Pond?

Fillingham's voice rang out from behind the school. "He's headed for the beach!"

She raced across Lakeshore Avenue to the inner school courtyard.

"This way!" Fillingham shouted from the shrubbery.

She ran in his direction, arms wide as she tried to keep her balance as the grass gave way to sand. The path turned, and she ran headlong into Fillingham. They rebounded off each other with grunts, Christine falling to one knee in the sand.

"He's taken off in a rowboat," Fillingham said as he took off, spraying her with sand. "I'll get the canoe!" he called over his shoulder.

She jogged southward until she reached the open beach that looked out onto Lake Ontario. Fifty feet from shore, she spied the dark outline of a rowboat, oars cycling swiftly in and out of the water, the smudge in the middle that was the rower.

The boat headed eastward; she was tempted to run along the sand and keep pace with it, but she needed to paddle the canoe with Fillingham. The water was illuminated by the muted glow of a half-moon partially hidden by cloud cover. She squinted as she tried to identify a recognizable trait—height, weight, gender, coloring, age—of the shadowed sailor.

"Can you see him still?"

She turned. Fillingham's voice came from underneath the canoe held over his head; he was jogging, as if the boat were no heavier than a firewood log.

"Yes," she answered.

With one move, he turned the canoe over and laid it on the water. Her shoes and pant legs instantly soaked as she splashed into the shallows, then crab-walked inside the bow of the boat. Fillingham pushed off and jumped in behind her. She grabbed a paddle and jabbed it into the water.

Fillingham grunted as he paddled frantically in the seat behind her. "Harder!" he commanded, like a frenzied coxswain.

For the next three minutes, Christine barely looked up, her world reduced to the stick of wood in her hand, the burn of her shoulder blades and the inky lake. She and Fillingham matched strokes, grunting with every dig, inhaling sharply when they pulled their paddles out of the water. They had a rhythm going, a frenetic pace that she wouldn't be able to maintain.

Sweat dribbled into her eye, and she blinked the sting away. The rowboat was pulling ahead as it passed Manitou Beach and steered toward the Center Island Pier that jutted out half a mile into the lake.

"I can't see him anymore!" she yelled. The rowboat had disappeared into the murky shadows underneath the pier. Had he gone left or right, or was he hiding behind a concrete pillar? Or had the rowboat continued eastward toward Ward's Island?

"Keep paddling," Fillingham said. "We'll look around when we get to the pier."

One minute later, darkness descended and they were under the pier.

"Stop paddling," he said. "Do you see anything?"

After a few seconds, her eyes adjusted to the dimness. The pier lights on top provided a yellow backdrop to the wooden beams, steel girders and concrete legs. "I don't think he's—"

"There!" Fillingham screamed. "Go! Go! Go!"

Grabbing her paddle, her arms burning with complaint, she thrust it into the water.

When their canoe emerged from underneath the pier, she scanned the horizon. Where was the rowboat? The half-moon had slipped behind clouds, and it was hard to discern the charcoal of the water from the dark hue of a boat's stern. Had the suspect beached the boat? Had they missed him under the pier?

"I see him!" Fillingham said, exultantly. "Eleven o'clock. Keep going." He steered their craft nearer to shore, where the water was calmer and they could skim over it faster.

She grimaced with the pain of repeated pull, her hand cramping in its grip around the paddle shaft. Her arms, face and clothes were soaked, water pluming with every dig. To her left, she spied the concrete breakwall that protected the two-mile boardwalk spanning the southern border of the Island. He couldn't beach the boat there—it would be impossible to scramble up the barrier. He must be heading for Ward's Island.

She heard the residents before she saw them—laughter, drums, the call of voices. The smoldering scent of burning wood reached her as she spied the red and yellow licks of light from a huge bonfire on Ward's Island Beach.

Gala Day celebrations.

The firelight momentarily illuminated people as they moved around the pit. Yellow dots of light, from lanterns and hand-held torches, danced in a staggered circle around the bonfire. Snatches of song reached her with a gust of wind.

"Keep going," Fillingham said between breaths. "We're gaining on him."

The suspect had stopped rowing. The man—if it was a man—was moving around inside the rowboat. Was he giving himself up?

A white spark lit the interior of the rowboat, evolving into a thin, glowing line.

A bright flash flew at their canoe.

"Duck!" she yelled as the stick exploded into a starburst of blue light beside the canoe.

The group on the beach had noticed nothing amiss. A few clapped at the fireworks.

"Paddle," she yelled to Fillingham. "Get closer." They had to keep this person away from the beach, the Islanders, the children.

Another fiery stick sailed through the air but was extinguished when it fell in the water ahead of them. The man ignited another rocket, averted his hooded face as it sparked, and sent it arcing toward their canoe.

It landed in between Christine and Fillingham, torpedoing inside their craft with flashes of white and red light until Fillingham grabbed it by the base and threw it out over the lake in white and red scribbles of light.

"Aaah!" Voices rose in appreciation from the beach.

"Jesus, he's trying to set us on fire," Fillingham said.

"Paddle close," she said. "I'll tackle him."

The canoe sliced through the water toward the rowboat. The hooded man moved around the boat like a pyrotechnic monk as he lit a trio of fireworks and, one by one, threw them at their watercraft. Geez, he must have gotten in the boat used for Gala Day firework celebrations. Christine kept her paddle across her knee, batting away the flaming batons like a goalie.

The canoe neared the rowboat—sixty feet, fifty, forty... The audience on the beach grew quiet, realizing something was wrong.

"Stop! Police!" she yelled as they circled the rowboat. Neither of them was in uniform. She wanted to ensure that the suspect knew they were officers—even if he was high on something. The hooded man paused, as if uncertain about his next move, a handful of lit firecrackers sparking in his grip, his chin showing dark and shaded in the light. Was that a beard?

"Toronto Police," Fillingham bellowed. "Dump the firecrackers in the water."

They zig-zagged beside the rowboat, waiting, as the wick on the firecrackers burned down. Gosh, they were going to explode in his face.

Suddenly, he dropped the fireworks into the bottom of the boat. Yellow, blue and white balls of light pinballed inside the hull, a few escaping in a spray of colored light. Smoke rose from the belly of the boat, clouding the suspect who stood like a character from Dante's *Inferno*.

There was a dull boom and the man stumbled, falling back onto the seat. His hood fell off, revealing a pale thin face, dark hair stuck damply to his head, a black mustache and the scruffy beginnings of a beard.

Davy Morgan—the mechanic from Algonquin Island Yacht Club. Ginny's boyfriend.

Fillingham paddled closer. Davy blinked through the smoke as if he were waking up. Licks of fire rose from the mound of pyrotechnics erupting in the boat's bottom.

"Jump, Davy!" Fillingham yelled above the squeal of an erupting rocket. Christine motioned to Fillingham to steer her closer to the fire-ravaged boat.

Davy looked at her. "I didn't know she'd be there."

They stared at each other through the wavering plumes of gray smoke. Davy was the marijuana grower. Her assailant.

And the killer.

"She was supposed to be working!" he wailed. "Why did she have to come?"

"It was an accident, Davy!" she shouted. "You didn't mean to hurt her. We know that. Let us help you. Step into the canoe." She waved him over.

"Tell her mother I'm sorry." He leaned forward, gathering unlit sticks of fireworks in his arm, then held them in a bundle against his chest. He was going to light himself on fire, burn himself to death.

"Now!" she yelled to Fillingham, and she rose from her seat into a crouch. The canoe thrust forward, and she leaped into the rowboat as Davy lit the wicks of the firecrackers. She ended up on top of him as sparks and fire licked around them. She grabbed him around the torso and thrust with her legs to propel them out of the rowboat—just as a thunderous bang sent them flying, a searing pain down the length of her calf.

Davy was torn out of her arms. She hit the lake with an "Oomph" and immediately submerged. Looking up through the water, it was like midday—the sky lit with punctuations of white, blue and yellow pinwheels of light, thunderous vibrations trembling the surrounding water.

She kicked frantically, shooting herself out of the water, treading so vigorously that her shoulders hovered above the waterline. Where was Davy? And Fillingham? She turned, scanning a semicircle of lake, looking for them.

The rowboat was a yellow and orange floating torch, spurting and burping colors. Behind it, the overturned canoe slid by, floating gently downwind, empty.

"Geoffrey!" she screamed. She started swimming toward the canoe one hundred yards away, trying to scoop her arms, straighten her legs to get there faster.

Suddenly, Fillingham popped out of the water, oar in hand, and then threw himself on the canoe hull.

"I'm fine, Christine," he yelled. "Find Morgan!"

She turned, whirlpooling herself as she searched for Davy in the yellow-orange light of the blazing boat.

There. Floating toward the shore—the dark hump of a back.

Eyes squeezed against her exhaustion, she swam over to the floating figure, her shoulders burning. Treading water, she turned him over. Davy was unconscious. She couldn't tell if he was breathing.

She curled her elbows under his arms like Fillingham had taught her and kicked backward toward land, Fillingham gliding in beside her in the righted canoe, sensing rather than seeing people run down the beach toward the water. Panting, she swam on her back, her long sleeves and pants dragging her down as she constantly checked that Davy's face was above water.

When she felt the sand beneath her toes, she stood up. Hands helped her, grabbing Davy, pulling her toward the beach—the sleeves of a uniform, of a firefighter, Mrs. Polotov's gentle tug. She let them take Davy out of her arms, everything happening in dark and light, dark and light, as people's torches bounced beams off the rippling water.

She walked out of the lake, slowed by her wet clothes, and turned to look at the velvet sky scribbled with red and green chalking of light. The rowboat was an inferno of crackling wood and sputtering explosions, floating out across the lake like a dead Norse warrior being cremated on the waves, releasing his soul for its journey over the seas.

Chapter 21

She opened her eyes. Fillingham was fast asleep, head propped on his arms as he leaned across the bottom of her hospital bed from his chair. He still wore the jeans and shirt he had on during the chase, wrinkled and smelling of lake water. The partners had been interviewed for an hour in the emergency ward by the two chagrined investigators, Allan and Fenwick, after being assessed by Dr. Jim. Subsequently, Christine was transferred upstairs to a private room, since only men were allowed in the four-bed police ward. By that time, it was two in the morning.

During the conversation with the investigators, she and Fillingham gave modified versions of how they had stumbled onto the marijuana patch last night while canoeing and chased the culprit, who later confessed to growing the crop and sabotaging the truck.

Fenwick's eyes narrowed. "Lots of lucky coincidences here."

"Right place, right time," Fillingham responded.

"Anything else to add to your *story*?" Fenwick asked.

Fillingham shook his head, blue eyes wide and credulous.

"Just good police work, I guess," Christine added.

Christine studied Fillingham's sleeping form on her bed cover. He was so still; she wasn't used to seeing him motionless. The nape of his neck looked tanned, the soft blond hairs disappearing into the collar of his shirt. She felt an urge to touch his neck, to feel his warmth under her fingertips, cover up his vulnerability.

He stirred, as if sensing her attention, and propped himself up on his elbows, blinking.

"That's a good look on you," she said, pointing to his face.

The explosion in the rowboat had singed his eyelashes and eyebrows and reddened his face, which was smudged with soot at the edges. His hair was burned black at the tips so that he looked like a blank-faced skunk.

Christine had second-degree burns on her calf. Dr. Jim said that the officers were lucky their clothes had been wet from paddling, since it protected their skin. The doctor was keeping her overnight for monitoring. She hadn't protested—they'd pumped her full of painkillers and she could relax now. Everything was okay. She and her partner were safe. They had caught the drug grower who was also her assailant and Ginny's killer. She still had a job. With Fillingham sitting beside her bed in her private room, she had let herself drift off to sleep.

As Fillingham stood up and stretched, she propped herself up in bed, feeling a lump under her palm. A small deerskin pouch edged out from under the pillow.

Hawk. He had handed her something when she stepped into an ambulance that had been ferried across the Inner Harbor. Davy Morgan was being loaded into the second ambulance. The scene on the beach was chaotic: flashing lights from emergency vehicles, the flickering bonfire, the rowboat sparking colors as it bobbed on the waves and Islanders milling around.

When Christine was moved upstairs from Emergency, she had tucked the pouch from Hawk underneath her pillow, out of Fillingham's view. She'd talk to Hawk after she was discharged, ask him what the gift signified, thank him for his thoughtfulness.

"You okay, Sixteen?" Fillingham asked. "You look flushed."

"Dozy from the medication, that's all."

"I gave Julie a call. She's coming down with Sarah before they go on day shift."

"Maybe your eyelashes will grow back by then."

His hairless eyebrows rose. "Doesn't affect my charm."

After a moment, she said, "Did you hear what the Islanders were saying while we were waiting for the ambulance?"

"What can they say?" He gestured widely. "Davy Morgan did it. All of it. He grew weed and sold it. He didn't want his profits affected if Islanders were forced to vacate, didn't want to lose his job at the yacht club. You scared him when you searched Trout Pond, so he knocked you out and removed your clothes to ensure you'd never come back there again."

"And he killed Ginny," Christine said.

"Davy cut the brake lines; Ginny died. He didn't mean to kill her, but he was out to hurt someone. To stop the demolitions."

"Are the Islanders relieved the murderer's been found?"

"Yes and no. It was a terrible thing for Davy to do, tamper with the truck, knowing someone could be hurt. But they also blame Metro Council for evicting residents in the first place."

"Have Ginny's parents been notified of the arrest?" she said.

He nodded. "Nancy Hamilton's up in Barrie, staying with her sister; they'll tell her in the morning. Daniel Rogers knows. They called him from the Center Island station."

"Teeny!"

Christine and Fillingham turned to the open door. Donna broke away from Wayne and her mother and ran toward the bed, dressed in her teddy bear pajamas over a pair of pants.

"Whoa!" Fillingham said, grabbing Donna before she threw herself on top of Christine and gently placed her on the edge of the bed beside her sister.

Donna squeezed her in a fierce hug. Christine gingerly hugged her back, mindful of the abrasions on the back of her arms. "Hey, Wayne." She motioned her brother over and squeezed his hand.

"Mom." Christine addressed her mother standing by the door. "I'm fine. You didn't have to come down."

"Two hospital calls in a month are a bit much." Her mom's hair was uncombed, her clothing wrinkled. She must have rolled out of bed after being notified of Christine's hospitalization, grabbed her kids and hopped in the waiting police car.

Christine introduced everyone.

Wayne turned to Fillingham. "What happened to your hair?"

Fillingham ran his hand through his hair from front to back, black flecks speckling his palm. "Good thing your sister likes me for more than my good looks."

She was about to make a sarcastic remark, but her partner was looking at her expectantly, eyes wide.

"Actually," Christine said, "I do like—"

"PW Lane. PC Fillingham. You have a visitor!" Julie called from the doorway. Behind her towered Deputy Chief Darlow.

Fillingham stood at attention beside her bed, shoulders back, arms at his side. Christine sat up taller, one arm encircled around her sister to prevent her from sliding off the bed.

Phyllis scurried over and pulled Donna off the bed. "Time to go."

"Mrs. Williams," the deputy said as Phyllis walked by with Donna and Wayne. After the three exited, Deputy Darlow stood in the middle of the room in a fitted charcoal-gray suit, white shirt and black tie. It was four in the morning, but he looked impeccable, his salt-and-pepper hair neatly parted to the side. "I'd like to speak with PW Lane."

"Yes, sir!" Fillingham said. "Permission to speak, sir."

The deputy nodded.

"PW Lane's investigative skills were integral in the arrest of Davy Morgan for Ginny Rogers' homicide."

"I know her attributes, Constable," Deputy Darlow said.

Fillingham hesitated. Behind the deputy, Julie winked at Fillingham and then motioned him out with her.

Fillingham exited the room, and Christine saw Julie crook her hand around his arm before they moved out of sight.

"I can stand, Deputy Darlow," she said, swinging her legs over to the edge of the bed.

"No need, PW. I only need a moment."

Was she in trouble again? Was he here to fire her, despite the arrest of the killer? "I'm fine, sir," she said as tucked her legs back under the covers. "They're keeping me in for observation, but I have a clean bill of health. Ask Dr. Jim. I'm good to go."

"I'm not here to discuss your medical diagnosis or your employment." He paused. "Your name has been put forward for a commendation."

Several seconds ticked by. Her job was safe. Her family was safe. "PC Fillingham was instrumental in the arrest," she said.

"He is being similarly recommended," Deputy Darlow said.

"I am honored, sir."

"Considering the difficulties you've faced," he said, his brown eyes looking into hers, "and the skills you have demonstrated, the chief will support your application to a station of your choice."

They were going to let her transfer downtown so that she could experience actual police work. Like she always wanted.

"Thank you, Deputy," she heard herself say. She paused. "Can I think about it?"

She didn't know what she thought about Toronto Island anymore—her resentment at her deployment had dissipated. The people, the scenery, even her partner, were growing on her. And she hadn't been bored for one second.

"As you like," he said, inclining his head. He took a step toward the door and turned around. "Anything you need, PW?"

She knew he was being polite, but she spoke up anyway. "There is one thing. PWs need summer-weight pants. It's impossible to chase a suspect in an A-line skirt."

The edge of his mouth quirked. "I'll see what I can do." He turned and left.

She closed her eyes. Images floating through her mind: the commendation note in her file, her ridiculous-looking partner without eyebrows. Her eyes fluttered open as she thought about Ginny's parents—would Davy Morgan's arrest make them feel better or worse?

Shifting in bed, her fingers touched the leather bag Hawk had given her. Closing her eyes again, she pictured the two of them with plates on their laps forking trout into their mouths. Her final thought before she slept was about Sergeant Bard. She would ask her sergeant if they could lunch at Clergy House on their next shift together. And she would tell her boss that, just for once, the bill was on him.

PRE-ORDER THE NEXT BOOK IN THE SERIES: MISSING

If you enjoyed FINAL LOOK, you can order the next book in the Christine Lane mystery series, MISSING, from your favorite online bookseller or from my website at DianneScottAuthor.com/books.

MISSING was a Finalist for the Excellence in Crime Writing Award from the Crime Writers of Canada.

FREE SHORT STORY!

If you want to read more about Christine Lane and her friends from the Women's Bureau, receive the free short story "Hello There" when you sign up for my monthly newsletter at DianneScottAuthor.com/Newsletter.

LEAVE A REVIEW

If you enjoyed FINAL LOOK, I invite you to leave a review at your favorite bookseller site. Reviews guide readers to my books and help me reach a new audience, so they are much appreciated.

ACKNOWLEDGMENTS

Final Look is the first book in my Christine Lane mystery series and has been years in the making. I have many people to acknowledge for their part in its creation.

My conversations with past and current residents of Toronto Island, including June Edwards, Alison Gzowski, Jimmy Jones and Jim Sanderson provided insights into the political, cultural and social milieu of Toronto Island in the 1960s. These Islanders opened my eyes to the landscape's beautiful geography, fascinating history and unique community.

For information on women in policing, I turned to the female officers who forged their early and challenging path in the Toronto Police Force in the 1950s, 1960s and 1970s. I thank Georgina Bellamy, Donna Brown, Ruth Burritt, Dorothy Taylor and Kay Wilson for information supplied through emails, conversations and in-person interviews, and I hope our conversations continue.

Final Look was supported by grants awarded by the Toronto Arts Council and the Ontario Arts Council. Diaspora Dialogues awarded me a rewarding mentorship with writer Marina Endicott. I also thank Tiffany Morris for her review of my manuscript.

I am blessed to have a writers group I've known for twenty years, and even if we don't get together as regularly, their encouragement continues. Thanks to Leanne Lieberman, Elizabeth McLeod, Roz Spafford, Ania Szado, Elsie Sze and the late Anne Warrick.

And finally, thanks to my father, Peter Scott, whose tales of policing Toronto Island inspired *Final Look,* and to my mother, Rose Marie Scott, for her lifelong support. Thanks to Michael for supporting the time, effort and expense involved in twenty-five years of following my bliss. And to my children, Claire and Matthew, who inspire me daily.

About the Author

Dianne Scott lives with her family in Toronto, Canada. Her mystery novel *Final Look* won the Crime Writers of Canada Arthur Ellis Award for best unpublished crime manuscript. Dianne's writing has appeared in the *Toronto Star*, the *Globe and Mail* and on CBC national radio. When she's not writing, Dianne is playing Sudoku (rather slowly), losing at gin rummy to her teenagers, walking Toronto neighborhoods or curled up reading beside her Bichon poodle.